Wild Souls

By
Faith Prince

This is a work of fiction. Any resemblance to actual persons, living or dead, or actual events is purely coincidental.

Cover Art by Vanesa Garkova

ISBN: 979-8-9881191-1-1

www.faithprinceauthor.com

Table of Contents

1

Soul Seer

Ethan

Everyone sees Kira and Luke standing in the classroom doorway, but only I can see the boa constrictor taut around her neck. As Luke pulls her closer, a shadow shrouds her light. His hand moves through her hair. Snake-like creatures erupt from his fingertips and slither across her scalp. I stand up at our lab table, fists clenched at my sides.

The bell rings. "See you later," she says and kisses him. As they separate, the snake unravels from her neck and glides back to Luke, coiling around his wrist.

"Later, babe." Luke walks away, a mass of dark scribbles and reptilian varmints following him. Kira glows like gold again. She slides into the seat beside me.

Ms. Anderson stands in front of the class. "It's time to get to work. Everyone should be finishing up the lab we started yesterday. If you have any questions, let me know."

I put my safety glasses on and pour the solution into the beaker. "So, um, what's going on with you and Luke?"

"He's my boyfriend." Kira smiles. "We've been hanging out for a few weeks, but we just made it official over the weekend."

"Oh." I pause. "I'm surprised."

"Me, too. He can have any girl he wants. I'm not sure how I got so lucky."

I shake my head. "That's not what I meant. You're way too good for him."

She laughs. "Yeah, right."

"I'm serious. You should stay away from him."

Kira's brows move together. "I don't understand. He's the class president. He'll probably be valedictorian. And he's gorgeous. What's the problem?"

The snakes. The darkness. The dread that wriggles up my spine whenever he's nearby. I can't say any of that out loud. She'll think I'm insane.

Kira drums her fingers on the table. "Ethan," she pauses. "I hope I haven't given you the wrong idea. You're not jealous, are you?"

"No, it's not like that," I say. "I appreciate that you're nice to me and that we're…" I pause, trying to think of how to describe our relationship. We chat during class, but it's not like we hang out outside of school.

"Friends," Kira finishes for me.

"Friends," I repeat after her. It feels weird coming off my tongue. I'm not used to saying it. "As a friend, I have to tell you. He's not a good person."

"How do you know? Have you ever even spoken to him?"

"No," I admit. I barely talk to anyone. Kira knows that. "But you have to trust me." I glance over at her. Apart from Luke, she's luminous as the sun, long golden tendrils stretching up towards the ceiling. A burgundy sparrow is perched on her shoulder, watching me through narrowed green eyes. She'll put up a good fight, that's for sure, but ultimately: snake food. "He'll pollute your soul," I say. "He'll destroy you."

She looks down at her notes. I sense the shift in her immediately. I took it too far. Now she thinks I belong in an asylum. Just like everyone else. We complete the lab in silence.

When the lunch bell rings, she doesn't say goodbye. She leaves the classroom without a word. I wait for the hallways to clear before I head outside. I walk into the woods, weaving through the trees until I reach my spot: a decrepit picnic table under a canopy of multi-colored leaves.

It's Friday, so Alex joins me. Most days, I eat alone. He plops down on the bench across from me, his brown bag crinkling as he digs inside of it. "Good afternoon, Ethan. It's a pleasure to see you again." Alex uses a script we learned seven years ago when our parents signed us up for the same social skills group. Even after my mom threw away a fortune on doctors and therapists, I'm still a mess, but at least I found my first friend in Alex. "How are you today?" Alex asks, his voice flat. No matter how hard our therapist tried, Alex never grasped using inflection in speech.

"Okay, I guess. What's new with you?" I'm careful not to make direct eye contact. As usual, Alex is encompassed by predictable patterns: geometric figures lined up in order of complexity, color wheels spinning in sync, twice counter-clockwise and once in reverse. Lights blink methodically, a complex code that I can't decipher.

"I'm creating a new app in Computer Science class."

"What kind of app?"

"It's a virtual experience app that uses technology similar to Mind-Reel. You know how when you use Mind-Reel, you're transported into someone else's perspective?"

I nod.

"Well, with my app, you can experience anywhere in the world: sights, sounds, and sensations, as though you're really there."

My brow furrows. "How is that different from Mind-Reel? When I plugged into a guy's reel from Italy, I walked through the colosseum and touched the limestone walls. I even felt the sweat rolling down my back."

"No." Alex shakes his head. "You felt the sweat rolling down HIS back. You were inside his perspective, experiencing a scene he already lived. You weren't able to alter his past experience or make conscious choices. In my app, you virtually go somewhere as yourself, and can control your experience."

"That's really cool."

"Yes, but there are challenges too. Like Mind-Reel, the session maxes out at five minutes. Any longer and users risk permanent brain damage."

"You can market it to people who want a more interactive way to scope out potential vacation spots." I take a bite of my sandwich.

"I think I'll call it Mind-Travel." As he goes on about the programming involved, I finish my lunch. "You're quiet," Alex observes.

"I lost a friend today."

"Who?"

"Kira Barner."

"Where did you lose her?" Alex asks.

"No, she's not missing. She just doesn't want to be my friend anymore."

"I should've known that." Alex's cheeks turn red. As brilliant as Alex is, he struggles to understand idioms. He's told me that when he messes up, he feels like an idiot. He shouldn't. I understand better than anyone that all brains aren't wired the same. "Why is she mad at you?"

I shrug. "It's kind of hard to explain." I don't tell anyone I can see souls anymore. No one ever believed me. I check my watch. "We should head back."

I keep my hoodie pulled low over my eyes. I focus on avoiding seeing souls and soul-animals for the rest of the day. Evil often lurks where I least expect it. Nowhere is safe.

When the final bell rings, I slip inside the library and hunker down at a back table. I can't enter that crowded hallway. Mobs are unbearable for me. This condition requires that I strategize my every move. Sometimes my life feels like an endless chess match.

When the building seems quiet, I walk to my locker, my footsteps echoing in the empty hallway. As I turn my lock, a familiar dread slithers up my spine. Luke is nearby. I keep my head inside my locker, hoping he'll pass by and not notice me.

"Ethan," he says.

My back is still to him. "What?" I dig inside my locker until I find my math textbook.

"Turn around," he says.

I don't. "What do you want?"

"I want to talk to you. Turn around."

In my peripheral vision, I see the snakes. One hisses in my ear. I drop my gaze to the floor. That usually helps block out the visions. But not now, not when Luke is in such close proximity, not when his rage is directed at me. Snakes circle my feet, staring up at me with red eyes. They're ready for a feast.

"I said turn around asshole."

My heart is pounding. I take a deep breath and spin around. "I don't know what your problem is—" I'm cut off by a blow to my stomach that knocks the wind out of me.

"That's for talking shit about me to my girl." He hits me again. "That's for being such a freak." Snakes coil around my wrists and pin me to the wall. I lurch against the restraints. I use all of my strength, but I can't break free. I'm helpless. His fist pounds into my rib cage. "And that's for even talking to my girl at all."

A snake sinks its fangs into my shoulder. Another tears into my leg. I shout and writhe in pain. The agony inflicted by my visions is as real to me as the physical punches.

You'd think he'd stop. I'm not fighting back. That only seems to incense him more. "And that's for being such a pussy!" He pummels my chest. I wonder if I'm going to be beaten to death in the school hallway. Of all the ways I imagined I'd go, this isn't one of them.

The girl comes out of nowhere. She shoves him—hard. "What the hell are you doing?" Shades of orange contour her frame, stretching into swirls of blue and violet. Luke's snakes move towards her, their fangs bared. Stars light up all around her, glittering against her purple waves. The snakes pause, almost like they're startled by her brightness. "What's your problem?"

"Mind your business," Luke says.

"I'm nosy!" The girl shouts. She pushes him again.

"YOU STUPID BITCH!" Luke's mass of darkness grows. Fury surges from him. The snakes hiss; their moment of hesitation is over. They spring towards the girl.

"Hey! What's going on here?" Austin Miller jogs down the hallway, his track t-shirt stained with sweat.

"She attacked me!" Luke says.

"Come on, don't yell at a girl. That's not like you," Austin says.

Luke's expression changes. Suddenly he's calm and composed, the demeanor that everyone else sees, the mask that's made him one of the most well-liked guys in our class. I still see the snakes. But I might be the only one. "You're right, man." He faces the girl. "I think we had a misunderstanding."

The girl squares on him. "I didn't misunderstand anything."

"Listen, I know you're upset," Luke says, his tone compassionate. "Maybe we can talk this out tomorrow when you're feeling more rational." He slaps Austin on the back. "See you later, man." And then he walks away.

The girl turns to me. "Are you okay?" she asks.

My body hurts like hell, but I nod. Her stars glisten among her vibrant colors. Her soul has its own pulse, a soft rumble that vibrates gently in my ears. I stare, speechless. She's beautiful. Jolts zig-zag down my spine.

The bell rings. If I don't make it out in time, I'll miss the late bus. "I've, um, gotta go," I say.

As I'm walking away, I realize that I never said thank you. I'm such an idiot. I look over my shoulder. Austin leans against the lockers, smiling as he talks to the girl. She's looking up at him, laughing. They're probably making fun of me. I turn back around.

As I head outside, Taylor Powell whizzes by, her brow tightly creased. Laser-like spikes poke through her skin and shoot into space. I duck to avoid being hit. On the sidewalk, Julien Acosta is encased within an enormous clock. He bites his lip, the clock's hands spinning erratically as the ticking grows louder and louder.

At the bus stop, a group waits. The mixture of souls overwhelms my senses. Neon colors, pastels, neutrals, and gray meld together until they're all one vomit-like mixture. Soul sounds collide until the thrum of a lullaby shifts into a piercing cry. A malevolent soul hides amidst the innocent faces. Red-eyed demons circle me, closing in.

I lower my chin and stare at the cracks on the sidewalk. The images subside. Luckily. Otherwise, I'd be wheeled away in a gurney, like all of the other times before.

People say there's good in everyone. They say good trumps evil. But they can't see what I see. They haven't watched virtue and good intentions get sucked into a vortex of malice and envy, swirling and intertwining, bumping against jagged edges and tearing open, spilling all over each other until you can't tell which is what anymore.

When I was younger and naive, I told doctors and therapists that I can see souls, thinking they could help me. I told them that although I've seen some beautiful souls, the ones that haunt me are vile and terrifying.

They all said that I'm crazy. Delusional. Suffering from hallucinations. That the grotesque and horrid images I see can't be real.

Sometimes, for the world's sake, I hope they're right.

2

Supermarket Dance Party

Jenna

As I veer around a blind curve, a massive pothole appears. I'm not sure that pothole aptly describes the ten-foot-wide concave depression that might swallow my vehicle whole. "Whoa!" I shout, swerving to the side. At that exact moment, a rabbit darts into the road.

I jerk the wheel too hard. My car drifts across the narrow path, careening towards a thicket of trees. I slam my foot down, the wheels screeching to a halt inches from a wide birch trunk. I exhale, my heart still pummeling against my chest. The rabbit scampers away, her puff-ball tail disappearing into the high grass.

In the passenger seat, Mia grips the oh-shit handlebar like it's a lifeline. "What the hell, Jenna?" Her face is ghost-white.

"Well, first, I was trying to avoid falling through the gigantic crater that looks like it could be a portal into the underworld. Then, a bunny hell-bent on ending her life sprinted into the road. I had a split second to decide that there isn't enough money I could donate to the SPCA or hours I could volunteer at an animal shelter that would help me sleep at night if I was complicit in the bunny's demise, even as an accidental accomplice."

Mia raises her brows. "What?"

"How could I cope when every night I'd dream of all the carrots that she'd never devour, the pastures she'd never prance through, the baby bunnies she'd never bear?"

"What have you been smoking?"

I have a strange sense of humor. So what? "What I'm trying to say is I love animals and have a particular fondness for furry woodland creatures."

"Um, okay." Mia points. "Make the next right. Carley's house is just ahead."

A small, half dilapidated red cottage comes into view. Carley is waiting outside, her hands stuffed inside her puffy jacket. I pull into the driveway, my tires stirring up clouds of dirt. Carley strides forward, glancing over her shoulder a few times, as though the house might follow her. She flings the back door open and slides inside. "Come on, let's go," she says.

"Where are we going?" I ask.

"Just get out of here," Carley says.

Sure, because when I suggested we hang out, driving aimlessly was exactly what I had in mind.

"What happened at school yesterday?" Carley asks. "I heard you broke up a fight."

"It wasn't exactly a fight. A bully was using someone as his punching bag. So, I pushed him."

"You pushed Luke Parker?" Mia straightens up in her seat.

I shrug. "Is that the jerk's name?"

"He's not a jerk," Carley says. "He's smart, athletic, hot as hell, and really nice, too. Ask anyone. Everyone likes Luke."

"Sure, if you choose to ignore the fact that he pummels people who are half his size, I'm sure he's a real stand-up guy. Also, I'd like to challenge your declaration that *everyone* likes him because I'm pretty sure that the guy who was having his face bashed in isn't a fan. Or does his opinion not count?"

"Not really," Carley chuckles. "Ethan Underwood deserves what he gets."

"Why do you say that?" I ask.

"Because he's psychotic. You're new here, so you don't understand. He's insane." As I back out of the driveway, Carley slips a small blue ring–sized box out from under her coat. On the side, block letters read: MIND-REEL.

"How do you like Roxbury so far?" Mia asks, changing the subject.

Driving down the poor excuse for a road, miles of farmland stretch ahead of us. Along the side, a black and white cow bends over the grass. A. Freaking. Cow. Her jowls flap, tongue popping in and out of her mouth as she chomps away. The next time my mom accuses me of eating like a cow, I'll demonstrate the disparity between my eager chewing and an actual cow. I'll even moo. I'm sure she'll enjoy that.

"Um, it's a lot different than New York City. It reminds me of, like Little House on the Prairie meets Children of the Corn." An image arises in my psyche; Carley shifting between cornstalks that tower over her, her auburn hair unkempt and straggly, eyes gleaming demonically. It's so absurd that I snort aloud.

Carley huffs in the backseat. Mia's posture stiffens. I cringe. I guess my new friends don't get my jokes.

"My dad won't let me use Mind-Reel," Carley says. In the rear-view mirror, I watch her open the box and slip the circular device in her ear. "He thinks it's dangerous. He's so overprotective. Now that I'm out, I want to do some reels." Carley leans over the center console, holding her phone out in front of her. "What reel should I try today?"

Mia points to the screen. "How about white-water rafting?"

"I've done that one before," Carley says. "Oh! I'll try this one. The steepest roller coaster in the world."

A flash of bright blue lights up the backseat, and I know Carley started the reel.

"Have you tried Mind-Reel?" Mia asks.

"Yeah, of course I love the fun reels," I say. "But lately I've been using it more as a research tool. I've been choosing reels of very sick people, just to see what their symptoms feel like."

"Why would you do that?" Mia looks appalled.

"I want to be a doctor one day," I explain. "I think it's important to be able to truly empathize with patients. Also, I've read that in the future, it will be common practice for doctors to use Mind-Reel technology to improve the accuracy of diagnoses. If a patient can't find the words to describe a particular feeling or sensation, what better way to assess their symptoms than to experience them yourself?"

Mia nods, securing an unruly brown curl behind her ear. "That's pretty cool."

"What about you?" I ask. "What are your favorite reels?"

"I can't use Mind-Reel. I have epilepsy. My doctor says it isn't safe." There's a thud in the back. Mia turns around and screams at the top of her lungs: a piercing, ear-rattling scream. I jump in my seat.

"What happened?" I pull over to the side of the road and spin around. Tall grasses sway in the wind and batter against my car.

Carley lays in the backseat, her face half-covered in blood. I crawl over the console and brush her hair out of her eyes. They're wide open, unblinking, life-less. Blood pours from her nose, dripping down her chin and onto the cloth seat. My heart is thumping in my chest. "Carley! Carley!" I shout, even though I know that yelling won't bring someone out of a reel. I grasp her wrist, feeling for a pulse. She's stiff as a board.

Carley's eyes flick open. "Whoa! That was crazy! That rollercoaster was awesome!" She smiles; her cheeks are red from excitement. Then, she notices me hovering over her, my hand still on her wrist. "What're you doing to me?" She pulls her arm away and sits up. Her eyes narrow.

"I was making sure that you didn't kick the oxygen habit."

"What?" Carley touches her face, pulls her hand away, and stares at the blood.

"I wasn't sure if you were having a rare, life-threatening reaction to Mind-Reel."

Mia digs inside her purse and hands Carley a wad of tissues. "I'm fine." Carley dabs her face and redirects her attention to her phone. "It's just a little nosebleed. Which reel should I do next?"

"I don't think you should do another one," Mia says. "The nosebleed isn't a good sign. My mom said Mind-Reel can cause brain damage."

"Oh, please," Carley says. "Where did she see that? National Inquirer?"

I jump in. "Scholarly scientific articles have reported that Mind-Reel induced nosebleeds can cause the user to become a zombie with an insatiable hunger for human brains."

"Huh?" Carley blinks. She raises her brows as she makes eye contact with Mia. Mia's eyes widen as she presses her lips together, her shoulders lifting in a half-shrug.

I'm not stupid. They think I'm weird. But I don't care. They'll learn to like me for me, or not. If there's one thing that I've learned from my dad, it's to be true to yourself. Live free and don't let anyone else define you. "Seriously, though, Carley. I read actual neuroscience magazines sometimes. There have been adverse reactions to Mind-Reel, including stroke and aneurysm. I don't think you should use it anymore today," I say.

"I agree," Mia says.

"Okay, I guess," Carley tosses Mind-Reel onto the backseat and folds her arms across her chest.

"Well, maybe we still can use Mind-Reel, but in another way," I say. "We could create our own reel and post it."

"Of what?" Carley asks. "Sitting in a car doing nothing? No one wants to see that."

"Yeah," Mia agrees. "There's nothing cool enough around here to create a reel from." I note that they're fine with insulting their town, but I'm not allowed to. It reminds me that I'm an outsider.

"I have an idea," I say. As I drive towards the center of town, Carley thrums her fingers on the back window.

"Where are we going?" she asks.

"You'll see," I say. A few minutes later, I pull into the grocery store's parking lot.

"What are we doing here?" Carley asks. "Don't tell me you're going to make a reel of grocery shopping."

"Not exactly," I say, my lips curving into a smile. I snatch Mind-Reel from the backseat and slip it inside my ear. "What I'm going to do is strip down to my tie-dye socks, and then streak up and down the aisles. If anyone tries to stop me, I'll throw tomatoes at them."

Mia's jaw hangs open. "Jenna, what? You can't do that."

After syncing my cell phone, I sign into my account. "You're right," I say. "It would be way cooler if I throw raw chicken drumsticks. Hopefully, Luke Parker is around, and I can nail him right between the eyes."

"Jenna, you can't. We'll all get in trouble." Carley sounds different: less sassy, almost frantic.

"Relax, I'm kidding," I say, hopping out of the car. Mia and Carley follow.

"What're you doing, then?" Carley asks.

I scroll through my phone until I find the file I'm looking for: *DanceMix*. The music begins as I click *Start Reel*.

"You'll see." My heart pounds as self-doubt threatens to consume me. Maybe this isn't a good idea after all. It's Saturday afternoon: prime grocery shopping hour. Dozens of people mill about. A toddler fusses, her little arms flailing as her mother straps her into a stroller. Another family walks towards the store's entrance, the brother and sister immersed in a tug-of-war over an iPad. "It's mine!" the girl shouts, ripping it from her brother's grasp.

"You've been using it all day!" the brother rebuts, lunging forward to reclaim the tablet. His sister snickers as she presses the iPad protectively against her chest.

Three teenage boys shuffle through the parking lot. As they move closer, one mumbles something about beer and fake IDs. I recognize the boy in the middle from my Biology class.

"Hey, Joey," I say.

Joey jolts, his eyes wide as he searches for who called his name. When they find me, he keeps walking, his expression impassive. "Oh, hi," he says, fiddling with strings that dangle from his hoodie.

Geez, people sure are friendly around here. Cold sweat pools on my clammy palms. Maybe I'm making a terrible mistake. "There's no such thing as mistakes, only good stories," I whisper under my breath, channeling my dad's carefree spirit. I picture him, his fingers running through his straggly beard, a mischievous grin on his face as he shares another self-caused debacle from his youth.

Thinking about my dad is like a hand clamping over my heart. When I saw him every day, I was quick to disregard his advice. Now that he's gone, I find myself seeking guidance through his memory all the time. It's funny how life works sometimes.

Sometimes I think that if I live the way he lives, that like magic, he'll come home. As though my actions can transform into an energy that propels itself through the universe, finding its way to my dad, wherever he is, and once it hits him, he'll miss me as much as I miss him.

"There are no mistakes, only good stories," my mind repeats. Committing social suicide during my first month in a new town would be the kind of epic blunder that could be passed down from generation to generation. And hey, if I pull it off, that would be pretty bad-ass too.

I step onto the sidewalk just outside the main doors to the supermarket. A pop song blares from my phone. I gulp a mouthful of oxygen, and my breath rattles on its way out. A few passersby glance my way. Either I'm paranoid or they're already giving me dirty looks.

Maybe living in the sticks caused a few to get stuck up their you-know-where. This may never work. But maybe wiggling around is exactly what the people of Roxbury need to dislodge their impacted sticks. I inhale and whisper, "I got this."

I raise my hands above my head and clap to the beat. "Hello, everyone! It's time for a Supermarket Dance Party!" The chorus starts, and my body reacts. Motor memory takes over. Although I was never good enough to make the dance team, my best friend Saja always did. While she fretted over national championships, practicing the routine in her living room, I joined her. I'll never have Saja's natural grace or fluidity, but I have the steps down, and I can shake and shimmy with the best of them (or at least I like to think so!).

I barely register the jerking heads and wide-eyed stares. I'm caught in the moment. The music and my body are no longer separate entities. The drums throb, pumping my heart. Chords circulate through my veins.

A few would-be shoppers detour from their errands to watch. The little boy who was fighting with his sister a few minutes earlier bounces and waves his arms, trying to mimic my steps. "Watch me," I instruct him, as the chorus begins. "Step right, crisscross, arms out, now turn." A small crowd hoots and camera phones are pulled out as the boy catches onto the choreography. The boy grins, and I step aside, allowing him the spotlight.

A couple more kids join him: a toddler who waddles and claps off-beat, a girl who jumps until her pink bows slide down her pigtails. The boy calls his father, "Daddy, daddy! Come on!" A couple of older women nudge a reluctant red-faced man forward. "Daddy, dance with me!" The man bends his knees tentatively and jerks his hips. I can't tell if he's dancing, twitching, or trying to hold his pee. Still, his son beams up at him. The song ends, and the dozen or so of us burst into applause.

As our group disperses, I remove Mind-Reel from my ear. The boy tugs on my pant leg. "Can we do it again?" he asks.

His mother shakes her head. "Not now. We have to get groceries," she says, then turns to me. "Thank you," she mouths. Her kids play a hand game, seeming to forget their earlier iPad feud.

I head back to my car, my cheeks strained from smiling so wide. It turned out awesome—I can't wait to post and share my reel with Saja. I scan the parking lot, searching for Mia and Carley. They didn't make an appearance at the dance party. Their loss. A little dancing is good for the soul.

I open the driver's side door and peer inside. Carley's ducked down in the backseat. Mia is beside her. "The attention whore is back." Carley glares at me and lunges forward, plucking Mind-Reel from my grasp.

My heart drops into my stomach. "What's your problem?" I start up the engine. "Everyone had a good time."

"The problem is that you looked pathetic. It's embarrassing."

I swallow hard. My eyes burn as tears threaten to spill. I blink them away.

"Take me home," Carley says. It's not a request. It's a demand.

I consider throwing Carley out of my car and wishing her luck hitching a ride. I'm not sure why I don't. Something about her tone makes the hair on the back of my neck stand on end. - When Carley tells you to do something, you just do it.

I park in Carley's driveway, and she slams the door behind her. Dirt swirls around her feet as she stalks away. For the rest of the drive, Mia stares at her hands. She shifts in her seat, crossing and un-crossing her legs. I pull in front of Mia's house, tapping on the steering wheel to break the awkward silence.

Mia tugs on the latch. One of her legs hangs outside the vehicle before she turns around. "Carley isn't usually like that," she says.

"I'm sure," I mutter.

"Her dad…" Mia's voice trails off as if carefully choosing her words. "Her dad can be tough. It's just, she has to watch out so she doesn't get in trouble, you know? Sometimes he gets mad over things."

"I wouldn't do anything to get you guys in trouble." I shake my head. "Everyone has their own family shit to deal with. I know I have my share, but I've never used it as an excuse to be a jerk." As soon as I say it, I wish I hadn't. I really should keep my thoughts to myself sometimes. Mia has been friends with Carley for years. She isn't going to take my side.

"See you," Mia says. The door clicks shut.

3

Hi, Jenna

Ethan

I've always wished that I could be someone else, even for five minutes. Mind-Reel granted me that wish.

My mom was the first to tell me about Mind-Reel. She read about it in one of her million magazine subscriptions on how to raise a special-needs child. "Psychologists say that it can help people feel more connected," she said. "Will you try it?" Her voice dipped as she waited for my response, fiercely hanging onto another thread of hope, another chance that I could become the son she wanted.

As soon as I said, "Okay," she was gone. An hour later, she rushed through the front door, the plastic bag crinkling as she tore Mind-Reel from its package. "Here it is!" She held up the plastic earpiece like it was a magic wand. Maybe if she waved it and said "Abracadabra," I'd evaporate and then rematerialize. I'd be brand new and shiny, the son she ordered but never received. If only it was that easy.

I disappeared into my bedroom, playing reel after reel, fascinated. Through someone else's eyes, faces weren't muddled by colors and designs. No creatures. No flying objects. No strange sounds or tastes. Instead, I could make out the color of their eyes, the shape of their jaws, and the curve of their noses.

Each reel I experienced made me feel more and more hopeless. Instead of helping me feel more connected to others, Mind-Reel confirmed just how defective I am. I retreated deeper, convinced that I'm beyond any kind of help.

After a few weeks, my mother realized that her latest remedy was yet another failure. That *I'm* a failure, most likely permanently. Then, even the hallway and locked doors between us couldn't restrain the waves of despair. Her disappointment rattled my bed frame, its weight heaving down into my lungs. I let her down, again.

Since then, Mind-Reel collected dust, buried under a pile of clothes in my closet. And yet, tonight, I'm drawn towards it again. I'm not sure why. Maybe it's the girl. I can't stop thinking about her. She rescued me. I close my eyes and picture her: bright-white stars blazing through an orange and amethyst sky.

Maybe I gave up too quickly on Mind-Reel. Maybe it could help me. If there's even the slightest chance I could be normal, I'll try anything.

I log into Mind-Reel and browse through the latest reels by category. I never choose the "Thrill-seekers" reels. Instead, I'm intrigued by the more mundane reels, the daily happenings that everyone else takes for granted, but I've never experienced. In the past, I plugged into reels of a son having dinner with his family at a restaurant, a player's pickup beach volleyball game, a pedestrian walking down a city street.

Tonight, I choose a reel of a more romantic nature. I become someone else, someone who can talk to a girl and take her to a dance. I hold her close, inhaling the scent of her cherry shampoo. She gazes up at me, adoration in her big brown eyes. Euphoria surges through me. The reel dissipates, and I'm back inside my bedroom. Alone.

I wonder if a girl will ever look at me that way. Not just any girl. Amethyst girl. That pretty girl in the reel has nothing on her.

Another category catches my eye. *Local Reels- Check out reels of people you know!* I click the link and scroll through reels uploaded within a five-mile radius.

I don't know what I'm searching for until I find it. My breath catches in my throat. The reel is called *Supermarket Dance Party.* Beside the title is a tiny photo of the reel's creator and her username, *Jennalivesfree.*

It's *her.* Amethyst girl. Her name is Jenna. In the thumbnail photo, I can't see the swirling purples. I can't feel the zig-zagging jolts. When I saw her in the hallway, half of her face was obstructed by waves of color. But I still *know.*

This isn't the first time I've recognized someone in a photo who was hidden by their aura. It seems that some latent part of my brain does see past the auras, subconsciously registering physical appearances. I study her: the rosy cheeks, turned-up nose, prominent eyebrows.

For the briefest moment, I'm thankful for my disorder, for the moments when I saw her true essence: the majestic blues, the vibrant oranges, melding together.

In the hallway, she was magnificent. In the thumbnail photo, she's just another girl. Don't get me wrong; I think she's pretty. It's just that no exterior features—even the most exquisite mouth, nose, or cheekbones—can measure up to *all* that she is.

I click on the reel. A moment later, I'm Jenna, walking through the supermarket parking lot, my cell phone blasting a pop song. Passersby shoot disdainful looks. Children scream and fight. Still, the world is good.

I'm Jenna, and she's afraid. My heart thumps louder than the electric bass. My palms are slick with sweat. My breaths are shallow; my head feels fuzzy. I whisper, "I got this."

I'm Jenna, and she's the bravest person I've ever met. I clap my hands above my head. I dance like the music was born inside me, as if my movements control the melody, as if my gestures produce the beat, as if my shoulder shakes affect the tempo and not the other way around. As if I stop moving, the music will cease to play. My energy magnetizes those around me; they gather like moths to a flame.

Something like electricity fires through my veins as the children emulate my moves. There's laughter, shrieks, and cheers: a chaotic euphony that sounds like pure joy to me.

I'm Jenna, and she's proud. It wasn't my intention to put on a show or bring attention to myself (that was only a means to an end). My goal was to shake things up (pun intended!) in this small town, to bring some novelty to even the most routine part of their days. Mission: Achieved!

Suddenly I'm Ethan, and that sucks. So, I hide inside my room, replaying Jenna's reel over and over and over and over again, until my ears pop and my head throbs and I decide that continuing might not bide well for my health.

Every time I use Mind-Reel it amazes me how each person uniquely interprets their surroundings. Whether we see it or not, the aura that surrounds each of us acts as a filter through which we perceive the world.

Although the swirling colors and sparkling white lights are invisible to Jenna, they still shape her vision. Jenna peers through a screen that, although translucent to her, tints every molecule in its field with vibrancy.

The differences are subtle: the sun just an iota brighter, colors a bit more vivid, the wind gusts almost melodic. Still, it's all of these tiny variations that add up to the bigger picture: a person who chooses to focus on the positive, whose storage of optimism serves as her strength.

I collapse into my bed, feeling empty and sick. I want to live. I'm breathing, but I'm not alive. At least, not in the way Jenna is.

I reach for my laptop and open it on my chest. A red dot lights up next to Jenna's thumbnail photo. *Jennalivesfree is online!* Another link invites me to *Connect with your friends on Mind-Reel! Click here to Direct Message Jennalivesfree.*

I click here. A text box pops up. This is my chance to direct message Jenna. I have no idea what to say. I stare at that text box for forty-five minutes.

I type a few words and then delete them. I stare some more. Type. Delete. Stare. I pray for some witty, groundbreaking, sweep-her-off-her-feet idea to come to me. Type. Delete. Stare. It never comes. I don't believe she'd ever like me in real life. What am I supposed to say? "Hi, Jenna, it's me, Ethan, the loser that you saved in the hallway. Yes, that's right, I'm the weakling who can't even defend himself. I'm sure you've heard by now that I'm a freak. But I think you're amazing."

I'm not sure why I'm even doing this. I should just shut off the computer and go to bed. I type. "Hi, Jenna." I stare. I don't delete. My finger hovers over the enter key.

4

Saja in Love

Jenna

It's the day after the supermarket fiasco, and I'm still stressing over it, which isn't like me. I need Saja. I call her again, for the third time in the past two hours. Patience isn't one of my stronger points. Her voicemail picks up. "Hey, stranger! I miss you, but I'm starting to think that you don't miss me. I feel like a borderline stalker the way I've been blowing up your phone. What the hell, as long as I've gone this far, I might as well go all the way. If you don't call me back, I'll track you down, find you, and kidnap your ass. Bahahaha!" I make my best impression of an evil witch's cackle and then disconnect the call.

"Meow!" My black and gold tabby cat, Purrscilla, rubs against my calf. I scoop her into my arms and she purrs against my chest, her gentle vibrations soothing me. As I unlatch the front door, she leaps onto the porch. Acorns crunch under my feet as I stroll into the yard, Purrscilla prancing beside me.

A myriad of colorful leaves floats gracefully through the atmosphere. Birds fly overhead, chattering to one another. Purrscilla sits upright, her gaze following as birds swoop from tree to tree. Back home, she'd done the same; only bird-watching wasn't nearly as exciting through a city window. At least this move worked out for one of us.

My phone buzzes in my pocket. Saja. "Finally!"

"I'm sorry. You know I miss you so much! But please don't kidnap my ass. It's kind of important to me. It provides a nice cushion every time I sit down. But even more essential, I'm not sure I could twerk effectively without it."

"I'll take pity on your ass this time. Next time, you might not be so lucky." I lay down, stretching out my legs, grass tickling my ears. Burnt orange and ruby red sail through the sky.

"Oh, divine mercy! My ass has been spared!" We both burst into hysterics. "So, what's new? How are the cornfields and country boys treating you?"

"Oh, just fine and dandy," I mutter in my best country accent.

"That doesn't sound good," Saja says. "What happened?"

"Ugh, I don't even know where to start," I say. "This town sucks so bad that even the bunnies are trying to off themselves."

"That's pretty bad. Details?"

"I bet rabid werewolves are friendlier than some of the people around here. Come to think of it, maybe they *are* werewolves. I could've sworn I heard howling during the last full moon. Shit, do you know where I can get a crossbow or a silver sword?"

"I can't help you with that. I don't want my PETA membership revoked. For real, though, how bad can these people be?"

"The only girls that'll hang out with me have no sense of humor and think I'm weirder than a rhino in a tutu."

"Hmmm. Well, you *are* weirder than a rhino in a tutu."

"Bad example. A rhino in a tutu rapping with a baby kangaroo beat-boxing on its back."

"Okay, that's got you beat."

I laugh. "Seriously, Saj. There's no one else like you. I don't know what else to do."

"About what? Finding another me? Well, she doesn't exist. I'm one of a kind, baby. I guess you could try to clone me, but I'm not going to lie, that would be hella creepy."

"Hmmm, not a bad idea though. Next time I'm at your house I might have to swipe your toothbrush for some DNA." Purrscilla sprawls out beside me, her paw kneading my knee.

"I don't think you'll have to take such extreme measures. It's only been a few weeks. It takes time to meet people."

"I've already met everyone," I grumble. "At least everyone who wasn't foaming at the mouth."

"How? Have you been walking up to strangers saying, 'Hi, my name is Jenna. Do you want to hang out'?"

"Yes!" I say.

"Oh," Saja chuckles. "You would. That's your problem. You're coming on too strong."

"If they can't appreciate my directness, we're not going to get along anyway."

Saja sighs. "So stubborn and impatient. You have to let these things happen organically."

I pluck a few strands of grass and toss them up like confetti. "Yeah, I guess. So, what's new with you?" A strong gust rattles the branches. More leaves escape their confines and enter free space, dancing with the wind, looking for a place to land.

Saja pauses. "Um, not much, really." I know her too well. Maybe it was the delay or the uncharacteristic lilt in her tone. She's lying.

"What're you hiding from me?" I jolt up, leaving my silhouette indented in the grass. Saja and I don't keep secrets from each other.

"Jenna, it's not like that. It's just… It doesn't seem right to talk about this amazing thing that's happened to me when you're all sad and stuff."

"I'm fine. Tell me now!"

"I'm in love."

"Haha, good one. No, seriously, what's going on?"

"His name is Javi. We met at the coffee shop on 8th and Park. He was writing poetry and I was drinking a raspberry-infused espresso."

"That's cool, but love? How long have you known him?"

"A few weeks, but it only took us one day to fall in love."

"What?" I shriek. Purrscilla startles; her ears pin back. "Are you sure your espresso wasn't infused with a little something extra? Like crack-cocaine?"

"I know it sounds crazy, but I love him."

"Oh, that's awesome." I hate that the words feel hollow exiting my lips. I should be happy for Saja. "Tell me more about him."

According to Saja, her boyfriend is the world's greatest kisser and has the best body in the galaxy. Everything about him is amazing: his smile, his writing, the way he balances a pencil behind his ear, and furrows his brow when he's deep in thought. "I'm sorry, have I been going on and on?"

"Nope, not at all. I'm dying to hear every detail. What else? Let me guess! He has the sexiest back moles in all of existence, their hairiness is such a turn-on. Oh, and his foot fungus is absolutely exquisite!"

"Do I really sound that crazy?"

"Do you remember when Alayna started dating Nick?" I ask. Last year, our friend Alayna fell in love for the first time. Throughout their early courtship, Saja and I were subjected to hours of nonstop gushing about Nick. If Alayna ever ran out of things to say about Nick, she'd start repeating the same stuff over and over. When Alayna wasn't around, Saja and I theorized that Nick was a hypnotist and our friend had been brain-jacked.

"Oh my God! Am I that bad?" Saja asks.

"Worse," I say. As time went on, we saw Alayna less and less. It seemed that our company couldn't compare to the all-incredible Nick. Our daily jaunts eventually dwindled to bi-monthly coffee dates when Nick was working. Even then, part of her was absent, her phone stretched in front of her as she snapped another duck-faced selfie. Alayna nodded and laughed on cue, but she continuously checked her phone, her eyes lighting up only when Nick responded to her selfie with a heart emoji.

"Oh God, no!" Saja says. "Is there any help left for me? One kiss and I was done for."

"A lobotomy may be the only option." I wonder if Saja will suffer from the same syndrome as Alayna. Will she also slowly disappear from my life? I'm not sure how I'll ever get over losing her.

"Javi just got here. I've got to go! I'll talk to you soon! Love you!"

The call disconnects. I turn to face the big empty house, feeling lonelier than ever. Sunlight and tree shadows obscure the plank-wood siding. An assortment of windchimes dangles above the porch. They sway as Mother Nature composes her symphony, low gong-like bells complementing soprano tinkles.

When I first saw the house, I thought: *This is the perfect place for my parents to fall in love again.* Yes, they're separated, but they've broken up and gotten back together many times.

My dad has been gone for ninety-four days. He'll probably call any day now. I imagine his voice saying, "Jenna, how about a burger with your old man?" At the diner, we'll fill up on greasy food and sugary desserts. I'll give him hell about disappearing, and he'll apologize like he means it. When he drops me off, he'll come inside. And this time, he'll stay. Forever. I just know it.

I slide my phone out of my pocket and call my dad. It rings and rings. I get his voicemail. I try again. He doesn't pick up. I dig my hands into the grass, ripping a few blades up from their roots.

My mom's Jeep rolls up the driveway. She hops out and opens the back latch, revealing a trunk full of groceries. I walk over. "Hey, Mom," I say, avoiding eye contact as I hang grocery bags from my wrists. Last night, we nearly tore each other's heads off, and I'm not in the mood for another argument

I lug the bags inside and toss them on the counter. As my mom closes the front door with her foot, paper bags rustling in her arms, I jet upstairs. "I have a ton of homework," I lie, taking the steps two at a time.

I open my laptop and log into Mind-Reel. A new comment from *QueenSaja* reads, "Hot damn! Who taught you those moves? You must've had one fly-ass instructor!" I grin as I respond, "Flyer than a rocket ship speeding into uncharted galaxies."

I check out Saja's new reels and browse for a while. Then, I notice a red light blinking in the corner of my screen. I click it, and a pop-up box appears. *You have a Mind-Reel Direct Message from Soulseer23. To accept this message, click here.*

Soulseer23? I wonder who that could be.

"Jenna!" My mom yells from downstairs. "Dinner's ready!" Every muscle in my body stiffens. I'm still not ready for another Dad bash-fest, but I can't avoid her forever. I close my laptop and go downstairs.

At the kitchen table, she sets a whopping plate of spaghetti and meatballs in front of me. Lately, mom's been on a vegetarian kick. For the past few weeks, I've been subjected to meat substitutes accompanied by obscure vegetables, followed by some herbal tea concoction.

Tonight, she prepared my favorite. It could be a peace offering or a ploy. It's unsettling not knowing which.

"How's school?" Mom asks. She stands over me, a block of cheese in her fist. She strikes it on a metal grater repeatedly, shredding parmesan onto my pasta.

"Fine," I say. I grab my glass of ice water and take a big gulp. "How's work?" My strategy: focus the conversation on her. If I keep her mind off dad, then I won't be subjected to another interrogation to try to find out if I know dad's whereabouts, or worst of all, another attempt to force me to choose sides, and lay on the guilt trip when I refuse.

"Today was difficult. Two kids came into the ER. They were badly beaten by their father. It was heartbreaking to see." She stabs the spaghetti, her wrist spinning round and round, round and round, creating a massive nest. "But even though they were bruised and bloodied, their bones broken, they kept defending their father." The nest slides off the fork, disappearing into the bowl. "I'm not sure why kids always make excuses for their parents, no matter how awful they are."

I groan and drop my gaze to my lap. I see where this is going. "Mom, don't start," I warn. My hands ball up into fists, tearing into my napkin. "Dad never abused us."

"I never said that he did," Mom says, her tone innocent. "Funny that you should bring him up. Have you heard from him lately?" She punctures a meatball. Red sauce squirts out like guts. A splotch lands on her collar. She dabs at it with a napkin, but that only seems to spread the mess, leaving a dark stain.

"No, he's busy. He's on tour," I say. "You know that."

"Oh, really," Mom says. "Because when he stormed out of our lives, he didn't mention anything about a tour. In fact, I clearly remember his last words being 'I'm tired of your nagging' before he slammed the door. As far as my memory serves, this whole 'tour,'" she makes air quotes, "wasn't brought to my attention until months later."

"Well, maybe he couldn't focus on his music with all of the arguing!" She isn't wrong. I know she isn't wrong. Somehow that makes me angrier. "And now he's on the road making something of himself and his band so just let it go, okay? The tour's a big success."

"Is that what he tells you?" My mom smirks. "Because as far as I can tell, our bank accounts are flowing in the wrong direction."

"Mom, please," I plead. "Just stop." Apparently, Plan A is a colossal failure. Time to launch Plan B. I hunch over my plate and start wolfing food into my mouth. She can't expect me to respond while my mouth is stuffed.

"If this tour is so 'successful'," she makes air quotes again, "why is all of the money dwindling from the colossal trust fund his daddy left him?"

I shove my plate aside. So much for Plan B. "I'm done with this conversation." I stand, my chair toppling and crashing on the floor behind me. "And until you respect that, I'm done talking to you!"

"Keep on defending him! That's all you ever do!"

I run up the stairs and into my bedroom, slamming the door as hard as I can behind me. I press my back against the door, sliding to the floor, my cheeks hot, pulse pounding. I can't take it anymore. My mother is out of line. I'm so sick of her trying to get me to take her side.

I suck in a deep breath. I hate that she's so angry. All I want is my dad to come back and my parents to be together. Is that too much to ask?

I open my laptop, Purrscilla curling up beside me. The screen is the same as when I left it. *You have a Mind-Reel Direct Message from Soulseer23. To accept this message, click here.*

I don't know who it is, but the username intrigues me. It could be anyone—including a super creep. Whatever. It's not like I have anything better to do. I click accept.

5

I'm funny online

Ethan

Soulseer23: *Hi, Jenna*

Jennalivesfree: *Hi, Soulseer. Cool username. Can you see my soul?*

I'm an imbecile. When I sent the message, I didn't remember my stupid username. I have no idea what twisted fallacy of thought provoked me to choose that idiotic username. I guess I assumed that no one would ever see it. Now, I kind of revealed my biggest secret to a stranger.

I try to think fast. The seconds seem to tick double-time. I wonder what Jenna would say if the tables were turned. I envision Jenna: bold, confident, and carefree. She isn't fearless, but she doesn't allow fear to consume her. Jenna wouldn't show if she was flustered. She'd play along.

Soulseer23: *Yes, I can.*

Jennalivesfree: *What does my soul look like?*

Soulseer23: *Like an endless sparkling sunset drifting along a deep, starry indigo ocean. It's beautiful.*

Jennalivesfree: *Wow, you're good. I've heard my share of one-liners, but that takes the cake.*

Soulseer23: *That's cuz it wasn't a line. But I'll accept the cake. I never pass up cake.*

Jennalivesfree: *Me either. I'm totally craving strawberry shortcake right now.*

Soulseer23: *You didn't win the cake. I did.*

Jennalivesfree: *Haha. You're funny.*

Jenna thinks I'm funny! I resist the urge to spring into the air and cheer.

Jennalivesfree: *Who are you? Do we know each other?*

Damnit. For one sweet moment, I was a balloon, floating above the clouds. I burst as quickly as I blew up, rubber scraps plunging back to earth. I don't know what to say. If I tell her I'm the loser she saved in the hallway, this conversation will be over before it begins.

Jennalivesfree: *HELLO? Are you there?*

I consider shutting off the computer and disappearing. I've gone too far with this already. But then I remember that Jenna thinks that I'm funny. I imagine her laughing, a deep, hearty laugh, a laugh that makes her belly bounce and her cheeks ache. I want to be the one to make her laugh like that. Even if it may only be through a computer screen.

Soulseer23: *I go to Roxbury HS. I've seen you around.*

Jennalivesfree: *Oh, you've seen me. So, are you a secret admirer?*

My cheeks flush. I put my foot in my mouth again. I'd probably be better off spending forty-five minutes composing every response. Now she thinks I'm some kind of stalker.

Maybe I should just own it, and she'll think I'm confident and sexy. One can hope…

Soulseer23: Something like that.

Jennalivesfree: I'm flattered, but I don't bite. Next time say what's up.

Soulseer23: Yeah, I'd like to. What does your username mean?

Jennalivesfree: Live free. Be free. Do what feels right. Accept people for who they are and don't try to change them.

Soulseer23: That's a nice idea, but I don't think I can accept all people for who they are.

Jennalivesfree: Why's that?

Soulseer23: I can see everyone's souls, remember? Some people are evil.

Jennalivesfree: That could be a chicken and egg situation, don't you think?

Soulseer23: I don't follow.

Jennalivesfree: Are they not accepted because they are evil, or do they become evil because they weren't accepted? I believe the latter.

If that's true, my soul would be a nefarious, hideous monstrosity. But it isn't. My soul has changed over the years, yes. When I was a kid, I looked into the mirror and saw earthy colors: forest green, sienna, and even gold. Now, I avoid my reflection, but there are times that I unintentionally catch a glimpse. Pillars of stones, slate-like boulders, and slabs of concrete make me now. But still, there are no hellions, no malignant fiends, and no brutish beasts. I'm not much, but at least I'm not evil. But I can't say any of this to Jenna.

Soulseer23: *Souls can change over time, but I think there's something different about a soul that has the capacity to turn evil.*

Jennalivesfree: *Something inherent?*

Soulseer23: *I don't see what else it could be.*

Jennalivesfree: *Have you ever seen a baby with an evil soul?*

She brings up a good point. My cousin Skyler's soul looks like fuchsia missiles spewing multi-colored glitter. I wonder if there's any circumstance that could cause Skyler's missiles to trade their glitter for dynamite.

Soulseer23: *Not yet. My baby cousin's soul looks like a rainbow glitter bomb.*

Jennalivesfree: *That's such a creative way to describe it! Babies are so sweet and precious. Although I have to admit that glitter has become my worst nightmare. Use it once, and it haunts you for the rest of your life. A year ago, I customized my Keds with glitter stripes. Just last week, I found a few specks where the sun don't shine. And the other morning I woke up with one in my eye. You know I found out there's actually an online company that will mail glitter to your enemies.*

Soulseer23: *For real?*

Jennalivesfree: *I'm not even kidding. Google it.*

Soulseer23: *Shipyourenemiesglitter.com. You'd better stay on my good side!*

Jennalivesfree: *Haha. That would be evil! Which reminds me that we were discussing the origin of evil and got sidetracked. So, where do you think evil comes from?*

Soulseer23: *I'm not sure. Maybe evil is like a parasite, a contagious infection that latches on over time. Souls that touch* *often have a tendency of bleeding onto one another and changing each other over the years.*

Jennalivesfree: *That's an interesting theory. Hey, do you want to video chat? I want to see you while we ponder all the mysteries of the human psyche.*

A moment later, a pop-up box shows on my screen. *Jennalivesfree has invited you to video chat. To accept, click here.*

I'm frozen for a few moments. I can't refuse. She'll know something's up. I'm also not ready to tell her who I am. Even with all her talk about acceptance, I don't believe she could be interested in a freak like me. Maybe she'll accept me, but she'll also feel bad for me. I don't want our friendship to be born out of pity.

I rummage through my desk drawers until I find a roll of scotch tape and a notepad. I tear off a corner scrap from the notepad, press it over the webcam lens with one hand, and secure it with the scotch tape with the other. This isn't my proudest moment, but I don't know what else I can do. I click accept.

Jenna appears on my screen. Her hair is pulled back in a messy ponytail, wayward tendrils frame her heart-shaped face. Through the computer, I can't see her aura, although if I focus, I can detect the slightest shimmer.

"Hey," I say.

"Oh, hi," Jenna says. "You're there. I can't see you. Can you see me?"

"Yeah," I say.

A crease appears between Jenna's brows as she clicks her mouse. "This is weird," she says. "I can hear you, but I can't see you."

"Hmmm. My webcam is on. I just checked." I'm not lying. My webcam *is* on. The fact that the lens is covered by a tiny piece of opaque paper is a detail I neglected to mention. "Can you see me now?"

"Not unless you look like a big black void," Jenna says.

"Not usually," I joke. "I must have forgotten to take off my invisibility cloak."

"A fellow Potter fan!" Jenna smiles, and the cutest little dimple indents her right cheek. "Although, technically, you're incorrect. The purpose of the invisibility cloak is to become invisible, meaning that you'd blend into your surroundings, whatever they may be. So, unless you've fallen inside a black hole, your invisibility cloak wouldn't have this effect."

"You're right," I say. "I guess my webcam is broken."

"Well, this isn't fair," Jenna says, folding her arms across her chest.

"I'm sorry," I say. "I understand if you don't want to talk anymore." Please, please, please still want to talk to me.

"No, I didn't mean that," Jenna says, her brown eyes widening. "I like talking to you. I hope we can be friends. But first, there are some things that you should know. One: I've been known to do outlandish things, even in public. If you embarrass easily, we probably won't get along. Two: for the most part, I say whatever pops into my head. I won't filter my thoughts or opinions to please you, but I do try to be cognizant of not offending anyone. Three: I'll apologize if I'm wrong, but I won't apologize for being who I am."

"Okay, that's cool."

"Awesome, I'm glad we got that out of the way. Now we can resume."

"Did I just, like, consent to your terms and conditions?"

Jenna laughs. "You did. So now it's your turn."

"My turn?"

"Are there any stipulations associated with your friendship?"

Yes, I think, there's a few. There's a high probability that I'll melt down in a crowded area, so no sporting events, concerts, or really any venue where I might be exposed to other living human beings. Also, absolutely no eye contact. That won't be safe for you.

"I'd rather not..." I pause. "Um—"

"Let me finish for you," Jenna says, apparently growing impatient with my loss for words. "You'd rather start off our relationship under false pretenses by showing me only your very best qualities. Inevitably, your flaws will come out, but slowly over a long period, when hopefully I'll already like you enough not to care."

"Um, how'd you know?" I ask.

"Because you're not the first male specimen I've encountered," Jenna says. "I've dealt with your kind before." The light in her eyes and tone of her voice lets me know she's teasing.

"It's not that I want to deceive you," I say. "It's just, I'm, um, I don't know, insecure, I guess."

"You all are!" Jenna says. "I think it's written somewhere in your DNA. You and your fragile egos." Jenna shakes her head. "Although I've got to admit, I'm impressed that you admitted your insecurity so readily. That's a step in the right direction. I'll crack you soon enough."

"I'm not sure I like the idea of being cracked."

"I didn't mean that I was going to crack you in the face. Crack can have many meanings. Well, what I meant was crack you, like an egg. Open you up, figure you out."

"You might find that I'm a tough nut to crack."

"Give me time, and I'll crack your code. But for now, let's chat about enigmatic and fantastical things." Jenna says.

"Sounds good to me."

And so, we talk. We talk about souls and spirits and parallel universes. Jenna asks a lot of questions. She seems to have an infinite supply. None of her questions are generic. She doesn't ask, "What's your favorite color?" or "What kind of music do you like?" Her questions are deeper, more thought-provoking. "What would you do if an alien spaceship landed in your backyard?" and "Do you believe in reincarnation?"

As our conversation continues, I'm surprised by how much I like answering them. Other than, "What's your problem?" I haven't been asked many questions over the years. Now that I have the opportunity, I like talking about myself. Jenna wants to know me—my thoughts, my ideas, my opinions, and my philosophies.

I've spent most of my life hiding, guarded, head down, and walls up around me. Even I forgot there's so much more to me than that. Although my experiences with the outside world are limited, I've read a ton of books, watched even more movies, and listened to hundreds of hours of music and podcasts. Along the way, I developed a unique outlook, viewpoints, and theories that are my own and worth sharing. I'm not just a freak. I'm more than that.

As the hours pass like seconds, I can't believe that I've done just as much talking, maybe even *more* talking than

Jenna. We discover that we're both die-hard Yankee fans and are discussing the likelihood of them making the World Series when I check the clock.

"Did you know it's four in the morning?" I ask.

"What?" She jerks her head and gapes at the clock. "That's crazy. I had no idea."

"My alarm goes off in three hours."

"Yeah, same. I guess we should try to get a couple hours of sleep."

"I guess so," I say.

"But I don't really want to go," she says.

"Me either."

"I really like your voice," she says.

"I like yours, too." Jenna's voice is throaty, almost sultry.

"So, I guess this is goodnight, um, oh man, I just realized that you never told me your name!"

"Oh, um, yeah, I guess I never did," I say, my mind racing with ideas on how to get out of this one. I'm the only Ethan in school. If I tell her my name, she'll find out who I am.

"What is it?" Jenna asks.

"What's what?" I ask back, a pathetic attempt at buying time.

"Your name!" she says.

"Oh, um, um, Michael." I'm becoming an expert at lying without lying. Michael is my middle name. Jenna hadn't specified that she wants to know my first name. I know it's a stretch, but I'm also getting better at justifying my misdoings when it comes to preserving my relationship with Jenna.

"Michael," Jenna repeats. "Do people call you Mike?"

"No," I say. Still not a liar! Okay, I know, I know. I'm a liar. Like I said before, these are not my proudest moments.

"Okay, goodnight, Michael. I really enjoyed talking to you. Will you find me tomorrow at lunch?"

"Um, yeah," I say, because what else can I say? "Goodnight, Jenna."

I close my computer and pull my blanket over my head. I should just disappear, never talk to Jenna again, and save myself a lot of heartache.

And yet, I know that I can't do that. I want her to get to know me, the real me, not the part of me that's flawed. I want to know everything about her, even the smallest details that seem not to matter, but they'd matter to me. And then, in my wildest dreams, we'd fall in love.

But first I have to meet her for lunch in a crowded cafeteria. I have less than eight hours to figure out how I'm supposed to pull that off.

6

Michael who?

Jenna

"Jenna, wake up!" I drift in and out of consciousness, vaguely aware of my mom shouting over a blaring alarm. "Jenna, it's time to get up!"

I sleep like the dead. One of these days, I might be mistaken for a vampire and get staked in the heart. "I'm trying," I mutter, willing my eyes to open even as the peaceful comfort of slumber descends upon me, rendering me powerless, my limbs immobilized.

"Jenna!" I can sleep through almost anything. After all, I'd spent my entire life in a busy city. From infancy, alarms, police sirens, horns, and drunken shouts were the lullaby that rocked me into oblivion. "You're going to be late for school!"

School. Today. Memories of last night's conversation rush through my groggy brain. Michael. I shoot upright in bed, swing my legs over the side and jump to my feet.

My mom's brow furrows. "That was a quick turnaround," she says. I'm already racing around my bedroom, foraging through my drawers for my lucky Yankees t-shirt. "Jenna, I wanted to say that I'm sorry about last night." My mom shifts her weight from one foot to the other. She holds a teacup in each hand, offering one to me. "This tea helps diffuse stress and tensions."

I grab the teacup and take a sip. "It works." I shake out my shoulders. "No more tension."

"I've just been, you know, stressed. Starting a new job, moving to a new place… I just haven't been myself lately. But you're right, it isn't fair to ask you to take sides."

I study my tea. "Damn," I grin. "What is this magical potion? I might need to keep a secret stash for the next time you get crabby."

Mom laughs and pulls me in for a hug. I hug her back, my eyes widening as I notice the clock. I pull away. "Mom, it's cool. We're good." I grab a towel from the top of my dresser. "I have to shower. I might sleep like the undead, but that doesn't mean that I want to look like one." Especially not today.

I stand under the stream of hot water, clouds of white steam filling up the shower stall as I replay highlights of last night's conversation in my mind. I loved how he was game to answer all of my obscure questions. His responses were clever, thoughtful, and often funny. Michael even seemed excited to participate, which was refreshing. The last time I went on a date, the guy groaned every time I asked him anything that required more than a one-word response. Needless to say, that was our first and last date.

Most guys just don't get me. But maybe Michael will. I blast pop music all the way to school, singing at the top of my lungs and shoulder-shimmying as I pull into the parking lot.

As I walk toward my locker, my heart flutters. I told Michael to meet me at lunch, but maybe he'll find me before then. As I open my locker, anticipation courses hot through my veins. He could be watching me right now. Any moment now, he could approach and say, "Hey, Jenna, it's me."

I smooth my hair and walk to first period. I stand tall, my eyes darting from face to face, examining eyes and chins and lips and smiles, all the time wondering, are you Michael? Are you? Or you? I regret not asking what he looks like but discussing all the mystical things seemed so much more important at the time.

In between third and fourth period, Austin stops me in the hallway. "Hey, Jenna," he says. "Staying out of trouble?"

"So far," I say. "But the day is still young."

The boy who I saw getting beat up on Friday walks down the hallway. He stares at the floor, his hands wringing. I want to say hi and make sure he's okay, but he's moving too fast.

"What's his deal?" I ask.

"Who?" Austin jerks his head. "Oh, Ethan Underwood?" He shrugs. "He has mental problems."

I glance over my shoulder. When Ethan turns at the end of the hallway, I catch a peripheral view. Blonde waves fall over his eyes. A wireless earbud dangles from his ear. He probably wouldn't have heard me even if I said hi. Besides, he seems like the kind of guy who doesn't want to be bothered. It's a shame, really. He's cute.

The bell rings. "See you later, Austin." I jet to class.

When the lunch bell rings, my nerves lurch into overdrive. In just a few short minutes, I'll meet Michael. I enter the cafeteria, my heart pounding every time a boy passes by. I grab a tray and slide it along the lunch bar, my palms clammy as I scoop chicken fingers onto my plate. I pay, leave the line and lean against the cafeteria wall, my tray digging into my abdomen. I scan the tables, rows and rows of students laughing, sipping soda, and dabbing their French fries into ketchup.

A boy I don't recognize walks toward me. My breath hitches as I make eye contact with him, willing him to stop and say, "Hey, Jenna. Nice chat last night." Instead, he averts his eyes and joins another group of unfamiliar boys, greeting each of them with a special handshake.

When I told Saja I already met everyone in Roxbury, I knew I was overdramatizing, but I hadn't realized how much. Right now, I feel like everyone is a stranger. Where is Michael? My temper flares.

"Hey, Jenna." I spin around. Mia secures an unruly black curl behind her ear. "You can come sit with us," she says.

At that moment, I realize how I must look to Mia. The last time I saw her Carley was possessed by an evil demon inspired by the movie *Mean Girls*. When Mia saw me standing alone, probably looking awkward as hell, she must've thought I'd feel unwelcome at her table and have nowhere else to go. What Mia doesn't understand is that I have no problem butting into any conversation in this whole damn place. But I want to sit with Michael.

Unfortunately, Michael is Mia in all caps. (In other words, MIA. I can't help myself. I love puns!) "Okay, but I hope the demon has been excised from Carley's soul. I don't have time to perform an exorcism. My chicken is getting cold." We make our way toward the table. Carley is facing Elexis, engaged in conversation. When I'm sure Carley isn't watching, I bow my head and cross myself. Mia giggles.

As I pull out a seat, Carley glances up. Even though she doesn't say hi, I can already tell that she's over the supermarket dance party. She doesn't even need to say a word. If Carley doesn't want you around, she'll make sure you know. I doubt the demon was banished, but it seems to be dormant, at least at the moment.

I shove a piece of lukewarm chicken in my mouth as I scroll through my phone. I don't have Michael's phone number, so I can't call or text him. My only way of contacting him is through Mind-Reel. I log into the Mind-Reel app. Soulseer23 is offline. I message him, "Where are you? Take off your invisibility cloak and show yourself."

"Big game tonight," Elexis says, jutting her chin towards my Yankees t-shirt.

"Yeah," I say, my gaze roaming from table to table.

"If we win, we clinch a spot in the playoffs," Elexis says.

"Yeah," I say again.

"You're not too talkative," Elexis observes. "Is everything okay?"

"Not exactly," I admit.

"What's wrong?" Mia asks, her eyebrows lifting.

"I met this guy on Mind-Reel last night. He said he goes to school here. I told him to meet me at lunch, but there's no sign of him yet."

"That sucks," Mia says. "Sounds like a catfish."

"You think?" I ask. "Maybe he's shy."

"What's his name?" Carley leans forwards.

"Michael," I say.

"Michael what?" Carley asks.

"I don't know," I say, realizing how idiotic I sound. Why didn't I ask? "How many Michaels can there be?"

"I can think of two Mikes," Elexis says. "Chang and Welsh."

"There's also Michael Tavarez," Mia says.

"Tav?" Elexis asks. "No one calls him Michael."

"It can't be Tav," Carley says. "Tav's been texting me the past few days. He's not trying to hit up other girls." She purses her lips, considering, then pulls her phone out of her backpack. "I'll ask him right now."

I cross my fingers under the table, silently praying that Tav isn't my Michael. After Saturday, Carley and I are still on tenuous ground. If Tav is my Michael, that ground might just split open, revealing a gaping hell-mouth from which she-devil Carley emerges, hurling fireballs and pitchforks my way.

A few moments later, a boy with curly hair and a masculine jawline pulls up a chair beside Carley. "What's this about?" he asks, reading from his phone. "I need to speak to you immediately."

"Did you contact Jenna last night?" Carley asks.

Tav's brow furrows. "Who's Jenna?"

"It's not him," I say. Tav jerks his head towards me. Carley's eyes widen with confusion. "I'd recognize his voice," I explain. "Where are Chang and Welsh?" I'm not going to wait around anymore. That's just not my style.

Elexis points out Mike Chang, and I'm on my way, crossing the cafeteria at supersonic speeds. Mike Chang seems like a nice guy, but he isn't my Michael. Besides, I'd only known him for about three minutes before it became fairly obvious that he's crazy about his friend Kristin. After Kristin directs me towards the table where Michael Welsh usually sits, I lean forward and whisper in Mike Chang's ear, "Stop being a wuss and tell her that you're madly in love with her. She's clearly into you, too."

Michael Welsh is absent. His friends tell me they were all playing online video games from 9pm until the wee hours of the morning, and Michael often skips school to sleep in after marathon gaming sessions. I blink as the alibi sinks in. Michael Welsh is not my Michael either.

The bell rings. My stomach drops. My neck swivels: frantic, jerky movements. Strangers rush by. Carley and Mia catch up with me as I merge with the crowd heading out the cafeteria doors. "What happened?" Mia asks. "Did you find him?"

I shrug, pretending it's no big deal. "Not yet. There has to be another Michael."

"I don't know of any," Carley says.

"But…" My voice drifts off. Last night, I felt an undeniable connection to him. But I can't make sense of why he isn't here today. Maybe he's a creep and a liar. Maybe he doesn't even go to school here.

I dig my phone out of my pocket and sign into my Mind-Reel app. Soulseer23 is still offline. He hasn't checked my last message.

I message him again. "I spent my entire lunch looking for you. Catfishing and standing people up you meet online isn't cool. I'm not sure what game you're playing, but you won't win. I will find out who you are."

1

The Comeback

Ethan

I'm an idiot. Worse than an idiot. I'm a lying, pathetic, despicable wimp. At the very least, if I wasn't the lowest scum of the earth, I would've sent a message to let her know that I wasn't in the cafeteria during lunch. Then she wouldn't have wasted her entire lunch hour searching for me.

I lean back in my desk chair, laptop open on my desk, hand pressed against my forehead. I read her messages for the hundred millionth time.

There's a knock on my bedroom door. "Ethan, are you okay? You barely ate at dinner." My mom's anxiety is like steel wool scrubbing off my skin.

"I'm fine, Mom," I can't stand it when she feels this way, especially when it's my fault. "I just have a lot of homework," I say. The scratching sensation eases.

"Okay, honey. I won't bother you." The sound of her footsteps disappears down the hall.

In the darkening room, my open laptop casts a beam of light across my face. I should probably just leave Jenna alone. She might even hate me already. But some for reason, I can't just let it go. I need to apologize. Even if she wants nothing to do with me, I have to tell her how I feel.

Soulseer23: *I'm sorry.*

Jennalivesfree: *Wow, look who finally resurfaced. What are you, a vampire? You only seem to emerge between dusk and dawn.*

Soulseer23: *Would that get me off the hook?*

Jennalivesfree: *Hardly. I was always Team Jacob.*

Soulseer23: *But I'm not talking about lame sparkly vampires. I'm talking about old-school bad-ass vampires like Dracula or Blade.*

Jennalivesfree: *Blade can go outside during daylight, so he would've met me in the cafeteria. Which brings us back to the topic of concern. What happened today?*

I stare at the screen until it looks blurry, my heart thumping in my chest.

Jennalivesfree: *Helllloooo? Have you disappeared again? You have thirty seconds to explain yourself before I sign off.*

Soulseer23: *It's kind of complicated.*

Jennalivesfree has invited you to video chat. To accept, click here.

The tiny piece of paper still obstructs my webcam. I inhale in a gulp of oxygen and click accept. Jenna appears on my screen, and my lips instantly curve up. For a few moments, I forget my nerves. I just watch her, smiling like a dope.

"Hello?" Jenna says, her brows moving together as she reaches for her mouse. "Are you there?"

"Hi," I say. "I'm here."

"Hi Michael," she says, and I feel a hard pang in my chest. It hurts, hearing her call me by another name. More than anything, I want to hear her say my name. I imagine Ethan rolling off her lips, and chills race down my spine. "In my experience, complicated excuses can be quite verbose and may be better presented orally. I also figured that if you tried to type all that out, you may be putting yourself at risk for a hand cramp and possibly even carpal tunnel syndrome."

I grin. "I appreciate the concern. My joints thank you." I pause, blood rushing through my ears as I try to formulate my defense. I beg my brain to function, but I keep blanking out. "Um," I say. "Um, um…"

"Game's back on. Wait until the next commercial. I can't focus right now."

"Game?" I ask.

"What kind of fan are you?" Jenna accuses. "Yankees-Red Sox, hello! It's the last inning. Yankees are down by two, and we're up to bat. Two outs, man on second."

I grab my remote and flick on the television. I'd been so preoccupied that I completely forgot the game. Aaron Judge takes his position at bat, digging his cleats into the dirt. "Come on, Judge," I say. Then, he slams one into left field. The ball bounces away from a frenzied fielder as Judge rounds first base. "Yes! All rise!" I jump to my feet and Jenna smiles, striking a pretend gavel.

There are batters on first and third base when Gardner trots to the plate. The Yankees have a chance to win this.

After two strikes, Jenna and I are both silent. This next pitch means everything. As the pitcher releases, I watch, my teeth clenched, the ball seeming to rotate in slow motion. Crack! Gardner blasts it into the upper deck in right. "Gardy went yardy!" I shout as the players score, winning the game and clinching the Yankees spot in the playoffs.

Jenna performs a celebration dance around her bedroom: her shoulders popping and head sliding back and forth. When she returns to her seat beside the computer, she's flushed and out of breath.

"I can't believe they just pulled that off," I say.

"I can. I knew they'd come back," she pants. "Anyways, what were you saying before we got distracted by this epic victory?"

"Hmmm," I say. "Don't remember. Maybe we should just talk about something else?"

"Nice try, buddy," Jenna's voice takes on a playful scolding tone. "I am stoked that the Yankees won, but that doesn't mean I forgot you blew me off today."

"I'm sorry. I didn't mean to," I say.

"Then why did you?" Jenna asks.

I have no idea how to explain that I can't enter the cafeteria. Every time I've tried, I was bombarded by heinous creatures and flying sinister objects. I'd have to tell her that when I mentioned I see souls, I meant it literally. She'd have to understand that seeing souls is not as cool as it sounds. Of course, there are good souls— I've seen many beautiful, enchanting, even mesmerizing souls. But those aren't the souls that swarm aggressively, consuming my being every time I enter a crowded place.

If I say any of this, she'll think I'm insane and run for the hills. "Hello!" Jenna says. "Are you there? I'm not getting any younger. This question shouldn't be that hard."

"I'm sorry. But, but... I was scared." It isn't a lie. "You might not like me in person."

"You shouldn't be scared," Jenna says, her voice softening. "I already like you. A lot. Even if you're twinning with a clown-faced ogre, I'll still like you."

Great. Now she thinks I'm hideous. "That's not it," I say. "I'm just, I, um, I really like you Jenna and I don't want to ruin everything."

"You won't," The way she says it, with such confidence, almost makes me believe it. "Listen, I get it, you're feeling self-conscious. I've felt that way before."

"You have?" I ask.

"Yeah, for like two or three seconds." Jenna laughs. "Seriously, though, I get self-conscious too. Everyone does. I just don't let it overpower me."

"Yeah, I admire that about you," I say. "I think you're incredible."

Jenna smiles, and that adorable dimple emerges on her right cheek. "You're sweet," she says.

"Does that mean you forgive me?" I ask.

"That depends," Jenna says. "Are you going to chat with me about all of the mystical things?"

"I would love to," I say. We discuss the mystery of the Bermuda triangle. I believe the missing persons were victims of bad weather or technical malfunctions. Jenna thinks they were sucked inside a portal that led to the lost city of Atlantis. Today, they've all been granted immortality and are living like royalty in a utopian magical land.

Jenna tells me she believes shooting stars have magical powers. Once, when her dad was gone for too long, she spotted a shooting star and wished for his return. The following morning, Jenna was still in bed when she heard his key jiggling inside the front doorknob. Jenna sprung to her feet, whispered "Thank you" to the brightening sky outside her window, raced down the hallway, and flung herself into his arms. Lately, Jenna spends a lot of time scanning the sky, waiting for that streak of light, for the heavenly body that might bring her dad home again. Even through the computer, I can feel how much Jenna misses her dad. Whenever she talks about him, my chest aches, like a piece of my heart is caving in on itself.

It's been years since I've talked about my dad, but with Jenna, it's easy to open up. I tell her that he left us one summer day without warning, and we never heard from him again. I only know he's alive and has a new family from spying on Facebook. I don't tell her that I'm the reason he left. My outbursts were too much for him to handle. He wanted a normal son. I didn't fit the bill. Based on his smiling Facebook photos, his new son hasn't disappointed him.

"It's three-thirty in the morning, and we barely slept last night." Jenna rubs her eyes. "I'm exhausted, but I love talking to you."

"I love talking to you too," I say.

"So then let's talk again tomorrow," Jenna says. "At lunch."

"I, um, I can't," I won't let her waste another lunch period trying to find me.

"What's your problem?"

"It's just that, um, there's too many people around and…"

"So, you don't want to meet me at school because you're worried about people gossiping?"

"Um, sort of. That's part of it."

Jenna rolls her eyes. "Just so you know, I couldn't care less what anyone says, but if it makes you more comfortable, we can meet outside of school. How about Vinny's pizza?"

"Um, I can't," I say.

"I'm starting to think that you don't want to meet me," Her voice fades.

"No, of course I want to meet you. I don't want you to think that."

"Then come to Vinny's pizza tomorrow at six," Jenna says, her eyes wide, her lips parted.

"Okay," I hear myself saying.

"Awesome," Jenna smiles even as her eyelids droop. "Goodnight, Michael."

"Goodnight," I say. The screen turns black. Hours pass. Birds chirp outside my window. The sun's rays permeate the glass, flitting across my bedsheets. When my alarm sounds, I'm still awake.

8

Winged Hyenas

Ethan

Kira slides into the chair beside me. I cringe. It's happening faster than I expected. I can see the snake bites on her collarbones; strangulation marks on her neck. Her soul animal, the burgundy sparrow, clings to her shoulder, looking sick. Half of her feathers are gone; the ones that remain are bent and missing barbs.

"Kira, are you okay?" I ask.

She stares at the table. "I'm fine."

"Kira," I pause, not sure how far to take this. "I care about you, okay? If something's wrong, you can tell me."

Her chin rises. For the briefest moment, I see the flicker of her golden sunshine. She opens her mouth as if to speak. Then snaps it shut. "I'm fine," she repeats.

In between classes, I feel Jenna's presence in the hallway. The electricity jolts down my spine, and I can't help myself. I look up and catch a glimpse of her white stars and shining blue waves.

Puffs of green smoke materialize as Carley Jenkins falls in step beside her. Carley whispers something to Jenna and they both laugh. Carley's green invades her edges, polluting the vibrant blues-violets, muddying them into a dulled olive.

Carley waves as she disappears through a classroom door, the putrid greens following her inside. Jenna glows again like amethysts. For now.

I wonder why good people choose to associate with bad people. Maybe they don't realize how much other people's energy can transform their own. Do they feel it happening slowly over time and allow it? Or are they unaware until one morning they wake up, irrevocably changed?

Jenna sees me and offers a friendly smile, her lips curling up beneath the indigo haze. I can't help but smile back, grinning stupidly in the hallway, forgetting to keep my head down, completely unaware of any soul other than hers. I want to tell her right here and now, "It's me. My name isn't Michael. I'm sorry I lied." But I don't. I'm a coward. She walks by.

When the lunch bell rings, I take two left turns and walk down the hallway toward the cafeteria. I pass the crowded lunchroom and enter the computer lab three doors down. Alex stares at a screen, a sandwich in his hand.

"Hey, Alex," I say, pulling up a chair beside him.

"Hey. I wasn't expecting you." He rakes his hand through his hair, leaving it standing on end. I know that schedule changes can fluster him, and I suddenly feel bad.

"Sorry. I just wanted to talk for a few minutes," I say. "What are you up to?"

"I'm working on Mind-Travel," Alex says. "Mr. Soto said he may nominate me to participate in the Young App

Developers fair. High school students compete from all around the country, and this year it's being held in New York."

"That's awesome!"

"Yes, but there's a chance he may choose someone else."

"Who could possibly beat you?"

"Luke Parker," Alex says.

My blood heats in my veins. "What's his project about?"

"I don't know. He's very secretive about it. The only person who's seen it is Mr. Soto, and he's very impressed."

I clench my fists. "You'll destroy him. You're a genius!"

"Luke and I have the same IQ."

"Nothing about you is the same as Luke!"

"Sometimes it's hard to recognize things that are the same. Did you know that both diamond and graphite are made entirely of carbon?" Alex asks. "The only difference between your pencil tip and a sparkly diamond is atomic structure. In diamonds, the carbon atoms bond in three dimensions, while the graphite forms in layers. The hardest known natural mineral and one of the softest are actually the same."

This makes me think of Jenna. She's the diamond: precious, sparkling, and strong. I'm a lump of graphite: weak and crumbling under pressure. Maybe if I peel back some of my layers, I'll find something that shines underneath. Something that could make me worthy of Jenna.

"Alex," I start, then pause. Alex has zero experience with girls, not to mention that social interaction isn't his forte. But I don't have anyone else to turn to for advice and this is the reason I interrupted his project time. "This girl I like invited me to Vinny's pizza. I don't know what to do."

"You like this girl, and you like pizza," Alex says. "I'm not sure I understand the problem."

"It's just... You know I have problems being around a lot of people. What if I freak out?"

Alex nods. He also has difficulty in crowded settings. At school assemblies, he used to sit in the back row, rocking, his ears covered by noise-canceling headphones. It's taken him years to learn to tolerate noisy settings, and he still doesn't like them. "Vinny's Pizzeria is approximately seven-hundred square feet. I think that the environment is small and controlled enough to avoid triggering hyperacusis. Based on my assessment of this setting and observations of your behavioral patterns, you have a high probability of success."

Except that my problem isn't hyperacusis. It only takes one nefarious soul to ruin everything for me. But I can't say that. "I'm just… I'm scared that she won't like me."

"She wouldn't have proposed pizza if she didn't like you."

"Yeah, until I totally blow it," I say. "What would you do if you were in my situation?"

"I wouldn't go to Vinny's pizza," Alex says.

"I thought you said I have a chance!" I throw my hands up.

"I have celiac disease and Vinny doesn't make gluten-free pizza. If I eat there, I'll get sick."

"What do you think I should do?" I re-phrase.

Alex turns bright red, realizing his mistake. "I think you should go. If she doesn't like you, that's her loss."

"She smiled at me in the hallway," I say.

"It seems like she likes you, and you like her," Alex says. "I don't see any reason for you not to go."

I stand up, swinging my backpack over my shoulder. "I think you're right," I say, moving towards the door. "Now get back to work and kick Luke's ass! His snakes can't help him with this!" Alex furrows his brow as I back out of the classroom door.

A few hours later, I approach my mom in our living room. Pastel pink and pale-yellow surround her slight frame as she lounges on the living room couch, reading a paperback. I clear my throat. "Um, Mom," I say. "Can you give me a ride to Vinny's pizza?"

She glances up. "Are you meeting Alex?"

"Um, no," I say. "Another friend."

Her colors brighten as she lowers her book to her lap. "Who?" Why are parents so nosy? And how pathetic is it that I only have one friend?

"Someone new to town," I say, keeping it as vague as possible. Part of me is bursting to talk about Jenna. I could go on and on about her for hours. But if I tell my mom too much, she'll become too invested. Then, if I fail, if Jenna doesn't like me, she'll be crushed.

When we pull into the parking lot, I check the time. As planned, we're fifteen minutes early. I want my mother to be gone before Jenna arrives for two reasons. One: it's embarrassing that I don't have my driver's license yet. It's too scary: the possibility of having an attack while on the road. Besides, it's not like my mom can afford to buy me a car. I know she struggles to make ends meet as a single parent. Two: I want to get there first, to settle into my surroundings and pull myself together before Jenna arrives.

I can't get out of the car. My legs feel like lead, my shoes like suction cups adhered to the floorboard. I don't think I can go through with it.

Then, I close my eyes and envision Jenna: vibrant blue, shimmering orange, blazing white stars, incandescent energy.

All that she possesses: her boldness, her courage, her volition, is all that I lack. Since I can't find my own strength, I channel hers. I imagine her teasing smile, the cute little dimple on her cheek, her throaty voice when she says, "I love talking to you."

I tear my resisting feet from the vehicle and step onto the concrete.

"Have fun with your friend, honey!" The glee in my mom's voice makes me cringe. "Call me if you need a ride home," she practically sings. If her son eating with another human is enough to elate her, I'm pitiful.

As my mom drives away, I drag my legs across the gravel, feeling their heaviness with every step. As I draw closer, I feel her. I panic. This isn't going according to plan. I'm supposed to arrive first, to get my bearings. The zaps of energy tingle along my hairline. The hum of her rhythmic melody reverberates within my ear canal. From there, I don't propel myself. I surrender to her essence. She carries me the rest of the way.

At the pizzeria's storefront, fear consumes me all over again. My heart beats faster than a runaway train and then I'm inside the runaway train, grasping onto the walls as a frenzied conductor pumps on malfunctioning brakes, a cliff just ahead. Yet, I can still feel her; she enters the train, unafraid, and although we accelerate, the precipice drawing closer, I feel safe. And then I lift my head, raise my chin up against that store window. Jenna is just on the other side of the window. She's even more striking up close. Her colors braid and unbraid, twisting and knotting around me, buzzing with crystalline light.

She sees me. She smiles. She lifts her hand. Her fingers flutter.

We launch over the edge together, floating through the train's window, holding hands, soaring, and then plunging fast, gloriously together. As I watch her through the glass, my lips parted in awe, my veins thrumming with a blissful delirium. For a few moments, I forget who and where I am. I forget that I'm the town loser, a freak, a pathetic joke.

I'm almost tempted to make direct eye contact, but luckily, I still have some sensibility. I point my gaze at her lips, admire her smile and the cute dimple on her right cheek. I immerse myself in the free-fall, the wind rushing between my fingertips, and the wind is all the colors of the night sky and the sunset, billowing together like the sails of a ship, gliding gracefully over the white crests of a stormy sea.

I wave right back to her. She tosses her hair behind her shoulders. Her smile widens. For those few moments, it's only me and her, nothing else in the world matters.

Something sharp jabs me in the side, and a dark tar-like substance closes in on me. I know who it is immediately. It's not the first time that I've encountered Cole's soul. In second grade, his winged hyenas surrounded me, their pointy teeth stabbing into my flesh, their loud wings flapping a piercing cry. I ran off the playground and into my teacher's arms, shaking and sputtering, flailing and wrenching, unable to shake the creatures from my body. That was the fourth time during that school year that I'd been inconsolable. The counselors, the teachers, the principal—they didn't understand. They couldn't see the varmints who feasted on my skin. As the paramedics strapped me to the gurney and the wails continued to erupt from my throat, the teachers exchanged pitying glances.

Of course, it had to be Cole. Of all of the billions of people, of all the infinite places, of all of the incalculable coordinates on this earth, the one and only Cole McFadden has to pass by my exact location at this exact moment. I doubt that even mathematical-genius Alex Tavarez could have determined the minuscule statistical improbability of this unfavorable occurrence. The universe must hate me more than I hate myself.

The hyenas hang back, cackling as they let the tar-like substance do their dirty work. The thick resin forces itself into my mouth, sucking the air from my lungs as the hyenas advance. I duck, but the hyenas are faster. One clamps down on my shoulder, and another tears into my shin. The tar oozes further through the passageways of my body, searing each cell it moves through.

I'd like to kick myself for letting my guard down. If only I'd been more alert, I would've sensed Cole coming, and maybe I could've been more prepared. Oh, who am I kidding? Cole's demons would've beaten me anyway.

Fight or flight mode kicks in. But I don't know how to fight something that isn't even tangible, figment beasts that somehow inflict pain more real than any I've ever felt. Before I can even make a conscious decision, I hear my sneakers colliding with the concrete. I run and I run and I run and I run and I run.

9

Vinny's Pizza

Jenna

I stare at the white spot on the window where his breath had been. Just a second ago, Ethan Underwood was here. He looked at me through coffee-brown eyes framed by long black lashes. Wisps of dirty-blonde waves peeked out from beneath his hoodie. He waved. He smiled. He didn't seem so psycho to me.

I watched the scene unfold as the two boys approached him from behind. I recognized Tav from school, but I didn't know the other boy—the boy who elbowed Ethan. I still didn't understand why or where Ethan went. Why he looked so scared. Why everyone is always picking on him.

The bell jangles overhead as Tav pushes open the pizzeria's door, the other red-headed boy trailing behind him. "Hey," Tav says, recognizing me as he walks inside. "Jenna, right?"

I square myself towards the two boys, my hands clenched at my side. My face flushes—my insides boil like the devil's pitchfork dipped in holy water. If staring daggers was a real thing, the red-headed jerk would be Swiss cheese. "Why did you elbow Ethan?"

Tav's eyes widen as he raises his hands as though he's under arrest. "What? I don't know what you're talking about."

"Not you," I wave my hand dismissively. "Him." I point at the redhead.

The redhead leans against the wall and his hands slip inside his jeans pockets, a nonchalant grin on his face. "Simmer down, sweetie. I didn't do nothing."

"I'm not your sweetie," I say, moving forward, contemplating slapping that arrogant expression off his slimy face. "Not even in your wildest dreams." Tav moves between us, gently placing his hand on my shoulder.

"Cole, what did you do?" Tav asks. His eyes narrow as he locks eyes with the other boy. Tav's exasperated tone tells me this isn't the first time he's had to mediate on Cole's behalf.

"I didn't do nothing," Cole repeats. "Don't listen to this crazy bitch."

"If you think that using derogatory language designed to insult, intimidate and silence females is going to shut me up, then you're both wrong and pathetic," I say.

"Jenna, tell me what happened," Tav says.

"Bro, nothing happened!" Cole's fists are balled up at his sides. Red splotches materialize on his neck, and a vein bulges on his forehead. I guess it only takes one insult to rile up the prick-head. Poor little fragile bully ego. Tav ignores him, his eyes focused on mine.

I inhale, my insides still exploding with red-hot waves of fury. "I was watching through the window when this guy," I point at Cole, "elbowed Ethan, and then, and then..." I can't explain it. "He did… I don't know what, but he did something terrible that scared Ethan."

"I didn't see him elbow anyone," Tav says.

"That's because Cole was behind you!" I say. "Why do you think Ethan ran away?"

Cole smirks. "Because he's bat-shit insane. Ever since pre-school, no one could control him. That loser's been chased by invisible shit since the day he was born."

I shake my head. "No, that's not true." I have no idea why I feel so strongly to defend an almost stranger, but I do.

"He's a freeaaakkk!" Cole's arms stretch out like Frankenstein, his eyes wide and gleeful.

Tav glares at his friend. "He has a disability," Tav snaps, his voice dropping an octave, his tone threatening. "Like my brother."

"Listen, man, I didn't say nothing about your brother," Cole says.

"Cole, can you get our pizza?" Tav nods towards the counter. For a few moments, Cole scowls. Tav stands tall, arms rigid, his chest puffed out. Next to Tav's muscular physique, Cole looks puny. The biggest part of Cole is his ugly mouth. The boys stare at each other, a stand-off of sorts.

Cole sighs, his shoulders dropping. "Alright, man." As he trudges past, his elbow juts out, inches from my side. He's not close enough to make contact, but the message is clear. Asshole.

As Cole approaches the register, Tav leans closer to me. "I'm sorry about that. Cole can be a real ass sometimes."

"Yeah, I noticed," I mutter. "Why do you hang out with him?"

"I've known him since I was, like, three," Tav says, as if that explains everything. "How do you know Ethan?"

"I don't know him well," I admit. "But I don't understand why everyone hates him so much."

"I don't hate him. I think Ethan's a good kid. He's friends with my brother, Alex. My brother has autism. Ethan comes over and plays video games sometimes."

"Does Ethan have autism, too?" I ask.

"I'm not sure. Something is going on with him. I don't know what it is exactly. People worry that he could be dangerous, but I don't think so."

Cole saunters past, a pizza box supported by his palms. "Let's go, bro," he says.

"See you around, Jenna," Tav says, with a quick salute as he heads towards the exit.

"Hey, Cole," I say.

Cole turns, his back against the door. "What?"

"I'll see you later tonight," I say, producing a coy smile.

"Huh?" Cole asks.

"Much later. When you're in bed."

"Oh yeah?" Cole raises his eyebrows.

"I didn't get a chance to tell you about my superpower," I say. "I'd much rather show you."

"Really?" Cole smiles suggestively. "In that case, I'll keep my bedroom window unlocked."

"No need," I say. "I don't need an entrance to sneak inside your dreams."

"What?" Cole's brow furrows.

"I've met every person that has ever crossed me in their dreams," I explain. "Then, let's just say that the lines between dream and reality blur, and it doesn't ever turn out well for my enemies."

Cole's mouth twists. "What do you think that you're some kind of female Freddy Krueger or something?"

I use my most demonic sing-song voice. "One, two, Jenna's coming for you…"

Cole snorts. "Lunatic," he mutters. "You and Ethan Underwood are perfect for one another."

"Three, four, better lock your door…"

Cole swings around too fast, accidentally banging his shoulder against the doorframe. "Bye, freak!"

I hope when he lays down tonight, his heart will race as he closes his eyes. I hope that each time he feels himself drifting into a dream, he jolts upright in bed, my image looming over him. The scumbag deserves to lose a few hours of sleep.

I slide back into the booth and check the time. 6:05. Michael's not here yet. It was the first time I was early for something in my entire life. And now he's late.

Minutes pass like eons. I can feel my hair turning gray, arthritis weaseling its way into my neck. At 6:09, I sign into Mind-Reel.

Jennalivesfree: Where are you? I'm waiting.

Jennalivesfree: If you don't answer in 5 seconds or less, I'm going to assume that on your way to meet me, a brain-sucking zombie feasted on your cerebellum, and then fed your remains to his pack of pet werewolves.

Jennalivesfree: It's been 5 seconds. Should I call the authorities?

Jennalivesfree: Helloooo?? Are you alive?

Jennalivesfree: *You're now 25 minutes late, and I'm officially pissed off.*

Jennalivesfree: *I can't believe that I've waited this long. Even the waitress is giving me sympathetic looks. Where the hell are you?*

He's standing me up. Again. Tears sting inside the corners of my eyes. I feel like a fool. I should've known. All the signs were there: his webcam not working, his reluctance to meet up in person. He probably doesn't even go to Roxbury High School. He might even be some old, creepy man.

And yet—he knows what Ms. Anderson's class is doing in Chemistry this week (although we aren't in the same period). And he doesn't sound old.

Last night, when I told Michael how much I miss my dad, he cared. His breath sharpened; his voice turned gravelly. It was almost like he could feel my pain.

Michael misses his dad too. Although he didn't say it, I got the impression that he blames himself for his dad's absence. As though he'd done something wrong—something that drove him away. As though he's ashamed of who he is.

I envision Ethan Underwood outside the restaurant window. He approached so cautiously—his hands stuffed inside his pockets, neck craned towards the ground, shoulders slumped inside his oversized sweatshirt.

Jennalivesfree: *Was that you outside before? Is your name Ethan Underwood?*

10

A cloud of dust

Ethan

Cole's hyenas are gone, fading once I'm a few blocks away. I run all the way home. The light is on in the kitchen, but I can't go inside yet. I'm not ready to face my mother. I can't bear to watch the colors of her aura turn drab, to feel the ache of her worry in my gut.

Instead, I tiptoe through the backyard and slip inside the dense thicket that surrounds our property. Moving through weeds and brush, thorns puncture my shirt, but I don't care. Leaves crunch under my sneakers. An owl hoots. A squirrel scampers up a tree. I drift effortlessly through the heavy tangle of bark and greenery that I know better than the back of my hand. I stop when I come to my spot, a long flat rock that borders a gurgling creek. I stretch myself out along the rock and check my phone.

Jenna has blown up my phone with Mind-Reel messages. I read her messages again and again. Especially the last one. *Is your name Ethan Underwood?*

She's angry. Rightfully so. I don't deserve her, not as a friend or in any other capacity in my life. As much as it kills me, I have to end it with her.

Soulseer23: *I'm sorry that I ruined your night. I won't bother you again.*

I shut off my phone. A frog croaks. Here, in the middle of the woods, far away from any humans, is the only place where I find peace.

An opossum sips from the creek. She bends over, her tongue darting into the water, unaware of my nearby presence. I take a few moments to gawk; she's something to behold. Thousands of squiggly lines rise from her, made from vibrant colors: neon pink, bright violet, sunflower yellow. She isn't what one would expect from an opossum; but then again, those who we expect the least from are those who surprise us the most.

I lean forward to get a better look, snapping a twig beneath my foot. The opossum shifts and bares her teeth. Her squiggly lines grow longer, extending high above her. She scampers away, an exquisite multi-color mane stretching out behind her, like a wavy rainbow following her as she disappears into the long grass.

I stay there for an hour, thinking about Jenna. I create another life in my head. In a parallel universe, I take Jenna by the hand and lead her out of Vinny's pizzeria. We vanish into the woods, breathless as we make our way up and over rock walls. We run until there's no sign of society, nothing to remind us of what we left behind. I use branches to build a shelter; Jenna weaves its roof from leaves and twigs. During the days, we fish, swim, climb trees, explore the forest and befriend the animals. At night, I hold her close. Staring up at the stars, we chat about all of the mystical things.

It could be perfect. I'd run away with Jenna in a heartbeat. Only it wouldn't be fair to her. Jenna's smart, funny, goal-oriented, and has so much to share with the world. It would be selfish of me to force her into reclusion, to keep her all for myself. Also, I couldn't leave my mom behind.

I picture my mom, pacing across the kitchen, checking the time, worrying that I've fallen into another one of my fits. At least I spared her that much tonight. I scoot off the rock and walk back to my house.

I push through the front door. My mom bounces into the room, her colors glimmering as she greets me. "How did it go, honey?"

I shrug. Her face falls. A murky residue coats her pastels, as though a gray cloud descended upon her. "Oh, honey." She puts her hand on my shoulder. "Do you want to talk about it?"

I shake my head. "I'm sorry," I say. All I ever do is fuck everything up. I go upstairs to my bedroom and shut the door.

I collapse onto my bed and pull the blankets over my head. Maybe if I hide for long enough, I'll disappear. Maybe the humiliation gouging my stomach and clawing my brain will eat me alive. Tomorrow morning, my mom will peel apart my self-made cocoon, and inside I'll be nothing but a cloud of dust.

11

Carpe Diem

Jenna

I arrive at school the next morning with a mission: find Ethan Underwood. I scour the hallways, craning my neck over groups of students, searching high and low for the boy I saw outside the pizzeria. Carley leans against her locker. Mia and Elexis huddle around her, laughing over a video on Mia's phone.

"Hey!" I say. "Have you seen Ethan Underwood? I need to find him."

Carley's face squishes up into a parody of disgust. "Why?"

"Because I think he's the guy I've been talking to online," I say. Mia's mouth forms an 'o'.

"Ethan Underwood talks?" Elexis asks, her eyes wide. "I don't think I've ever heard his voice."

"I've heard his scream." Carley snickers. "Jenna, I know you're new here so maybe you don't understand. Ethan Underwood's got major problems. You should stay far away from him."

"I didn't ask for your opinion. I asked if you know where he is." Any second now, the bell will ring.

"Thankfully not," Carley says. "Hopefully he fell off a cliff somewhere." She giggles.

I spin around, marching away with my fists clenched at my side. I don't have time for this. I need to find Ethan. In the middle of the hallway, I freeze, turning in every direction. Students swarm by, swinging their backpacks over their shoulders, groups splitting apart to move past me, creating a narrow ravine in the hallway.

The bell rings. My shoulders drop in defeat as I shift direction toward my first period class. "Take off your invisibility cloak, Ethan," I murmur under my breath, studying each face that moves by. I think about his reluctance to meet in person, about Cole and Carley and Elexis's reactions when I've mentioned his name. "I like you," I say, remembering our long, obscure conversations. "I don't care what anyone else thinks of you. Look at me, talking to myself in the hallways. You see, I'm crazy too." I grin.

From behind, a finger taps my shoulder. At that moment, I imagine our connection is so strong that somehow he heard me, my voice echoing in his thoughts, my soul pulling on his, like a magnet, drawing him to me. I turn, my heart clenching.

Instead, there's Mia, a stack of books held close to her chest. "Hey," Mia says. "I just wanted to tell you… um, about Ethan Underwood. I've passed him on my way to lunch. He leaves the building. He goes out the back door by the gym."

"Thanks," I say, and slip inside my first period class.

When the lunch bell rings, I spring out of my seat and sprint into the hallway. Students stare, but I don't care. Since my class is on the other side of the school, I have to make sure that I don't miss Ethan. As I zip around the corner, the back door comes into view. I see the boy's profile, his chin pointing at the floor. He pushes the door open, his back facing me as the door slams shut behind him.

I slow down, breathing heavily. For a few seconds, I doubt myself. Maybe Ethan isn't Michael. Maybe he's mentally disturbed or deranged or whatever everyone thinks about him. But something tells me that isn't the case.

My heart races as I fling open the back door. "Ethan!" I call as I step onto the sidewalk. He moves fast; he's already a good distance ahead of me. "Ethan!" I yell again. He disappears into the woods bordering the school.

I jog to catch up. Following a boy who might be insane into the thicket is unwise. This scenario is ripe for a horror movie plot, and I'm doing every stupid thing that I scream at the actresses for doing.

As my feet move forward, I wonder if I'm possessed. Nah, I'm just doing what my dad taught me: carpe diem. Seize the day. If only he seized more of those moments with me. I shake my head, removing my dad from my thoughts. Right now, I have one focus. Follow Ethan Underwood.

Ethan maneuvers quickly over rocks and through bushes. My breathing labors as I struggle to keep up. It's like he knows I'm trailing him and is trying to lose me. I duck beneath a tree branch and step over an abandoned hornet's nest. Ethan stands beside an old picnic table, his head bowed down.

"Jenna," he says. I don't know how he knows it's me; his gaze never left the ground. The second he speaks, relief floods through me. Ethan is Michael. I would've recognized his voice anywhere.

"I followed you," I blurt out.

"I know," Ethan says.

"You lied to me. Your name isn't Michael."

"I'm sorry." He stares at his sneakers, rolling twigs beneath his soles.

"Why did you lie?" I ask, stepping closer.

"Because I didn't want you to know the truth," he says. "That I'm a freak." His voice breaks at the end.

"No, you're not," I say, moving closer than I intended, closing the gap between us. I can feel his breath, our torsos practically touching.

"Everyone says so," Ethan murmurs, his voice softer than before.

"I don't believe what everyone says, and neither should you." I place my hand beneath his chin, prodding it upwards. "Look at me," I say.

Ethan jumps back. "I can't."

I'm not sure what happened. Maybe I'm coming on too strong. "I'm sorry."

"No, I'm sorry." Ethan digs his hands inside his jeans pockets. "This is why I'm a freak. It's why I said we shouldn't talk anymore."

I don't understand. He could have autism or an eye condition or a psychiatric disorder, and it wouldn't matter to me. As much as I want an answer, I decide not to prod. When he's ready, he'll tell me. I gesture to the wooden table. "Is this where you eat?"

"Yes," Ethan says.

"Do you mind if I join?" I ask.

"You want to?" he asks. "I mean, I wouldn't blame you if you didn't."

I plop onto the bench and retrieve my lunch from my backpack. "Yes, I want to eat lunch with the awesome guy that I love talking to so much that I've forgone two nights of sleep."

Ethan stands nearby, shifting from foot to foot.

"Just in case I wasn't perfectly clear, that's you," I say. "Sit your butt down and eat with me." I ramble on and on while Ethan stares at his uneaten sandwich. I can pretty much talk to a wall, so this isn't the difficult part. It hurts remembering the spark we had over the computer. Our witty banter, shared humor, and endless flow of words seem to have vanished. Poof and disappeared, like a fickle ghost.

After a while, Ethan looks up. Although he's not looking directly at me, at least I can see his face. Even in the chilly air, sweat beads along his brow. His dirty-blonde hair is damp and matted against his forehead. I keep jabbering about everything under the sun, pretending that I'm not studying his face: the angular curve of his jaw, straight nose, eyes the color of coffee.

Finally, he cracks a smile and interjects a few brief comments into my blabber. A few minutes later, he's full-on talking again, and the Ethan I met online is back. I'm laughing so hard that I choke on a piece of turkey and soda shoots out of my nose. Now that's what I call a great conversation.

"Last summer I read two of my mom's nursing textbooks in my spare time," I tell him. "I'm going to study pre-med in college. I want to be a surgeon one day."

"Really?" Ethan says. "You're so into the fantastical and supernatural. I didn't take you for a science person."

"Why can't I be both?" I ask.

Ethan shrugs. "I mean, sure, I guess you can be. I'm just surprised that's all."

"To me, they aren't different at all. Medicine is just a form of magic that we know the most about, that's all. Think about antibiotics. They're pills that contain tiny warriors that fight off infections that used to kill millions of people. If that's not a magical potion, I don't know what is."

"You make me see things differently," Ethan says. "That's one of the many things I like about you, Jenna."

"You do the same for me," I say. "So, what do you want to be?"

He looks down. "I don't know. Probably nothing."

"Nothing? Are you independently wealthy?" I joke.

Ethan clenches his fists. "A few years ago, my mom took me to see a therapist. Another one of her many attempts to fix me. After a session, I waited in the hallway while my mom spoke to the therapist. The walls were thin. I heard everything." Ethan sucks in a shaky breath. "The therapist told my mom that I would most likely never be employable and that I'll just have to collect permanent disability for the rest of my life."

My jaw drops. "That's awful!"

Ethan shrugs. "She may be right."

"She's not," I place my hand over his. He stares at our hands. I can feel the energy between us; it's electric. I intertwine my fingers through his.

Underneath the canopy of autumn leaves, school feels a million miles away. Drops of dew sparkle in the sunlight. Even the air seems to shimmer.

Ethan checks his watch. "We need to go back."

I can't hide my disappointment. I hoped that time would stop, at least for us, and we could stay in the woods for hours and hours, while the rest of the world melted away. Ethan leads the way back through the brush. As I push through the branches and place my feet on the sidewalk, I can't shake the feeling that I just passed into another realm, that the magic inside the woods can't come through here.

Ethan darts ahead, his long legs stretching out in quick strides. "Hey! Don't forget that I'm vertically challenged. I can't walk that fast." I say, jogging to keep up. "What's wrong? Do you have to pee or something?"

"You don't want to be seen with me," Ethan says.

"I don't appreciate you telling me what I want," I say. "Also, if you think you're a mind-reader, your skills need some honing." I lace my arm through his. "Now let's walk back to school together, and not at a break-neck speed, please. Contrary to popular opinion, I'm not actually Supergirl, although I do look damn good in a cape."

Ethan stops. "Jenna… If people see you with me… They're going to talk."

"Let them talk. Our forefathers died for our right to freedom of speech."

"But… I don't think you understand. I'm a pariah. I don't want anyone to treat you differently."

I shrug. "Their opinions don't matter to me." I pull him towards the school. "Let's go."

* * *

A few hours later, my biology notebook lays open on Mia's kitchen table. She reads a question from the review sheet. I search through my mental catalog of biology terms but come up blank. All I can see in my mind's eye is Ethan, his tentative smile that faltered several times before it fully emerged, breathing warmth into the chilly autumn air, breaking through like the sun trickling between the leaves.

The doorbell rings and Carley marches into the kitchen. I resist the urge to groan. After the way she talked about Ethan, she's the last person I want to see. If only I possessed the power of teleportation, I would've been out of there in a nanosecond. I'd be sprawled out on a beach towel, ocean breeze cooling my sun-kissed skin, Ethan by my side…

Carley swings open the refrigerator and rummages around

"What's up?" Mia asks. "I didn't know you were coming over. Jenna and I are studying for our Bio test."

"I had to get out of there," Carley grumbles. Her auburn hair is matted with scraps of leaves; mud is caked onto the soles of her sneakers. It must've been a long hike through the woods to get here.

"Is everything okay?" Mia asks.

"The usual. Dad's drunk and yelling at everyone." She pulls a bottle of pink wine out of the refrigerator. "Rosé, anyone?"

Mia stands. "Carley, we can't. That's my mom's."

Carley shrugs. "It's been in the fridge for ages. She'll never notice. Your parents won't be home from work for hours."

I can see Mia backing down, her shoulders falling as she moves away from the refrigerator. Carley sets the bottle down, combing through a drawer until she retrieves a corkscrew. I stand up. "Carley, stop," I say. "Mia could get in trouble."

Carley rolls her eyes. "I think I know Mia's parents better than you do. I've been friends with her my whole life. You've known Mia for what? Five minutes. So seriously, stay out of it. I've had a rough day. I need something to relax."

Carley pours the pink liquid into a glass, raises it to her lips, and takes a sip. I shake my head. "It's ironic that you're upset about your dad drinking, but your response is to start drinking yourself. That doesn't make a lot of sense."

Carley squares on me. "You know what really doesn't make sense? Going into the woods with a known psychopath."

"First of all, Ethan is not a psychopath. Negatively labeling a person because he seems different is ignorant. Second of all, diverting the topic to put me on the defensive doesn't make you right."

"You're such a know-it-all, but you don't know anything about Ethan. He *is* a psychopath, and he's ruined people's lives. If you look him in the eye, bad things will happen to you."

"Oh, please," I laugh. "And if you touch my pinky finger, rabid monkeys will fly out of your butt."

"I'm serious, Jenna. I've known Ethan since pre-school. He's dangerous."

"Oh, really?" I press my hands onto my hips. "Enlighten me."

"There's so many stories. I don't even know where to start." Carley says.

"I only want to hear hard facts. Spare me rumors or anecdotal observations."

"Okay, in third grade, Ethan Underwood and I were in Ms. Lynch's class. One day, Ms. Lynch's necklace disappeared. Apparently, it was a family heirloom that meant a lot to her. The chain had broken during class, and she put it in her desk drawer. At the end of the day, it was gone. She searched the classroom and asked all of the students if they'd seen it, but no one claimed to know anything.

"The next day, Isabella Stephano and I were playing truth-or-dare. I dared her to look Ethan in the eye. We cornered him, caught him when he least expected it. Isabella looked right at him. He tried to look away, but I held his head in place. You should have seen the scene he caused! He was screaming like a dying animal."

Fury boils in my gut. "And how does this make him a psycho? This only proves that you're a bully."

"I'm not done yet," Carley says, taking another swig of wine. "The next day, Ethan accused Isabella of stealing the necklace. Ms. Lynch searched her backpack. When she did, the necklace was found exactly where Ethan said it would be, inside a hidden pocket."

"So," I shrug. "Isabella is not only a bully but also a thief. I'm glad Ethan called her out."

"No, that's not how it happened!" Carley says. "Isn't it obvious? Ethan stole the necklace and then blamed Isabella to get back at her."

"About as obvious as the purpose of Stonehenge. Did it ever occur to you that maybe Isabella did steal the necklace? Or do you twist every story to fit your "Ethan Underwood is a maniac" narrative?"

"That's just one of a thousand creepy stories! Mia, do you remember when he accused Mr. Brophy of touching girls?"

Mia is seated at the table. She's still as a statue; her back rigid against the floral cushion. She stares at her textbook, wringing her hands. "Will you guys please stop? I'm trying to study."

Carley ignores her. "Mr. Brophy was the nicest guy in the world, and rich too. He bought a huge lot right up the way and built a big house and a ginormous pool. Since he didn't have his own family, Mr. Brophy welcomed everyone to his house. All summer long, the neighborhood kids would swim in his pool.

"My brothers and I would go there when my dad was being crazy, which was a lot. He'd strike up the grill and make hot dogs for all of us. He was a great guy. Mia used to hang out over there, too."

Carley glances over at Mia for support, but she's still pretending to be engrossed in her textbook. "Anyways, when we were in fifth grade, Ethan Underwood made up a disgusting lie about Mr. Brophy. He even called the police. When the police didn't do anything because there was no evidence whatsoever, he bashed Mr. Brophy all over social media. His reputation was shot. The poor man was so devastated that he sold his house and moved away."

"How do you know he wasn't guilty?" I ask.

"Jenna, I was at Mr. Brophy's house almost every day for two summers. He never once laid a hand on me. Ethan Underwood didn't even know Mr. Brophy. He couldn't even explain how he came up with his story."

"Why would Ethan make it up?"

"Because he's insane!" Carley flings her hands up. "He's delusional and fucked up in the head. Who knows why he does the things he does? All I know is that I'm staying far away from him. Elexis and I already talked about this, and we decided that we're not hanging out with you anymore if you're going to be around him."

I shrug. "Then I guess you won't be seeing me anymore."

Carley smirks, lifts her glass to her lips, and downs the rest of her wine. "You're right about that. So why do I still see you right now?" Viciousness encapsulates her, tension emanating throughout the room, spreading like smoke.

But I'm not backing down. "Because I'm here to study with Mia."

Carley faces Mia. "Are you really going to let her stay here and speak to me this way?"

Mia ruffles her hands through her hair; curls fall in front of her eyes. Her eyes look glassy. I really hope that she isn't going to cry. I'm not sure what we said to make her so upset. "I don't, I, um, I mean, can't you guys just drop this?"

"No," Carley says. "Either she goes, or I go."

Mia shifts her gaze from Carley to me, her forehead creasing.

"Seriously, Mia. Are you going to make me go home right now? You know how crazy my dad gets when he's drinking."

Mia's fingers twist into her curls. "Um, no, but—"

I toss my textbook inside my backpack and swing it over my shoulder. "I'm going to head out." I face Carley. "Not because you want me to, but because I can see how uncomfortable Mia feels right now. A good friend wouldn't put her in the position to have to choose."

I spin on my heel and walk out on the only girlfriends I have in this godforsaken two-horse town.

12

Force field

Ethan

The following morning, Kira pokes me in the arm. "Hey," she whispers. "I hear you've been hanging out with the new girl."

I'm surprised she's speaking to me. "News travels fast."

"I think she's cute." Kira smiles. A mass of black scribbles covers most of her glow, but I can still see golden strands shining underneath.

"She's beautiful," I say.

I hear the snakes hiss and then one slides down my spine. "Kira," Luke walks into the lab. "You didn't meet me at my locker."

Kira jolts to her feet. "I'm sorry," she says. "I thought you were mad at me."

He stands next to her, studying her. "I don't approve of the way you spoke to me last night," he says.

Kira looks down at her feet. "I'm sorry." A snake wriggles around her neck.

"But that doesn't mean that you can just blow me off and not come to my locker this morning."

Kira's face reddens, her hands out in front of her. "But you were so mad! I didn't know what to do."

"You have to use your common sense, Kira." He taps the side of her head, a little too hard. "You should have met me. I was waiting for you."

"I'm so sorry," Kira says. "It won't happen again."

As he kisses the top of her head, the snake tightens around her throat. "I know it won't. I can see you learned your lesson." When the bells ring, Luke leaves the classroom, but the snake stays behind, its fangs digging into Kira's jugular.

"Hey, are you okay?" I whisper as our teacher begins the lesson.

"Fine," Kira mumbles.

"Are you sure? You don't seem fine."

"I'm fine," Kira repeats, not bothering to disguise the annoyance in her tone. "Just stay out of it, Ethan."

"I want to help you."

"You can help me by minding your business."

At lunchtime, I settle on the old wooden bench. My brown paper bag crinkles as I reach inside and pull out my sandwich. Just yesterday, Jenna was at this table with me. When she smiled, I felt a rush of orange heat before her indigo swooped in like a cool breeze. When she laughed, stars swirled and glistened around me.

I wonder if she'll join me again today. A strong gust of wind captures my lunch bag; it floats into the sky and lands on a pile of leaves. As I bend over to retrieve it, another gale batters against my ear, tousling my hair, my sweatshirt billowing. I glance up at the darkening sky; gray clouds move over the canopy of rustling trees. A storm is on its way, closing in fast. I doubt Jenna will come out in this weather.

Shivers zig-zag up and down my spine, hot and cold, electric. My heart throbs and warm waves ebb and flow against my skin. Tendrils of blue-violet rope around the branches as Jenna steps between trees and into view.

"Hey," she says. A strong wind blasts through the woods. I secure my lunch bag with my palm as it balloons, threatening to fly away if I loosen my hold. "I wasn't sure that you'd be out here in this, but I'm glad you are." She slides into the seat across from me.

"I'm glad, too." This storm is nothing compared to the hell I'd experience inside the cafeteria, I think, but I don't say it aloud. I'm not ready to tell her everything, not yet. Sometimes, when the temperatures plummet, piles of snow rendering my rotting picnic table uninhabitable, I duck into the library. In the darkest corner, between bookshelves that tower to the ceiling, I eat alone. This winter, I wonder if Jenna might join me. I imagine us at that back table, inhaling the musky smell of old books as Jenna reaches for my hand.

A light drizzle begins, the mist sparkling in Jenna's aura. But why would *she* come out in this weather? Another thought occurs to me, one that has dread coursing through me. "Are your friends mad at you for hanging out with me?"

"Anyone who would be mad at me isn't really a friend."

"Jenna, this isn't what I want. I don't want to come between you and your friends."

Jenna shrugs. "Carley doesn't have much to offer as a friend anyway. Besides being beautiful, she doesn't have many redeeming qualities."

"You think Carley's beautiful?" I ask, incredulous.

"Yeah," Jenna says. "Come on. Unless you're blind, you have to know that Carley's gorgeous."

I envision Carley: the putrid green smoke and muddy splotches, and I think that everyone else must be blind. "I don't want you losing friends over me."

"I appreciate your concern, but Carley isn't someone that I want to be friends with anyway. I see some good in her, but her dark side overshadows the light."

"Like Two-Face?" I ask.

"Nah, more like there's a green-slime gurgling, jagged-yellow-teeth sneering, demon-faced succubus lurks inside her, just beneath her creamy flawless skin."

I laugh. "I've never heard descriptions quite like yours. Do you remember when you accused me of looking like a clown-faced ogre? That was a new one, too."

"That was only because I'd never seen your face. You can rest assured that I no longer suspect that you look like a clown-face ogre."

"That's good to hear," I say. "Because I lost a lot of sleep over that comment. Maybe that would explain why I never fit in. Maybe I really belong in the mountains with the ogres, or in a traveling circus with the clowns."

Jenna places her hand over mine. "Or maybe there's somewhere else where you belong."

A squall surges through, blowing Jenna's bag of chips across the table and onto the ground. We both scramble to our feet, but Jenna beats me. She stands in front of me, chips clutched against her chest. She steps closer, violet sparks whirring around me. Cold rain pelts us, but all I feel is heat.

She moves even closer, majestic violets encompassing us. Stars bounce off my shoulders, ricocheting from the trees. I can feel her eyes, studying me. I keep my eyes on the curve of her neck. Through the veil of colors, I can see her pulse, pattering away. "You're exquisite to me," Jenna says.

Exquisite is not a word I'd ever use to describe myself. It is, however, the perfect word to describe Jenna.

"It's like," Jenna starts, and then stops. "I don't know, this is going to sound weird. When I'm with you, I feel like I'm in a magnetic force field. Every atom around me is pushing me towards you."

I suck in a deep breath. Every word she says mirrors my feelings for her; if only I was articulate or brave enough to say it.

"But I like it," Jenna says. "It feels right. I'm trying to resist it because I don't want to scare you away."

She couldn't possibly scare me away. Is she out of her mind?

"I know, we barely know each other. I sound crazy, right?" Jenna says.

"No," I shake my head. "Not at all."

Jenna moves even closer. Every hair on my body sticks straight up. "I'm not good at holding back," Jenna says. "If I'm feeling something, I go for it. Act now, think later. Live free. But I don't want to do that with you. I don't want to make you uncomfortable and ruin everything."

She wraps her arms around my shoulders and presses her chest against mine. Our lips are inches apart. I'm speechless, reveling in the whirlpool of vibrant colors, the soft soothing melody that seems to synchronize with the beating of our hearts.

"If I'm too close, you can push me away," Jenna says.

I want to kiss her, but I'm too afraid. Luckily, Jenna is brave enough for both of us. Her lips press against mine. Euphoria bubbles hot in my veins, a sensation that overtakes each and every cell, one by one. Her blues and violets sink into my skin, their hues softening any sharp edges, easing away all tension or pain. Her stars shoot through me, exhilaration flooding in their wake.

When we finally separate, I realize that we're soaked. The world could've shattered around us, and I wouldn't have noticed. Rain plasters my hair to my scalp. Jenna's fingers are ice-cold against my neck. "That was incredible," I whisper.

Jenna lifts her chin to the sky; raindrops showering her cheeks. "The angels are crying." She smiles toward the heavens. "They must be happy tears. Nothing in the universe can be wrong right now."

And we kiss again.

13

Clairvoyance and Shaviah

Jenna

I pirouette around the kitchen counter, Purrscilla rubbing against my ankles. My phone buzzes in my pocket, and my heart flutters like angel wings in a hurricane. I hope it's Ethan.

Looking at the screen, my heart smacks against my ribcage. Dad! "Hey, stranger!" I say, ballerina twirling out of the kitchen and settling onto the couch.

"How's my beautiful daughter today?"

"Awesome, wonderful, amazing, and phenomenal. I'm on top of the world. This is probably what Wonder Woman felt like after she defeated Ares."

"So, you're liking the country better now?" Dad asks.

"I still miss the city," I admit. "But every day I find more reasons to like this area." I can think of a million reasons right now. Ethan and that kiss and Ethan and that kiss and Ethan and…

"I wanted to let you know that we're finishing up our tour. Just a couple more shows and I'll be on a plane back home." Dad says.

"Really?" I ask, the corners of my lips lifting. "I feel like you've been gone forever." Ninety-nine days, not that I've been counting or anything.

"I know. We're long overdue," Dad says. "I miss you, baby girl. Let me see, I'm flying in on Tuesday night. How about we hit a diner on Wednesday? I'll come pick you up around six?"

"Perfect," I wonder if all of this sudden good fortune is the result of stellar karma from risking my own life to spare that bunny, or if the planets have simply aligned in such a fashion that's unusually favorable to Taurus. Either way, I'll take it.

Just when I think things can't get any better, Saja announces that she's coming for an overnight visit. When she parks in front of my house on Saturday morning, I'm waiting outside. As soon as she steps out of her car, I maul her like a Chupacabra pouncing on its prey. I jump on her back, my legs gripping her waist, my arms wrapping over her shoulders. The sudden impact causes Saja to lose her balance, and we both topple to the ground. The sound of our laughter, dried leaves crumbling beneath us, and the wind chimes on the front porch intermingle to create the most magnificent melody.

"Geez, Jenna!" Saja says, between spouts of laughter. "Is body slamming an acceptable form of greeting out here in the country?"

"Only when my best friend in the entire galaxy shows up after an eternity apart."

"Slightly melodramatic," Saja smiles, rising to her feet and brushing brown bits from leaves off her jeans.

I stand beside her, sling my arm over her shoulder, and lead her to the house. "I thought that maybe you'd forget about me now that you have Javi."

"No way! I love Javi, but I still need my friends. And you, Jenna, are irreplaceable."

We spend the weekend like we used to: exploring our frontier and diving into our wild imaginations. The only difference is that instead of exploring the big city, we discover the wilderness in my backyard as we converse about life, love, and all of the creations inside our psyche.

As we walk along a winding trail, I tell Saja about Ethan and our amazing kiss. I tell her about his strange behaviors, how he was ostracized at school, and the accusations that Carley had made. As I speak out loud, the pieces seem to click together, and all of the clues I somehow missed before fall in place.

"I've figured it out!" I shout. A cardinal flies from her nest, a flurry of red wings decorating the periwinkle sky. "Ethan has a superpower! That's why he doesn't make eye contact!"

Saja giggles. "Yeah, he can like, shoot laser beams from his eyes."

"No, no," I say, my hand on Saja's arm. "I'm dead serious. I think if he makes eye contact, he sees things about people. That's how he knew that Isabella stole her teacher's necklace, and I bet that Brophy guy was molesting girls."

"I mean, I guess it's possible," Saja says. "Do you think he's psychic?"

I nod. "Yeah. I know it sounds crazy, but—"

"I don't know, Jenna," Saja says. "I know we love to chat about all this fantastical stuff, but this is real life, not a YA novel. I want you to be careful around this guy. I'm not sure if he's psychic or psycho."

From a logical standpoint, I know that she's right. It's more plausible that Ethan's eccentricities are the result of a mental illness than psychic ability. Though I must admit, I've never been the greatest fan of logic and even the most valid arguments would never convince me that Ethan isn't a superhero.

When my alarm goes off on Monday morning, I growl like a werewolf taking a silver bullet. My eyelids feel like they weigh a thousand tons; I struggle to pry them open. The night before, I lost track of time chatting with Ethan again. Even through the computer screen, he enraptures me completely. Our conversation lasted five hours and forty-six minutes, yet it felt like no time had passed at all. I mentally add making time fly faster than the speed of light to my growing list of Ethan's potential superpowers.

Even though it was nearly impossible to hold it in, I didn't ask him if he has psychic powers. I've decided I'll wait for Ethan to feel comfortable enough to tell me himself. Until then, I'll keep searching for clues that uncover the extent of his powers.

It seems to me that his voice is magical; I can't get enough of it. Just the sound of his laughter is enough to invigorate my soul. Could he be a vampire using mind control to make me feel so giddy? No, I've seen him eat food, so that can't be right. His smile bewitches me; every time his lips curve my heart launches into a tizzy. Could he be a wizard? My mind rakes through all the infinite possibilities as I get ready for school.

Somehow, I manage to make it to school looking halfway decent. Concealer has a magic all its own. Between third and fourth period, I'm inside a bathroom stall when I hear crying coming from another stall. The whimpers are audible even over the running faucet as I wash my hands.

As I shift from foot to foot, wondering if I should intervene, I notice another girl in the bathroom, long black braids to her waist. A crease emerges between her brows as she places her ear to the stall. "Hey, are you okay in there?" she asks, her voice soft.

"Fine," a choked voice answers.

"It's Shaviah. I'm here if you need to talk."

The late bell rings but I stay. "I'm fine," the voice repeats.

"You don't sound fine," Shaviah says. "Come out, and we'll talk about it." I hear the latch slide. The stall door swings open. A girl with burgundy hair steps out, mascara streaming down her face.

"Kira, I thought it was you. Are you okay?" Shaviah puts her arm around Kira's shoulders.

"I'm… I'm not sure," she says, wiping a tear. "Does this shirt make me look like a slut?"

I examine her pink V-neck sweater. It's form-fitting, but there's no cleavage. It barely even shows any collar bone.

"No!" Shaviah says. "Why would you ask that?"

Kira looks at the ground. "Someone told me that."

"Was that person a puritan who accidentally time-traveled here from the 17th century?" I ask. Kira notices me for the first time. She giggles and her eyebrow cocks into a quizzical expression. Even if she thinks I'm weird, I made her smile. Given the situation, I'll call that a win. "Don't worry about what some idiot says," I tell her. "You look great."

Kira shakes her head. "It's not that easy," she says. "It's someone I'm close with."

"Well, maybe reconsider how close you are with someone who talks to you like that," I say.

"I don't know…" Kira's voice trails off. "And it's just not the shirt… I just feel like, lately, this person has been criticizing everything I say or do. It just came out of nowhere. He used to be so nice to me. Now, he calls me stupid and ugly when he's mad."

"Is it Luke?" Shaviah asks.

Kira shakes her head too fast and raises her hands. "No, no, no, of course not." She swings her backpack over her shoulder, dropping her gaze to the floor. "Besides, I probably deserved it. I shouldn't have made him mad."

"You never deserve to be talked to that way," Shaviah says, shaking her head. "I'll never understand how human beings can treat someone they supposedly care about this way."

"Well, maybe this person isn't a human being. I mean, based on my limited knowledge of his behavior, it seems entirely possible that he's actually an evil mutant alien who masquerades as a human being and feeds off the misery he creates," I say.

Shaviah raises her brows, a curious expression on her face as she meets my eye. There's a long pause before she says, "I think that's a strong possibility."

"We should go," Kira says. "We're already late for class."

"What are you doing for lunch?" Shaviah asks Kira. "Come sit at my table. We're on the side by the double doors."

"Maybe," Kira looks thoughtful.

As the three of us enter the hallway, Shaviah turns to me. "I've heard about you. You're the girl who hangs out with Ethan Underwood, right?"

"Yep. I also answer to Jenna." I wait for Shaviah to lecture me about Ethan's mental issues and warn me to watch out for my safety like everyone else.

"Ethan… you know, he's always preferred to be alone. I'm glad he found someone he wants to hang with. That's cool." Shaviah says.

I smile. "I think so."

As we head in separate directions, Shaviah calls out, "Hey, Jenna, you're welcome to join us for lunch too, if you want."

When the lunch bell rings, I race across the school. Ethan stands outside the back doors, his neck craned forward, dark-blonde waves falling over his eyes, waiting for me. I burst through the doors, reach for his hand, and interlock my fingers with his.

"Hello," I say, and we walk towards the woods together, hand in hand, our steps in sync. "How's your day?"

He stares at our intertwined hands. "Right now, it couldn't be better," Ethan says. "What about you?"

"It's been an interesting day. I thought that Moaning Myrtle moved from Hogwarts to Roxbury," I say, referring to the character from Harry Potter, a series that Ethan and I have both reread a dozen times. "But it turned out that our bathroom wasn't being haunted. It was a human girl named Kira crying inside the stall. I wasn't sure what to do, but luckily a heroine named Shaviah came to the rescue. Shaviah seems awesome. I'd like to be friends with her."

"Is Kira okay?"

"I'm not sure. There's a toxic person in her life who's been hurting her," I say. "I could tell that Shaviah wants Kira to get out of that situation, so she invited Kira to sit with her at lunch." I pause. "Shaviah invited me to her lunch table too."

Ethan comes to such an abrupt stop that I'm jolted backward. "Why are you here?" he asks. "Go eat with Shaviah."

"Because I told you I'd meet you for lunch," I say.

"That doesn't matter," Ethan says, staring at his feet. He kicks a few pebbles across the sidewalk.

"I like spending time with you."

"I do, too. Of course, I do, Jenna." He takes a deep breath. "It's… It's just that it's not fair to you. I don't want you to isolate yourself and become a recluse like me."

"Isolating myself with you has been pretty awesome so far," I say.

"You might feel that now, but I know you well enough to know how important friends are to you." Ethan pauses. "Be honest. Do you want to eat with Shaviah?"

As much as I want to deny it, Ethan's right. Ever since Shaviah extended the invitation, I haven't stopped thinking about it. I love being with Ethan, but I want friends too. "I don't want to leave you all alone," I say.

"I'll be fine," Ethan says. "Go. If we keep stalling, lunch will be over before you get there."

"Okay," I relent, giving Ethan's hand one last squeeze. "I'll eat with Shaviah today. But even a pack of wild rabid werewolves won't keep me away tomorrow."

Ethan smiles. "Deal."

I lean in for a kiss. "I'll see you tomorrow," I promise. We pull apart, moving in separate directions. I glance over my shoulder one time, waving as I pull open the door. Ethan flashes one last smile but I can see the sadness in his eyes as the door closes between us.

14

Fake Love

Ethan

I'm worried about Kira. She looks worse than ever. When I try to talk to her, she ignores me. Her sparrow is gone, a possessive snake in its place. It hisses at me. I have to do something, but I don't know what. How do you help someone who doesn't want to be helped?

When the lunch bell rings, I'm worried that Jenna won't show. Maybe she had a blast with Shaviah at lunch yesterday and decided she doesn't want to hang out with a freak like me anymore. Last night, she didn't respond to my texts.

Jenna bounds around the corner, her stars blinking like strobe lights. She runs into my arms. "Hey," she says, pressing her lips against mine.

"Hey," I say. "It's good to see you."

"I'm sorry I didn't answer your texts last night," Jenna says. "I guess sleep deprivation finally caught up to me. I slept like Princess Aurora from seven o'clock until the sun rose this morning."

"It's okay. How was lunch with Shaviah?" I ask. Twigs crunch beneath my sneakers as we move towards the picnic table.

"Shaviah and her friends are really cool. Raven is writing a science fiction novel and is a total geek like me. Everly is boy-crazy, and Aaron is hilarious. This is going to sound strange, but I feel a connection with Shaviah, almost like a kinship. It feels like there's something inside us that's the same…not like sisters but maybe cousins or something…" Her voice trails off and she shakes her head. "I know it sounds weird. But I think you'd like the group. "

"Yeah, maybe," I say, sliding onto the old bench. "Did Kira come?"

Jenna shakes her head. "I wish she would've. I saw her across the cafeteria with some blonde guy. The way his hand was on her shoulder: it was like a vise grip. It gave me the creeps."

I sigh. "He creeps me out, too. I'm worried about Kira, but she won't listen to me."

"I'll try to talk to her," Jenna says and plops onto my lap. She kisses me. Chills sweep hot and cold up and down my spine. Every kiss is better than the last. We kiss and kiss and kiss. I never imagined that anything could feel this incredible. Jenna makes every iota of my being buzz with delirium.

When Jenna finally pulls away, she jumps to her feet. "Who are you?" Jenna asks, her hand on her chest.

Alex sits across from us, nonchalantly chewing his gluten-free sandwich. "My name is Alex Tavarez. It's a pleasure to make your acquaintance." Leave it to Alex to quietly observe a major make-out session and have no clue that was socially inappropriate.

"How did you like the show?" Jenna jokes.

Alex's brow furrows. "What show?"

"The one where I was examining Ethan's tonsils with my tongue."

Alex scratches his chin. "Is that what you were doing? I thought you were kissing."

I laugh. It's like Alex and Jenna speak different languages. "Jenna, this is my friend Alex. He eats with me twice a week. I was so distracted that I forgot what day it was."

Jenna sits down, opens her lunch bag, and pulls out a piece of pie. "My mom baked a vegan pumpkin pie. She hasn't mastered regular pies, so I'm not confident she'll do better with the vegan variety." Jenna shoves a big chunk of the pie in her mouth. As she swallows, her face twists into a grimace. "Ugh! Tastes like a pumpkin's ass!"

Alex looks genuinely perplexed. "I've never seen a pumpkin with buttocks."

Jenna's colorful, metaphorical dialogue and fascination with all of the mystical things doesn't quite mesh with Alex's literal and scientific perspective. For the time being, I'll be the translator. Over time, I hope they might learn to understand each other.

After lunch, Jenna whispers in my ear. "What're you doing after school? Do you want to hang out? Alone?"

I swallow. "Sure."

The rest of the day passes in a blur. When I get home, I vacuum, wipe down the kitchen, and order pizza. When the clock strikes five, my heart is racing. Flames lick my face and hot coals burn my insides, the heat intensifying with each second. My doorbell rings.

I jolt to my feet and unlock the door. Jenna fills my doorway, a wonder of light and energy, blue meteors circling shining amethysts. "Hey," I say. I lead her into the living room where Jenna promptly pops open the pizza box and tears off a slice.

"Where's your mom?" Jenna asks, her lips tearing into the cheesy dough.

"She's working. Ever since my dad left, she has to work two jobs. During the day, she's a receptionist for a construction company. Most nights she also waitresses at the diner."

We scarf down a few slices, and then Jenna asks for a tour of my house. After I show her around the first floor, Jenna asks to see the upstairs. Standing in the hallway, I push open the door to my bedroom. "This is my room."

Jenna peeks inside. Looking at my blank walls, a wave of embarrassment washes over me. For all these years, I've been nobody, my bare bedroom evidence of all of my shortcomings. Now I desperately wish that I'd been someone who could impress Jenna; somebody with a collection of cool artwork or rows of trophies lining their shelves. "And that's it for the tour," I say, turning back towards the stairs.

Jenna doesn't follow me. She marches into my room and collapses onto my bed, hair splaying out over my blue pillowcase. "What're you doing?" I ask, my heart thundering in my chest.

Jenna rolls onto her side, tosses her hair back, and flashes a flirty smile. "Want to make out?" she says.

I suck in a few unsteady breaths, willing my heart to slow down. I have to chill out, or Jenna will think I'm a loser.

I will my limbs to move, and a few moments later I manage to stagger through the doorway. I lower myself onto the bed, and stiffly stretch my legs out in front of me.

From the moment I lay down, she crawls on top of me, straddling me, kissing me. She runs her fingers through my hair, tugging on the ends, kissing me even harder. Then, she pulls away, staring at my face. I avert my gaze to avoid eye contact.

Jenna takes a deep breath. "I know this may sound crazy, but I'm going to say it anyway. If I feel something, I go for it. Carpe diem." She smiles. "I think I'm falling in love with you."

For a few moments, I'm shell-shocked. Jenna Farrell, the most amazing and beautiful creature to ever exist in this world, says she's falling in love with *me*, Ethan Underwood, a loser and a freak. How can this be true? The universe must be playing some kind of a sick joke on me.

I can't even fathom it.

Another thought hits me. How can she love me for me if she doesn't know who I am? I'm not sure if she understands that my condition is permanent, or if she'll be able to handle the long-term ramifications of being with someone like me.

"What's wrong?" Jenna asks. "I mean, it's okay if you don't feel the same way. I know it's soon." Her cheeks are bright red, and she looks away.

I'm at a loss for words. How can I accept her love when I don't trust that it's real? I don't want fake love. True love requires full disclosure and complete honesty. Truly knowing each other inside and out.

"Jenna," I say. "We don't know really know each other. There are things that you don't know about me."

"So then tell me. I want to know everything about you."

"I will, but…" I struggle to find the words. "I just can't."

"I see," Jenna says, standing up. She checks her watch. "It's getting late. I guess I should get going."

We share an awkward goodbye at the front door. When she leans in for a stiff hug, her oranges and indigos don't swirl around me. They keep their distance, an invisible wall separating them from me.

The door closes behind her, another wall between us. I saw the hurt on her face when she turned away. I should've explained better… I'm such an idiot. I just hope I didn't screw everything up for good.

15

Black Clouds and Torrential Rains

Jenna

When I wake up the next morning, my first thought is, *I made a fool of myself last night.* The humiliation actually makes me cringe. Tears burn in the corners of my eyes.

My second thought is: *My dad is coming to see me tonight!* I try to focus on that instead of dwelling on last night.

I eat lunch with Shaviah and her friends. Ethan and I agreed upon an every-other-day schedule. He always encourages me to spend time with my new friends. Probably so when he rejects me for good I won't be all alone.

I usually try to think positive, but it's hard right now. I can't believe that I told Ethan I'm falling in love with him so soon. I'm such an idiot. He probably thinks I'm a stage-five clinger.

After school, time seems to crawl slower than a shackled sloth. I count the seconds until dad will arrive. I close my eyes and picture him; his infectious smile, his calloused fingers strumming his old guitar. I miss him so much.

I've decided that the frenetic pace of the city overstimulated my dad, making it even harder for him to sit still. That's why he would blow through like a whirlwind, and when I blinked, he was gone again, swept up and away to somewhere else.

Tonight, in our yard, he'll feel free in the wide-open space. Unfettered by the claustrophobia-inducing city apartments and the labyrinth of buildings, my dad's adventurous spirit will have room to breathe.

After dinner, I'll bring him inside our country home. He'll take in the spacious rooms, their rustic details, the couch with two sunken-in cushions, and one that looked brand new. The well-worn floor will creak beneath his feet, and he'll never leave again. I can't wait.

When 6pm rolls around, I'm waiting on the front porch, Purrscilla curled up in my lap. By 6:15pm, I'm growing impatient, pacing like a caged lion, back and forth across the cedar planks. By 6:25pm, I've called my dad eighteen times and left five voice messages.

At 7pm, my mom asks me to come inside for dinner. I refuse, insisting that my dad is on his way. He must've hit traffic. Maybe he had an important meeting that ran late. He'll be here any minute. I know it.

By 7:30pm, the temperatures have dipped below freezing: an unseasonably cold night. I hold my hands to my lips; white breaths heat my numb fingertips. At 8pm, my mom tells me that I need to come inside before I freeze to death.

At 8:30pm, I come inside. I don't want to become hypothermic. "Jenna, you need to eat something," Mom says.

I take in a deep breath, holding back tears. "Okay," I say, trying to sound cheery. Mom is already angry enough at dad. If

I show how hurt I am, I'll be subjected to even more of her anti-dad rants. I can't deal with that. It's easier to pretend that everything is okay. In fact, everything is okay. It isn't a big deal.

"Did you hear from him?" Mom asks, sliding a plate in front of me.

"Yeah," I lie. "He got caught up with some important stuff."

"Sure," Mom says, settling into the seat across from me. "I'm sure it was urgent." The sarcasm in her tone can't be missed. Her phone buzzes. She smiles as she reads a text message.

"Is that dad?" I ask.

"Nope," she says. "I haven't heard from him in weeks."

"It'd better not be some other guy," I say. The one time my mom brought another man around I pitched a conniption that rivaled The Hulk.

"You don't get to dictate my love life," Mom says. "But if you must know, my sister shared a picture of her new kitten." Mom holds up her phone.

I grin. "I'm convinced that kittens are magical creatures sent from the heavens to lift our spirits. No matter how bad things seem, kittens always make it better."

Unfortunately, the kitten's magic is short-lived. By the time I crawl into bed, reality has set back in. In twenty-four hours, I was rejected twice. Tears spill down my cheeks.

I've never told anyone about all the times I cried. I've never admitted out loud how much my dad's disappearances hurt me. In the city, I broke down many times. All of those nights I fell asleep on a soaking wet pillow is between me and a spider named Charlotte. She spun her web in the far corner of my bedroom. We made a deal. As long as she kept my secret, we could coexist, and I wouldn't charge her rent. So far, she's proved trustworthy.

My mom thought that moving to the country would change things: that we wouldn't miss dad as much. She's wrong. Geography changes your physical location; it doesn't change your heart.

Tomorrow morning, I'll plaster a smile on my face. I've become an expert at pretending that I'm okay until I actually feel okay. I'll cover up my pain with quirky comments. I'll escape into daydreams about all of the mystical things and my future as a physician. And I'll be fine.

I check my phone one last time. No text messages. No missed calls. I close my eyes and will myself into oblivion.

The following day, black clouds and torrential rain match my mood. During the short walk from my front door to my car, my feet dredge through puddles and mud. Water seeps inside my sneakers; my socks are soaked. The soggy spaces between my toes itch. If only I had the power to fly I wouldn't have to worry about these mortal afflictions.

By fourth period, the rain shows no sign of letting up. I text Ethan.

Hey, I'm going to eat inside today. Even the mermaids are looking for umbrellas in this.
Okay. Is everything alright?
Yeah, fine.
I passed you in the hallway before. I just got a weird feeling that you're not okay.
How do you know what I am? I thought we don't know each other.

I immediately regret sending the text. Sometimes I'm too impulsive, like my dad.

I'm sorry. I'm just not in a good mood. I'll talk to you later.

After school, I run into Mia on my way to the parking lot. She holds her phone to her ear, her brow wrinkled.

"Hey, Mia," I say. "What's up?"

"Oh, hey," she says, lowering her phone. "I missed my bus. I'm trying to call my parents, but they're not picking up."

"Do you need a ride?"

"Yeah, actually. Thanks," Mia says.

A few minutes later, Mia settles into the passenger seat as I rev the engine. "So…" her voice trails off. "How's everything going with Ethan?"

"Okay, I guess." I twist my hair around my finger, remembering the sting of rejection. Then, a vision flickers in my psyche: his rumpled hair, his uncertain smile, the way his eyes light up when I take his hand. "I do like him. I know you and Carley think I'm crazy."

"I don't think you're crazy," Mia says.

I drive out of the parking lot. "You don't?" I ask. "I must've hallucinated that you were trying to convince me that Ethan is a psychotic freak."

"That was Carley, not me. I actually like Ethan. That's why I told you where to find him at lunch."

"You do?" My jaw hangs open. "I thought everyone in this whole town hated him."

"I don't think everyone hates him. I think they're afraid of him. Ethan knows things about people. Things that… people don't want known."

My fingers tremble against the steering wheel. This is the moment I've been waiting for. I need to find out what Mia knows. "How do you know?" I ask.

Mia doesn't respond. She stares out the passenger window, wringing her hands. Silence is a living, breathing thing. It's thick and serpentine, slithering throughout my car, squeezing into every empty crevice until it occupies all of the space, pressing against the glass, threatening to burst. This isn't ordinary silence; this is the kind of silence that reserves itself for moments when something is very, very wrong. I want to say something, anything to dissolve the heaviness that surrounds us, but words won't form in my throat. Finally, Mia speaks, "Because he knew about Mr. Brophy."

Realization sinks into me, and my heart is an ice cube melting in my chest, pumping frost through my veins. "Oh, Mia, I'm so sorry."

Mia's face falls into her palms; sobs escape from her throat. "No one else knows. Other than Ethan." Mia lifts her head and brushes the tears from her cheeks. "Ethan wanted me to go to the police. I wouldn't." Mia shakes her head. "Mr. Brophy said that he would hurt my family if I told anyone. He told me that it was my fault. He said that I seduced him."

Bile rises up in my throat. "No, Mia, nothing was your fault."

"But maybe I did do something wrong. Even Carley said that he never did anything to her. I was at his house a lot, more than any of the other kids. He made me feel so special." Mia's voice breaks. "But I shouldn't have gone over there alone in my bikini. He said that I tempted him."

I park in Mia's driveway, rain walloping against my windshield. "Don't let that sick bastard mind warp you into thinking that his barbaric actions were your fault! You were a child, and he was a deranged pedophile. That's the bottom line. There's nothing that you could've done differently that would've changed that."

Mia shrugs. "I guess, but I do regret not going to the police. And letting people think that Ethan was crazy when he was only defending me."

"You can still go to the police," I say.

"Yeah, right," Mia releases a bitter laugh. "They'll want to know why I waited so long, and why I didn't come forward before. They'll interrogate me; they'll call me a liar."

"You don't know that."

Mia shakes her head. "It's too late. I can't fix that now. But I can do something for Ethan. I owe him, after all. If it wasn't for Ethan, Mr. Brophy would've never moved away and I would've had to worry about seeing him around town, running into him in the supermarket..." Mia squeezes her eyes shut, as if even the thought of it is too much to bear. "That's why I told you where Ethan goes at lunch. It's also why I'm telling you this now. I don't want you to listen to any of the garbage that people talk about Ethan. None of it is true."

"I know," I say. "People hate what they can't understand."

"It's not just that," Mia says. "It's that... People work so hard on perfecting their façade, on creating an exterior that they're proud of, an outer coating for the rest of the world to see. But when Ethan Underwood looks at them, he sees right through that. He sees who they really are. That terrifies them."

I imagine Ethan's gaze piercing through me, my body translucent, his brown eyes seeing straight to my core. What do you see inside of me, Soulseer? "It terrifies me, too."

"It shouldn't. You're the only person I know who isn't pretending to be someone they're not."

Through the teeming rain, I see Mia's house. The driveway is empty. All of the windows are dark. "Are your parents' home?"

"No, they work late. Most nights they don't get home until I'm in bed."

"Do you mind if I come in? We could hang out for a while."

Mia's lips curve into a faint smile. "Sure, that sounds good."

16

All of our Secrets

Ethan

Jenna wants to know everything. She wants me to reveal my biggest secret, the one that I've kept for my entire life. And strangely, I want to tell her. I just don't have the words.

But with Mind-Reel, I don't need words. As twilight descends, I walk through the forest that is my backyard, climbing over dead branches and brush, onto the path that leads to the babbling brook. I sit on my rock, surveying the area. Within a few minutes, the bushes rustle and a familiar creature appears. It's the opossum, her beautiful squiggly neon lights streaming behind her. It's my lucky night.

I secure my Mind-Reel earpiece, log into the app, and for the very first time click "Create Reel." Between the tress, I glimpse a stag, silver flames bursting from his antlers in rhythm with a heavy metal/opera mash-up. Incredibly, I get the hell out of there unscathed.

The next morning, I text Jenna.

TGIF. What are you up to tonight?

Idk. I didn't want to commit to any plans because it's getting close to the full moon and there's a chance that I'll convert into my werewolf form.

Luckily, I'm pretty good with wild creatures. Actually, you'll understand that more once you see my reel. I made one for you last night.

Sweet! Is it posted on Mind-Reel? I'll check it out right now.

Actually, no. I didn't post it. It's a private reel. For your eyes only. It will help you understand my secret. I want to tell you everything.

Can you send it to me? I need to see it! Now!

I'd rather show you after school. You might have questions after you watch it. Can you hang out?

OMG after school? How am I supposed to wait that long? I might become the first documented case of death from being held in suspense.

You're strong, Jenna. I think you'll make it.

Haha. Okay, fine. Meet me in the parking lot at the end of the day. We can hang out at my house.

See you then.

At 3pm, we pull into Jenna's driveway, gravel flying as she jerks to a stop. "Show me now," she demands.

"Shouldn't we go inside first?"

"Okay, but that's the end of your stalling." I follow her up the steps, past the clanging wind chimes, and through the front door. She pulls me into the living room and leads me to the couch. "Now," she says.

"Okay." This is it. There's no turning back. I hand her my earpiece and start the reel. Jenna's eyes glaze over, her body stock-still, my palms dampening. She's in the reel, experiencing who I am. I have no idea how she'll react to my visions. Maybe she'll think I'm insane. I start to feel woozy and realize I've been holding my breath.

Finally, Jenna stirs, releasing a long breath as she removes the earpiece. "Wow," she says. "That deer's a bad-ass."

I laugh. "Yeah, but the opossum is my favorite."

"She's beautiful," Jenna agrees. "Was that her soul?"

"Something like that. It's her energy, and she doesn't always look exactly the same. Sometimes appearances change depending on the subject's state of mind."

"You're like a human mood ring."

"Sort of. But it's more complicated than that. Everyone has their own unique essence, and even though I may see slight changes in different circumstances, people's colors generally stay the same. When they do change, it's usually progressive, subtle shifts over very long periods."

Jenna nods. "But you don't just see energies. I heard and felt them, too."

"Yeah, I experience sight, sound, textures, smells, sometimes even pain. I never know what to expect when I come into contact with someone new."

"So that's why you don't like to be in public. You're accosted by all of these sensations. It must drive you crazy."

I swallow hard. Tears well up in my eyes, blurring my vision. It's the first time that anyone ever understood. "It's impossible to live with this." As much as I try to control my emotions, my voice breaks, exposing how weak I am. How defeated. I could've died of embarrassment. Jenna must think I'm the most pathetic person in existence. Way to go, loser.

I feel Jenna's arms wrap around me, her head on my shoulder. Electricity zaps up and down my spine. Silky strands of hair tickle underneath my chin. I inhale hard, sucking her into me, lights and stars and sparks and all.

"How do you function at all?" Jenna asks. "Like, at school?" Her voice conveys something like awe. Of me. In all of the hours that I spent imagining her possible reactions, I never cataloged this, not even in my 'best case scenarios' file. The most that I hoped for was acceptance. I hadn't dreamed of anything more. She traces my jawline, the curve around my ear. I tremble.

Jenna somehow feels admiration for me. I sense it in her delicate touch, in the purr-like undercurrent that accompanies her soothing melody, vibrating gently around me. Suddenly, I'm compelled to tell her everything, even the most embarrassing stuff.

"Over the years, I've learned some tricks," I explain. "Staring at the floor and trying to keep my mind occupied on other things helps. The more attention I pay to the visions, the more they seem to take over. The scariest stuff is always the hardest to block out.

"When I was younger, I was a mess. Several times a month, my mom had to pick me up at school because I was freaking out. A few times, the school nurse called the ambulance because my vitals were so out of whack, and I was inconsolable. I've been wheeled out on a stretcher more times than I can count… And believe me, the hospital is the absolute worst place in the world for someone like me.

"But luckily, I've gotten a lot better. It's still hard to be in crowded places, but I just avoid them if I can. For the few minutes in the hallways, I can hold it together. The cafeteria for an entire period…there's still no way."

"You've overcome so much…" Jenna's voice trails off. "You're incredible." She kisses me, her lips supple against mine.

"No, I'm not," I say, between kisses. "But I'm glad you think so."

"I think you're a superhero," Jenna says. She kisses my neck, and goosebumps rise on my flesh. Her breath is hot against my ear.

"More like a super freak," I say. "I'm going to tell you everything. There's more. I don't just see auras. When I look directly into someone's eyes, I see their most private moments."

Jenna nods, her brow furrows and then un-creases, as though she's found clarity on a very perplexing issue. "That's how you knew about Mr. Brophy. You looked into Mia's eyes."

I shake my head. "No, I looked into Mr. Brophy's." I remember the moment like it was yesterday. It's one of those experiences that I'll never forget, no matter how much time passes, no matter how many things happened between then and now, nothing can ever erase the horror of that moment.

I was in the backseat of my mother's car. As soon as my mother pulled into the gas station, I noticed the stench as we parked alongside the black BMW. A man in a suit pumped gas into his luxury vehicle. I held my breath, trying to ignore the odor, like a thousand rotting corpses were stuffed inside his trunk. I closed my eyes, but nothing could block out the sensation of a million cockroaches skittering across my flesh.

I heard the man talking to my mom. "Hello, isn't it a lovely day?" he said. The roaches' legs seemed to sharpen; tiny blades ripped into me. I opened one eye, just a tiny sliver. A ginormous cockroach crawled across my cheek, its glowing red eyes watching me, its antennae moving like a conductor's arms during the orchestra's crescendo. I shuddered and squeezed my eyes shut again.

"Yes, it's beautiful," my mom sounded happy, even flattered that this man had struck up a conversation with her.

"My name is Max Brophy," the man said. "It's a pleasure to meet you. Do you live in town?"

"Yes," my mom said. "My son and I."

"No husband?"

"Divorced," my mom said.

"I see. Well, I'm somewhat new to the area. I built a home up on Owl Head Road. Perhaps you've heard?"

There was no one in a ten-mile radius that hadn't heard, and Mr. Brophy knew that. In a small town, gossip spreads fast. Especially when a mystery man shows up out of the blue and builds a mansion that could arguably fit every Roxbury resident's home inside of it at once. "Oh, yes," my mother said. "I heard it's magnificent."

"Perhaps you'd like to come over sometime," Mr. Brophy said. "And of course, your son is welcome too."

"That would be wonderful," my mother said. I wanted to get out of the car and scream. I wanted to stand on the roof of my mother's old beat-up Toyota and shout, *She will not be going anywhere with you, ever! Go away and stay far away from both of us!* But I couldn't do that, so I just sat in the backseat, swatting demon cockroaches that I knew were real, but no one else would ever believe.

"I'd love to meet him. Is that him in the backseat?" I heard his footsteps, tap, tap, tap, against the concrete. My stomach heaved in revulsion, the retched odor intensifying as he moved closer.

"Oh, I don't think that's a great idea," my mother said, desperation in her voice. "My son… He's very shy."

"Don't worry. I'm great with kids," Mr. Brophy said. I heard the car door open, and the smell of rotting flesh burned my nostrils. I gagged. "Hello, there. What's your name?"

I couldn't have formulated a response if I wanted to. The cockroaches were in a frenzy. It took every ounce of effort I had to keep my sanity. I clenched my fists, my face twisted into a grimace. "Hey, buddy," Mr. Brophy's tone was meant to be soothing. "What's the matter?"

And then he touched my shoulder. It felt like needles piercing my bones. I yelped in pain, my eyes springing open as I flung myself backward. It was a rookie mistake. Everyone in this small town never dared to touch me. Someone spread a rumor in school that if you touched me, you'd be cursed for life. Even the adults steered clear of the poor emotionally disturbed boy, as though I was diseased, contagious.

Mr. Brophy's touch caught me off guard. His hazel eyes watched me with alarm as I snarled like a wild animal. I only caught his eye for one second. One second was all that it took.

I wasn't inside my mom's vehicle anymore; I was inside a rich man's bedroom. An elaborately sculpted bed frame held a king-sized mattress. Gold pillows with tassels were lined up alongside the massive headboard.

A girl sat at the edge of the bed; her two-piece swimsuit strewn on the glistening mahogany floors. Her eyes were wide with fear; her fingers moved rapidly through her mop of brown curls. I recognized her from school. Mia Boyne. I'd been in classes with her since pre-school, but we'd never spoken. Now

I was witnessing what was undoubtedly the most traumatic moment of her life.

The scene unfolded before me. I screamed for him to stop. I screamed and I screamed and I screamed but no one heard me. After all, there's nothing that anyone can do to prevent something that's already happened. There's no way to undo what's already done.

It was over an hour before I came back into my body. I later learned that my mom carried me upstairs and into bed, which was probably quite difficult for her considering that I was almost her height at the time. I was lucky no one called an ambulance. My mom knows how much I hate going to the hospital.

The next thing I remember, I was curled up in bed, my mom pressing cold washcloths against my forehead, singing a lullaby. I said, "Mom, please don't go to that man's house."

My mom sighed. "I don't think I'm invited anymore. Not after you puked all over his Versace shoes."

I recount the story to Jenna, sparing her the horrific details of the assault. Once I'm finished, I ask, "But how did you know?"

"Mia told me. She's grateful to you," Jenna says.

"She wouldn't go to the police. I wrote her a note and slipped it inside her desk. I told her that I would go to the police with her, but she wouldn't go."

"She was scared. Brophy threatened her."

"He's a monster." I close my eyes, remembering. "I went to the police myself, but no one believed me. What good did it do? What's the point of seeing these things if there's nothing I can do to help?"

"Brophy moved away," Jenna says. "Maybe after your accusation, he'll think twice before he tries that with someone else."

"Possibly." I'm not convinced. "So now you know why I can't look you in the eye."

"Why's that?" Jenna asks. "Do you think that I'm a secret ax murderer or something?"

"No, but it would be an invasion of privacy."

"Not if I want you to," Jenna says.

I shake my head. "No," I say, firmly. "You don't even know what I'd see. It's not fair to you."

"Hmmmm," Jenna says, intertwining her fingers with mine. "You might find out that every full moon I transform into a vampire mermaid who scours the sea for unsuspecting merman to drain dry. The only way to break the spell is for the Soulseer to look into my eyes, kiss me and find the perfect glass flipper that fits."

I laugh. "What's this? Dracula meets The Little Mermaid?"

"You forgot Cinderella and whatever our story will be called one day," Jenna says.

"Life isn't a fairy tale," I say.

My gaze is on the couch, but I can feel Jenna's eyes on me, burning me with their heat. "I believe more than ever that mine is," Jenna says. "I want you to look at me."

"Why?" I ask.

"Because now that I know all of your secrets, I want you to know all of mine. It feels right."

"But..." My voice trails off. "It's different. You're not going to have any control. I could see something that you blocked out or forgot or was so long ago that you don't even remember, but may humiliate you if it resurfaced."

"I don't embarrass easily," Jenna says. "Everyone says that they want to be accepted for who they are. Yet, we're scared to let anyone in completely. Do you see the flawed logic? How can any of us have what we truly desire if we live in fear of it?"

Jenna continues. "I'm human and so yes I'm scared. But I also know that the more we succumb to fear, the greater it becomes. The fear will grow bigger and bigger, magnifying, wedging itself into the space between us, so that even when we're touching we really aren't. Eventually, it will invade every joyful moment, the underlying fear that you may accidentally slip up and look my way."

Jenna's palms cradle my face. "Look at me," she repeats. "I want you to know all of me: the good, the bad, and everything in between."

"Are you sure?" I ask.

Jenna doesn't answer. She just uses her hands to lift my head. And I let her. My chin tilts upwards until my eyes are level with hers. Her face is obstructed. A whirlwind of colors and stars hide her features, swirling in rhythm with her purr-like melody. Then, through the whirlwind of colors, her eyes shine through. Dark and vulnerable and beautiful.

I'm not part of this world anymore. I'm a fly on the wall in a darkened theater. The lights come on; the music starts. The girls in red and white tutus twirl, their arms arched overhead like halos. One girl is seemingly unaware that she's a beat ahead of the rest, a huge smile on her face as she sashays across the stage. I immediately recognize her; a young Jenna, probably around seven years old. She's adorable.

Jenna scans the audience, her eyes stopping when she sees the woman, smiling and waving. Jenna shouts, "Hi, Mom!" for a moment seeming to forget that she's in the middle of a performance. Her smile falls when she spots the empty seat beside her mom.

On the walk home down the loud city block, Jenna's mom says, "Your father got caught up. He really wanted to be there."

Jenna shrugs. "I don't mind."

Inside her bedroom, later that night, Jenna tosses and turns restlessly, her blankets tangled from all the movement. Eventually, she gives up trying to sleep at all. She sits up on her bed, talking to a long-legged spider who dangles from a single pearl-white strand.

"Charlotte," Jenna whispers. "I don't know if my dad loves me." Tears stream down her reddened face. Charlotte climbs up into her web, a quiet presence in the corner. Jenna imagines that if her Charlotte knew how to write like the spider in *Charlotte's Web*, she'd weave a comforting message to Jenna. Somehow that makes Jenna feel better, and she finally falls asleep, her blankets knotted around her ankles, her final tear glowing in the moonlight.

A series of similar scenarios plays out in front of me; Jenna's dad missing her eighth birthday party, forgetting her middle school graduation, and then not showing up for the family's flight to Disney World, Jenna and her mother running through the airport and boarding the plane as a duo instead of a trio. And every time, Jenna says, "I don't mind," and then cries herself to sleep, wondering what she'd done wrong.

As I watch, I become angrier and angrier, so much so that my heart rate accelerates until my pulse roars at my temples. I want to kick Jenna's dad where the sun doesn't shine a couple of dozen times, but even that wouldn't be enough. The next time I see Jenna cry, my fury escalates to full-on enragement. When her dad shows up three hours late to Jenna's fourteenth birthday dinner at her favorite restaurant, I try to throw a piece of cake at him. My hands drift right through chocolate frosting like Patrick Swayze's character on *Ghost*.

I don't know how I can make this right, how I can erase all of this pain for Jenna. All I know is that when I return to the real world, I'm damn well going to try.

And then as suddenly as I was gone, I return. As Jenna's living room comes into focus, I feel her squeeze my hand. She's still beside me, studying me with her big eyes. "Do you hate me?" she asks, genuine worry in her voice. "I don't know what I could've done that was so terrible."

"You didn't do anything," I reassure her, pulling her closer to me and wrapping her up in my arms. "Why would you think that?"

"You looked so pissed off I could've sworn that steam was about to come out of your ears," Jenna says, climbing onto my lap.

"No, it wasn't you," I explain. "Your dad."

"Oh," Jenna draws in a deep breath. "What did you see?"

"Dance recitals, Disney World..." I run my fingers through her hair. "Your conversations with Charlotte."

"Oh," Jenna cringes. "Well, that *is* embarrassing. I can be overdramatic sometimes."

"You're not overdramatic. Your dad is a jerk."

"Yeah, I know he can be flaky. But I really don't mind," Jenna says.

"Jenna, you don't have to pretend with me," I say, cupping her face in my hands. "It's okay to not be okay sometimes." I kiss her softly, again and again.

Our faces are inches apart, her eyes, dark and hooded, probing into mine. It's a new level of intimacy, something I never imagined possible. "I'm looking right at you," I whisper. "And I'm still here."

"Maybe you've already seen everything," Jenna says.

I've always known that her eyes are dark, but now that I'm studying them, I notice subtleties that I couldn't possibly have before. Curled lashes frame milk-white irises that house the most beautiful brown eyes. I'd assumed her eyes were one color, but now I examine the nuances of shades; the lighter ring surrounding her pupils, the tiny green flecks that shine when you look close enough.

"That couldn't be further from the truth." I run my finger along her jaw, and electricity shoots through me. "I don't think that I could ever look long enough."

17

Pumpkin Chariots and Motorcycles

Jenna

It's one of those days that I never want to end; a moment in time that I wish would stretch into eternity, that the earth would stop orbiting the sun and that we could lay like this forever.

Ethan and I aren't part of this universe. It's like our brains have been sucked out of our skulls and we're existing inside a parallel utopia, tangled up and kissing and gazing at each other on the couch.

"Ahem! Jenna, did you want to introduce me to your friend?" My mom stands over us, hands on her hips, clearing her throat and speaking all too loudly.

We spring apart. "Hi, Mom," I. "I didn't hear you come in. This is Ethan."

"Um, h-hi," Ethan stutters, fiddling with a stray string hanging from a couch cushion. "S-sorry for um, um." His voice fades as he fumbles over his words and takes a shaky breath.

Mom stares at him, seemingly processing the stark difference between Ethan and some of the cocky jerks that I've dated in the past.

"Um, it's nice to meet you, Mrs. Farrell," Ethan mumbles, his face redder than a dragon's fire breath.

A few seconds seem to drag on for eons as my mom sizes him up. Her expression softens. "You're welcome to join us for dinner, Ethan," Mom says.

There aren't too many awkward silences during dinner, mostly thanks to me. Ethan kept his head bowed down and didn't talk too much, but he cleaned his plate which I'm sure my mom appreciated. He even ate a whole slice of her pumpkin-ass pie which to be honest I'm not entirely sure how he survived. I add stomach of steel to his growing list of superpowers.

After dinner, I invite Ethan upstairs to my bedroom to watch movies aka make-out. "Keep the door open!" my mom shouts from the bottom of the stairs. She's such a buzz-kill.

The movie is background noise. I curl up in his arms, my head resting on his chest as we chat.

"It was weird before," Ethan says. "Usually I feel it when someone enters the room, but I didn't even notice when your mom came in."

"Are you saying that my mom has no soul?"

"No," Ethan kisses me on the forehead. "What I'm saying is that I was so enamored with you that I was oblivious to anyone else. Once I snapped out of it, your mom's soul is quite lovely."

"What's her soul look like?"

"Flowers. Lots and lots of them. Orchids, tulips, lilies, and magnolias, all lined up in rows. Her smell is heavenly." Ethan pauses. "But there were a few parts of her garden that were… different."

"Different how?"

"I saw some weeds sprouting in places that otherwise looked well kept. And vines are stretching out over some of the flowers, and some of those vines have silver thorns, almost like some type of armor."

"Sounds right. She's nice and rosy until you piss her off. Then, she's a thorn bush."

"Oh, I believe it," Ethan says. "I felt a few jabbing me when she first appeared in the living room."

"It doesn't take a Soulseer to feel that. She can give a look that's the very definition of staring daggers. I often check for puncture wounds when she walks away."

A smile touches my lips as I imagine my mother sheathed in flowers, emanating the fragrance of sweet perfume. My expression changes as I think of the thorns, a protective barrier marring her perfect garden. I wonder if they existed before my dad. Or maybe he's hardened her over the years, changing the very essence of her soul.

The thought of my dad stirs up emotions that I don't want to feel, and so I cling harder to Ethan. "Talk to me about all of the mystical things," I request.

I ask Ethan if he believes in ghosts. He says he's not sure, but probably not. I tell him that I believe that the spirits of deceased loved ones linger around us all the time, watching over us, like guardian angels. After my grandmother died, I felt her touch all the time, a soft caress across my forehead and down the length of my hair. Grandma's gnarled fingers, bumpy and misshapen from arthritis, ran down the strands and then kneaded into my shoulders. Misplaced items reappeared in their place, even though I checked there a thousand times before.

As time wore on, my encounters with my grandmother changed as she crossed over. A touch that once felt real, like true pressure on my skin, became a quick brush of a feather. I clung to those rare moments, the times when I sensed grandma's presence: when the scent of her perfume swirled around me, when somehow the weightlessness of the air pressed into me, infused with grandma's energy. I'd suck in the deepest breath I could muster, pulling bits of grandma into my lungs, embedding her within my capillaries, pumping her into my cells. And although grandma doesn't come around anymore, I'm certain those pieces still live inside me, oxygen atoms that became part of my flesh.

Ethan doesn't look at me like I'm a crazy person. He nods thoughtfully. He tells me about his grandfather who passed away. When his dad bailed, his grandpa was around a lot, watching him while his mom worked long hours at the restaurant. They spent countless hours watching baseball games and playing cards. Near his grandpa, Ethan never worried about demons and devils. Instead, his closeness brought tranquility. His grandpa's aura was midnight woods and cicadas chirping: his silver glow like the moon stretching out languidly, its reflection glittering on a placid lake.

Ethan wonders aloud why his grandpa never visited him like my grandma. I can tell he's hurt by this. I suggest that his grandpa did come around, but maybe Ethan wasn't paying attention. Ethan's eyes look glassy as he thinks of all he might've missed out on while staring at the ground.

We talk about dreams and where the pyramids came from. We talk and talk and talk until it's almost midnight and my mom says Ethan needs to go home. "Come on, Mom! It's not even that late."

"It's late enough. In a few minutes, it will be tomorrow."

"Technically it's early then."

"Nice try, Jenna, but I'm tired and going to bed. That means that you won't have any supervision. Which means that Ethan needs to go home."

I sigh. "Fine. Just give us five minutes to say goodbye."

I swear that a time spell was set on us because five minutes passes in legit five seconds. As we say goodbye at the door, the clock strikes midnight. Ethan pulls me in for one more kiss. "I feel like Cinderella," I say.

"I'm not exactly Prince Charming."

"No, you're not. You're so much more."

A few days later, while the sun is a bright orange orb hovering between the trees, I'm battling the devil aka doing pre-calculus homework at the kitchen table while my mom washes dishes at the sink. My phone buzzes.

Hey Cinderella. What are you up to?

Attempting to use wizardry to solve math equations that were created by Satan himself

Wizardry? I haven't tried that strategy, although I have my own techniques for defeating diabolical equations.

I figured that mastering sorcery would be easier than figuring out why is there a log in my math problem. Logs belong in fireplaces and woods, not my math homework. This log might be the log that fuels the fires burning in the depths of hell.

The log does seem like a force that requires supernatural intervention. How's the magic working out for you?

It's not. I guess there's a reason that I never received an invitation to Hogwarts. All of these years I'd just been hoping that it was a clerical error and that my acceptance letter might turn up.

Haha

Seriously, though, if I can't get through pre-calc, how am I going to get through medical school?

If you need help, I'm not too bad at pre-calc. Maybe you could come over?

Let me check with my fairy godmother.

Great. I'd love to see your pumpkin chariot rolling up my driveway.

"Let me guess. You're texting Ethan," my mom says, circling a sponge around a plate.

"How'd you know?"

"That dopey grin on your face was a dead giveaway."

The roar of an engine fills our kitchen, the sound growing louder by the second. "What's that?" I ask. My mom drops the soapy dish into the sink. We both peer between the blind slats into the front yard.

My dad hops off his motorcycle. He takes off his helmet as he strolls to our door, his boots crunching leaves as he crosses our un-swept porch. I feel my pulse thrumming at my temples. The doorbell rings. Ding-dong!

My mom is paralyzed, staring through the slats. Ding-dong! Before I know what my feet are doing, they are flying through the vestibule. I fling open the door, still unsure if I want to clobber or kiss the man standing in front of me.

My dad leans against the porch railing, his hands in the pockets of his holey jeans. When he sees me, he smiles. "Jenna! How about that diner date?"

My arms are tight against my chest. "You're five days late."

"We ended up having to change our flight. Business stuff," Dad says.

"And you couldn't call?" Mom asks; her eyes boring into him.

"I lost my phone at the show the night before. I haven't had a chance to buy a new one," Dad says.

"And no one else had a phone you could borrow?"

My dad holds up his hands. "Whoa, Linda, hold it with the investigation. I got here as fast as I could."

"Do you know your daughter waited for you outside in the freezing cold for over two hours?" She's shouting now. A gust of air sweeps through the open door, the chill blowing underneath my sweater. I shiver. If I could choose any superpower, forget flying and telepathy. I'd ask for the ability to mute my mother as needed, like a button on a remote control.

"Aw, sweetheart, did you really?" Dad asks. I shrug. As tears well in my eyes, I shift my gaze to the floor. I blink the tears into submission and raise my head.

Any effort to disguise my sadness apparently failed miserably. "I'm sorry," he says. "I messed up." Every line on his face shows me that he means it.

An ordinary man wearing such a pained expression could invoke sympathy in even the most stone-hearted. Then, there's my dad, whose vulnerability is so at odds with his rugged appearance, that all of my anger melts away.

My dad is tough. Years ago, I sat beside him while a tattoo artist drilled into his neck. He didn't flinch. My dad is invincible. I still believe that my dad is a superhero. I don't see how that could ever change.

Today, that same tattoo folds and unfolds with each slow shake of his head. My name in cursive, *Jenna,* the "e" pulsating on his jugular. On the other side of his neck is one of his favorite sayings, *Live free.*

He watches me through clear brown eyes, his brows pushed together, a deep crease down his forehead. "I'm so sorry." My dad is strong and fearless and visionary and often sorry. But he only apologizes when he means it. I know that he means it. I can feel it down in my core. It takes all of my resolve to not tell him that I forgive him right then and there. My mom would've killed me.

"What can I do to make it up to you?" Dad asks.

"A milkshake would be a good start," I say, reaching into the coat closet. As I pull on my jacket, my mom stomps back into the kitchen. I hear her slamming kitchen cabinets as she puts away the clean dishes. A wave of guilt washes over me. Why do I always feel like I have to choose? Like going out with my dad is somehow being disloyal to my mom? I'm always in the middle. Nothing ever feels right when they aren't together. When we aren't all together, as a family.

"You ready, sweetheart?" my dad asks. I blink, realizing that I've been standing there, almost frozen, while my dad holds a helmet out in front of me. I secure the helmet as we step outside, the brisk fall air biting my cheeks.

"Born ready," I say. I text Ethan, *Sorry can't make it tonight. I'll come over tomorrow.*

"Good," my dad grins, a mischievous light replacing the sadness in his eyes. "Because we're going for a ride!"

I straddle his bike, my arms around my dad's waist. "Let's go!" I say, adrenaline already coursing through me. We speed around curves, up and down hills, my dad revving the engine, pushing his bike as hard as it will go. We zip through the mountains, multi-colored trees passing in a blur. The wind whips by, my hair straight out behind me as we merge onto the empty highway. The open road stretched out in front of us, the glowing orange half-sun getting swallowed up by the fields in the distance: that's all that exists anymore. We enter another dimension: one where time can't touch us, there is no beginning or end. There are no consequences; even a devil-possessed cheetah can't catch us. We are the fastest, the biggest, the baddest. Watch out world.

At the diner, I devour a milkshake and cheese fries while my dad talks about his travels. My dad has this way of describing things that makes me feel like I was there. Inside the majestic and ornate walls of St. Peter's Basilica, the Holy Ghost drifts through me, chills whizzing down my spine. In Ibiza, I taste the salty air and feel the pulse of the nightclubs. In the hustle and bustle of Las Ramblas, bodies brush past as peddlers lay out their trinkets. Suddenly, it feels like my dad and I haven't been apart at all.

My dad brings me home and we linger outside, rocking on the front porch swing, even though our breath is white, and my nose is numb. We talk and laugh and talk and laugh and I marvel over how easy it is to pick right up where we left off.

The front door creaks open, and my mom's head pops out. "Jenna, it's eleven o'clock on a school night. It's time to come in."

The night seemed to disappear in a heartbeat. I don't want my dad to leave. "You heard the queen. It's time for me to go," Dad says. "But I'll be back this weekend."

"Do you promise?" I asked.

"One hundred percent," he says "I promise." I know from past experience that his promises mean nothing. Still, I choose to believe him.

18

Absolutely, Insanely

Ethan

It's been days, but I still can't quite believe it. I told Jenna all of my secrets, and she still wants to hang out with me. I'm the luckiest person in the world.

Jenna comes over after school. It doesn't take very long to show Jenna that logarithms aren't nearly as evil as they seem. Jenna finishes the last equation and shoves her notebook into her book bag. "I'm demystified," she says. "I'm going to add mathematical wizardry to your list of superpowers." Jenna leans back, sinking into the oversized cushions on my couch.

I can't help but grin as I gaze into her brown eyes. Did I mention that I'm really lucky? "I hope that one of these days when you realize that I'm not a superhero you'll still like me."

"I'd like you even if you lost all of your superpowers," Jenna says. "But one day you'll realize that you truly are a superhero."

I shake my head but drop the subject. "How was your night with your dad?"

"Awesome. We had so much fun."

"Why aren't you still mad at him?" Because I sure as hell am.

Jenna shrugs. "He apologized. Besides, why wouldn't I want to move on from the negativity? What's the point of arguing?"

"You were pretty quick to tell off Cole and Carley."

"That's different..." Jenna's voice drifts off. "They're jerks."

"And your dad isn't?"

"I know that you think he is," Jenna says. "And I get why you think that. But it's hard to explain unless you know him. I can't stay mad at him."

"Is it because you're scared that he'll disappear again?"

Jenna looks down. "That's part of it, I guess."

"I don't like that he's hurt you."

"My dad is one of those people that radiates this amazing, infectious energy. If he's feeling good, everyone around him will feel incredible. It's impossible not to. And I guess that kind of makes up for some of the hurt he causes."

"Not to me," I say. No matter what Jenna says, I can't unsee the scenes that unfolded when I looked into her eyes. Even though she forgave him, it's going to take a hell of a lot more for me to do the same.

"He said he's coming back this weekend."

"Do you think he will?"

"I think so."

I can't bear to think about how Jenna would feel if he bails. If he doesn't show up, I'll be there. I'll show Jenna that she can count on me. "He'd better, or I might do something that will warrant my psycho reputation in this town."

"Calm down there Norman Bates," Jenna wraps her arms around my neck and presses against me until I'm on my back, her body on top of mine.

My heart races at two billion beats per minute. "I don't think that I can while you're on top of me."

"Even better." Jenna leans in to close the space between her lips and mine.

Jenna's dad must sense what's good for him because on Saturday he brings her to Six Flags. All day, I receive selfies of Jenna on rollercoasters and waterslides, grinning from ear to ear.

Wish you were here!
Me too.

But we both know the truth. I can't be there. I wouldn't even make it through the front gate.

Over the next few weeks, Jenna and I grow even closer. During waking hours, we don't go longer than a few hours without some form of contact. On nights we can't be together, we facetime until our eyelids droop and our voices fade into dreams.

Tonight, she curls up in my arms as a movie drones in the background. "It sucks that the Yankees were eliminated," I say. "I was really hoping to see them in the World Series."

"My dad was so bummed out. He's the reason I'm a die-hard fan."

"How's your dad's new place?" I ask.

"It's like a tiny hobbit home," Jenna laughs. "I'm not sure how he fits through the front door. Maybe a shrinking spell."

Jenna pauses. "But I'm so happy that he's close. Ever since he re-emerged from the abyss, he's really stepped it up."

It's true. Lately, when Jenna's dad says he's coming, he's been there and on time. So far, he's taken her to the movies, the zoo, snow tubing, and ice skating. He even rented a cottage in town. I still don't like the guy, but at least he's showing her a good time. Something I'd be doing if I didn't suck at life. "I'm glad that he's been more reliable," I say. "And I'm sorry that I can't take you out."

Jenna runs her fingers through my hair. "There's nothing to be sorry for."

"Yeah, there is. I want you to have fun with me too."

"I always have fun with you."

"Yeah, I'm sure you're having the time of your life while confined to our bedrooms or the woods. I'm worried that you're going to get bored."

"I could never get bored of you."

As I stare into her eyes, there's one thing I know for sure. I love Jenna. She is my first thought when I wake up, and the last before I drift into sleep. I love her colors and her courage and her smile and the way she twirls her hair between her fingers when she's nervous. I love how she makes me feel hot and cold and happy and electric and alive. I love everything about her. There isn't a single thing that I wouldn't do for her. I'll talk to her about all of the mystical things until my vocal cords explode if she wants me to.

And now that she knows all of me, it's okay for me to love her. Because now I know it's for real.

It's time for me to man up and say it. I take a breath, and touch her cheek. "Jenna, I love you."

She smiles, the cutest dimple indenting her right cheek, and my heart feels like it's going to burst. "Ethan, I am absolutely insanely in love with you."

I'm lost in an indigo fog as her lips touch mine. The gentle vibration of her soul song rumbles over me. "Madly. Completely. Passionately." I say.

Jenna climbs on top of me and shuts off the light. Even in the dark, her stars glitter all around me.

19

Home

Jenna

I'm writing a fairy tale.

Once upon a time, there was a strong, charismatic and handsome young king. He married his queen in a splendid affair, and a few years later a little princess was born. The king raised the princess to be fearless and carefree, like him.

There were a few times that the king had to go away. Although the princess missed her father very much, he'd taught her to be brave and confident. So, she raised her chin, hoping that she'd make him proud.

His most recent travels led him to far and distant lands. For months, the princess awaited his return. The princess had grown into a quirky young lady, and although she was proud of her eccentricities, she often felt she didn't belong in this world. She passed the time dreaming of mystical lands, places where reality and magic fit together like puzzle pieces.

Then, the princess met a boy. The boy believed that he was a frog. It only took one kiss for the princess to know that he was her prince. The boy claimed that whenever he looked at the princess she glimmered, her whole being illuminated by the purest of stars. The princess wondered if the stars were her own, or born from the effect of his gaze.

The princess and the boy fell deeply in love: insanely, absolutely. Still, the princess felt a familiar ache in the king's absence.

And then his majesty returned. The king took the princess on adrenaline-spiking adventures, appealing to her greatest delight. The queen, still embittered by the king's abandonment, refused to let the king inside the palace. The king, realizing that he'd been wrong to allow his voyages to sweep him away for so long, rented a peasant's cottage nearby to be close to the princess.

As the weeks passed, the princess could see the queen softening. In the end, although the queen tried to stay resolute, her anger proved no match for the king's charm. Just the other night, the queen took extra care with her hair and make-up. She invited the king and the boy to the palace for a royal dinner. The princess and the boy sat opposite his and her highness. As they feasted, they exchanged witty banter.

The king brushed his hand against the queen's when reaching for the cornbread. The queen flipped her hair. And the princess knew that they'd all be a family again. Soon enough. It was just a matter of time before they'd all live happily ever after.

But not everyone lives happily ever after. I see the girl on the bleachers, her burgundy hair falling in her face, her head in her hands.

"Hey, are you okay?" I ask, sitting beside her.

Kira looks up and wipes away a tear. "I'm fine."

"You're not a very good liar, you know," I say.

"I'm not good at anything anymore," she responds bitterly.

"Why do you think that?" I ask.

"I don't know…" Her voice trails off. "Lately I feel like I'm going crazy. Everything I say or do is wrong."

"Is that how he makes you feel?"

Kira stares straight ahead, almost zombie-like. "He insults me, and when I get upset, he tells me that I'm crazy or oversensitive or twisting his words and…" A tear rolls down her cheek. "I don't even know what's real anymore."

"There's a word for that. It's called gaslighting and it's a form of emotional abuse." I say. "You don't deserve that. You can walk away."

Kira checks her watch. "I got to go."

"Listen," I say, standing up. "If you need to talk, I'm here. Anytime, day or night. Or you can call Ethan. He cares about you a lot, you know?"

Kira nods. "Thanks, Jenna."

When I get home, I conduct an internet search and e-mail Kira articles about gaslighting, narcissists, and emotional abuse. I leave my phone number, hoping she'll call me after she reads them.

Later that evening, my phone rings. "Hello, my prince." I fall backward onto my bed, debating whether I should tell him about my interaction with Kira right away, or start our conversation on a more positive note. I choose the latter. "I've defeated Lucifer and all of his goblins."

"Does that mean you got your grade back on your pre-calculus quiz?" Ethan asks.

"A+!" I lift my arms in victory, my phone tucked under my chin.

"Awesome!" Ethan says. "I had a really nice time with your parents last night. Hopefully, I made a decent impression…" His voice trails off. "I hope they don't think I'm, you know, strange because I don't look at them."

"You're perfect," I say. I already explained to my parents that Ethan has a disorder where he can't make eye contact and if either of them have a problem with that, they are ignorant bigots. And that was the end of the subject.

"Okay, good," Ethan says, and I hear his breath release.

"I can't wait for Shaviah's Halloween party this weekend. I'm going to be a warrior princess."

"Sounds hot," Ethan says. "You'll have to send me pics."

"Or you could come with me," I say, even though I already know his answer.

"Jenna, I'd love to."

I hold my breath like I hold onto hope.

"But you know that I can't. I'm sorry," Ethan finishes.

I exhale, my chest deflating. "It's okay," I say. "I understand." And we change the topic.

I don't mind. I don't mind that Ethan couldn't come to Shaviah's Halloween party. I still kicked ass in my warrior outfit. November brings even more social action. Shaviah gets invited to a lot of events, and she always asks me to come along. As much as I love Ethan, I have to get out of the house sometimes. And so, I continue to divide my time between Ethan and my new friends.

I don't mind that Ethan missed Pete's keg party, even though he would've loved seeing Cole get so wasted that he puked all over himself. It's cool with me that Ethan didn't make it to Raven's birthday bash, even though he would've loved the hilarious games we played until the sun came up. I'm strong and independent. I don't need anyone to hold my hand. I don't mind. Not even a pinch. Really. Not even the itsiest-bitsiest amount. Not at all. Why am I getting the feeling that you don't believe me?

Saja's birthday is December 2nd. It wouldn't have mattered if I moved to Outer Mongolia, there's no way I would miss it. Even if an avalanche of Satan's burning hot coals descends on me, pinning me to the ground beneath the scorching rubble, I'll climb through inch by inch until I reach the top. Then, I'll speed to Saja, smiling through the pain of third-degree burns as I wish her a happy birthday.

Ethan kisses me goodbye on his doorstep. "I'm sorry," he says. "I wish I could come. But, you know, the city, all the commotion and people..."

"I know," I say. "You don't have to explain." And I begin the three-hour trek to New York City. Alone.

Later that evening, I glide through a sea of people, the glittering lights of an eighty-foot-tall gargantuan Christmas tree shining above me. "Check me out!" Saja twirls, her skates creating figures eights beneath her. "I'm ready to try out for the Olympics." She spins around, lifting one leg mid-twirl. She tumbles forward, hitting the ice face first.

"You might be better off trying out for the next season of Wipeout," I crouch by her side. "Are you okay?"

She rolls over, her black coat and leggings coated with ice shavings. "Ta-da!" Saja lifts her arms, and bursts into a fit of giggles.

I offer my hand. As I attempt to pull her up, she tugs me down hard. I land on top of her, our bodies a tangled heap of arms and legs sprawled across the ice.

Alayna stands over us, doubled over with laughter. She pulls out her phone and snaps a few pictures. "Your Olympic-level skills are now documented on Instagram," she says.

Saja rolls out from under me and pushes herself up from her knees to her feet. "Sorry, Jenna," she says through bouts of laughter. "Let me help you up."

As soon as I have a grip on her hand, I yank her back down. "Payback's a bitch," I say, as Saja falls onto me in an oomph! We are both hysterical when I hold my hand out to Alayna. "Help me," I say in my most pleading tone.

Alayna shakes her head. "I'm not falling for that one."

"No pun intended," I finish for her.

Javi and Nick skid to a stop in front of us. "Whoa, what happened?" Javi asks.

Saja and I both point at each other.

Javi pulls his girlfriend to her feet and kisses her forehead. "I can't leave you alone for five minutes," he says.

"Not with this troublemaker around," Saja says.

Nick holds Alayna's hand, and Saja links arms with Javi as we start another loop around the rink. I lag behind, brushing ice dust from my sleeves. Saja glances back, offering me her other hand. I wave her off. "It's cool. I don't mind being the fifth wheel."

I slow down and take it all in – the bright lights, the carolers chanting, the smell of street meat sizzling, the herds of people buzzing by, the sounds of horns and conversations and Christmas bells blending together. New York City is a living, breathing, familiar thing, a chaotic energy that is both comforting and intoxicating to me. Tonight, I'm not flying solo. New York is my date.

After the dinner was served, candles were blown out, and the cake was devoured, it was time for the girls to have an old-fashioned slumber party. Alayna and I roll out sleeping bags on Saja's bedroom floor.

"I'm surprised you came out tonight," I say, realizing the harshness of my words a moment too late. "I mean, I just haven't seen you in a long time, is all. I wasn't sure if you and Nick ran off to join a cult or if you were living in the wilderness amongst a pack of wild wolves or if you'd become zombies and quarantined yourselves to protect humanity from the infection."

"We had a lot of theories," Saja agrees.

Alayna looks at the floor. "I'm sorry," she says. "I haven't been a good friend. I got too caught up in my relationship."

Saja puts a hand on her shoulder. "It happens."

"I'm going to do better," Alayna says.

"I'm glad," I say. "Because I missed you!"

Alayna looks up, smiling. "I missed you, too. I can't wait to meet your new boyfriend! Tell me all about him!"

"Well, let me see, he's perfect and incredible and the most flawless specimen ever created by God, and oh, did I mention that he's the epitome of absolute perfection?"

Alayna punches me lightly on my arm, knowing that I'm mocking her, but her eyes are laughing. "How did you meet?" she asks.

"We met on Mind-Reel," I say. "He liked my reel and then he messaged me."

"Have you guys tried Mind-Merge yet?" Saja asks.

"What's Mind-Merge?" I ask.

"It's a new app that's compatible with Mind-Reel," Saja says. "You actually merge minds."

"Wow," I say. "It's like something out of a sci-fi novel. How does it work?"

"I tried it with Javi. We synced our individual Mind-Reels to Mind Merge and then I saw how I look through his eyes. I know that he's attracted to me, but damn! I almost didn't recognize myself," Saja says.

"What did you look like?" Alayna asks.

"Like an Egyptian goddess," Saja says. "And I also found out that I'm an unbelievable kisser. Which I figured, but it's still nice to get actual confirmation." Saja grins.

"Let me get this straight," I say. "You synced your Mind-Reel with Javi's and made out with him, but you felt what it was like to make out with yourself?"

"Sort of," Saja laughs. "I experienced what Javi feels when he kisses me."

My brow wrinkles. "I'm confused. If he was experiencing your perspective while you were experiencing his perspective, then you would be experiencing his perspective of your perspective which would actually just be your own perspective through his perspective and I'm getting really confused." I shake my head. "My brain hurts."

"Both perspectives merge into one," Saja explains. "I felt what I felt and what he felt simultaneously. When we kissed… I felt the familiar sensation of his soft lips on mine, tender as always…but then I felt something else too. First, I tasted something sweet, and then I realized it was my cherry lip gloss. Then, I felt all heady and giddy kind of like when you're at the very peak of a rollercoaster before the first drop. Then it all kind of blended together and we were one person: one heart, one soul. As corny as that sounds, it was true."

"That sounds incredible," Alayna says. "I'll have to try it with Nick."

I crawl into my sleeping bag, and a few minutes later Saja shuts the lights. Alayna breathes softly beside me. I can hear the city on the other side of the brick wall: a man shouting, a siren blaring, cars rolling past.

The city stirs something deep inside me: a sense of nostalgia. These streets are where I created a myriad of memories, happy and sad, crazy and spontaneous, first times and last times. I can't help but feel sentimental when I'm caught inside its grip.

And yet, it isn't home. Not anymore. Now, home is wrapped up in Ethan's arms, an owl hooting over a cicada symphony, the wind whistling through oak branches and tall grass, the moon glowing brightly in a starry sky.

If the city is enchanting, the country is another realm entirely, a place where magic and fairy tales truly exist.

I had a great weekend with my friends. But I can't wait to go home tomorrow.

20

Mind-Merge

Ethan

My phone buzzes and I open the picture message. Jenna stands in front of a mammoth Christmas tree; its height dwarfed by the skyscrapers in the background. I recognize Rockefeller Center. I've seen its famous tree dozens of times in photos: flat and two-dimensional. I've never seen the city as Jenna describes it: the music and laughter, the constant flow of traffic, wind tunnels sweeping between the colossal buildings, billowing coats open like sails on a ship.

And I never will.

In the picture, Jenna isn't alone. I'd been so focused on her that it took a few moments for me to register the four other people in the photo. On Jenna's left, a boy's arms are wrapped around a blonde girl's waist. To the right, a girl with long dark hair has her tongue hanging out of her mouth, an athletic leg kicking up high. Beside her, a boy laughs, his arm around the dark-haired girl's shoulders.

Two couples and my girlfriend. I let that sink in for a few moments. Jenna told me she was going to hang out with her friends. She didn't mention that everyone would be coupled up.

My phone buzzes.

I'm in a sleeping bag at Saja's thinking about my superhero before I drift into dreamland.

I'm not a superhero.

I'll keep telling you that you're a superhero until you believe it.

I don't deserve your compliments and I don't deserve you.

What's wrong?

I feel so horrible that I couldn't go with you.

I already told you that I don't mind. I love you.

I love you too.

I can't wait to see you tomorrow. Goodnight!

The next day Jenna jumps into my arms and bombards me with kisses, the sun shining behind her. "I missed you," she says.

My mom's at work. We spend the day in my bed. We lay side by side, her hands in my hair, her brown eyes probing mine. It's heaven. Jenna tells me about Mind-Merge.

"Do you want to try it?" she asks. "Saja said that it brought her and Javi closer."

"Sure. It sounds cool," I say. Before Jenna, I never imagined feeling this close to anyone. When she presses against me, I feel our hearts beat in unison. Her hand moves down my body, and I feel my cells bursts open, their DNA unwinding and intertwining with hers. And yet, I can't get close enough.

Jenna downloads the Mind-Merge app to both of our phones. I slide my earpiece into place. She does the same. My phone vibrates in my hand. A question appears on its screen, "Jennalivesfree would like to Mind-Merge with you. Click here to accept her request." I click here.

A blinking red light appears "WARNING!" Blink. "WARNING!" Blink. "WARNING!"

Mind-Merge has been linked with adverse side effects including headache, fatigue, and dizziness. Generally, these symptoms resolve within minutes to an hour after disconnecting from Mind-Merge. However, more serious complications may occur. Please check with your doctor to make sure that you are healthy enough to use Mind-Merge. In rare cases, severe reactions such as seizures, stroke, coma, and brain damage have been reported. As Mind-Merge is a new technology, long-term side effects have yet to be studied. Long-term or permanent neurological or psychological changes may occur.

By clicking below, I acknowledge that I have read the above statements. I am aware of the potential hazards associated with using Mind-Merge and assume responsibility for any adverse occurrence that may result as a consequence of using this technology.

A wave of uncertainty sweeps over me. "Um, Jenna?" She looks up from her phone. "I didn't know we had to sign a waiver. Is this even safe?"

"I'm sure it's fine. Everything requires a contract nowadays. Pretty soon attorneys will follow us around everywhere, clipboard in hand, monitoring our every move. They'll make us sign before we step on a crack on the sidewalk, lest our mother's back breaks and we decide to sue the city," Jenna says.

I grin. "They'll make us sign every time we kiss, just in case one of us is carrying a communicable disease."

Jenna presses her lips against mine. "We'd have to sign one billion times a day which would eventually lead to hand trauma." She kisses me again. "Then we can sue them for pain, suffering, and orthopedist bills."

I laugh and click below, signing my rights away. It's just a legality created by our law-suit happy culture. Right?

Mind-Merge between Jennalivesfree and Soulseer23 will begin now. The session will automatically terminate after thirty minutes. To end the session sooner, either party may say "Mind-Merge Exit." Once "Mind-Merge Exit" is processed by our voice-activated system, the session will abort.

Bright blue lightning bolts move under my skin, hot and fast. Bolts zig-zag across Jenna's forehead and down her neck. The bolts jump out of her skin, lurching through the space between us. As I watch, more and more bolts leap across the chasm, thousands of electric blue cords crackling between us, connecting us.

Everything goes black. I can feel something pulling on my insides, something pushing into my brain. My vision returns, like a blink that lasted a half of a second too long.

A handsome guy appears, seemingly from out of nowhere. His hair is rumpled like he just got out of bed. Soft dirty-blonde waves fall over his forehead and tangle with impossibly long dark eyelashes. His eyes are chocolate brown, the kindest eyes I've ever seen. What is he doing inside my bedroom? And why is he wearing my old t-shirt, the soft one that's fraying at the edges, and I always wear on Sundays when I'm lounging around the house?

My jaw drops open. His jaw drops open. He has a strong, masculine jaw. My brow furrows. His brow furrows. I point. He points. "Is that me?" I ask, incredulous. "No freaking way."

Jenna reappears: indigo and orange and bright silver stars. She smiles; her stars glittering. "This is so cool," she says. "Like an endless sparkling sunset drifting along a deep, starry indigo ocean."

My brows move together. "That sounds familiar. Did I say that?"

Jenna nods. "Our first conversation."

"You remember," I say.

"I remember everything you've said." Jenna runs her finger along my (very masculine) jawline. "You've always fascinated me. From the very beginning, I knew you were something special."

I feel the truth in her words. Her emotions are a tidal wave, bottomless in their depth, crashing hot onto my shorelines and then pulling me under, rinsing me with cooling comfort. She adores me. She trusts me. She loves me. Truly, absolutely, insanely. Unconditionally.

Her arms fold around my neck. I pull her closer. We kiss. I feel that soft rumble, that melodic hum that soothes me. "I think you're making me purr," Jenna says.

"That's part of your soul sound," I explain.

Jenna smiles. She has the most amazing smile. Or is that my smile? I'm her and she's me and together we are everything I never dared to hope for. Jenna reaches up, tendrils of colors curling around her finger, stars bouncing off her palm. "I wish I could go there."

"Where?" I ask.

"To my soul," she says. "If it were a place."

"If I could take you there, I would," I say. I imagine us in another realm, amongst her colors and stars, far away from the real world. I stare into her eyes, which were now half hers and half mine, willing it to exist.

The colors swirl around us, a tornado that encompasses us. I notice more colors mixing in: greens and yellows and browns, colors that were part of my soul before I built the big gray barrier. Honey and chestnut and violet and deep-sea blue move in opaque streaks around us.

I can't tell if we're in my bedroom anymore. All I can see are the colors of the whirlwind, spinning faster and faster. Jenna clings to me. Or I cling to her. I still can't tell. The wind blows our hair this way and that. I have the sense of falling, of being pulled through time and space.

The sensation stops abruptly. The colors around us fall away. Jenna is still wrapped up in my arms, her breath hot against my cheek. Above us, a tangerine sun glows in an indigo sky. Below me, my sneakers sink into glittery sand. Each pebble of sand is a different shade of blue: cobalt, sapphire, turquoise.

"Where are we?" I whisper, even though I already know.

"We're inside my soul," Jenna says. "You brought me here."

"Impossible," I say.

"Nothing is impossible." Jenna is already kicking off her shoes and socks, digging her toes into the blue sand. "Let's go for a swim." Jenna runs down the beach and towards the ocean. The waves are like none that I've ever seen before. Their crests soar up into the sky, white foam eclipsing the glowing hot sun. With each surge, sparks of energy escape, crackling as the water pours across the sand.

Along the way, Jenna sheds her t-shirt and jeans, leaving a trail of clothes behind her. "Come on!" She calls out to me.

Stripped down to our underwear and holding hands, Jenna leads us into the sea. The orange sun is hot on our bare skin, but the water is revitalizing. It reminds me of times that I held Jenna in my arms, the heat followed by the cooling comfort.

In the distance is a city skyline: buildings with hundreds of windows, the lights inside flashing on and off, skyscrapers with antennas that radiate pure white light.

"The city," Jenna says, following my gaze. "It's a part of me." She rolls her neck all the way back, her chin tipped up towards the sky. "Wow," she breaths.

I dip my head back and see the constellations above. Millions of stars connect to create a map of the human body: lights that create every bone and muscle, glittering as the heart pumps and shooting stars race through veins.

"There's the liver," Jenna points, "and the pancreas. See all of those little explosions in the brain? Those are neurons firing. That's what our thoughts look like."

"Incredible," I say.

"I told you magic and medicine are one and the same."

An enormous wave swells above us, interrupting my anatomy lesson. My stomach drops. "Oh, shit," I say.

"Jump!" Jenna says. We ride the wave, gliding down its steep slope. The rush of speed, the exhilaration, has us heaving with laughter as we're grounded again.

"That was awesome!" Jenna says. This place is hers. Everything here is a reflection of her: unique, wild, unpredictable, intelligent, and buzzing with energy.

Jenna swims further out into the ocean. I follow her. We swim and swim and swim until we can't see the shore. "Where are we going?" I ask, my arms burning from the effort.

Jenna points to a boat in the distance; a white yacht drifting over the waves. "My dad's on that boat."

"How do you know?"

"I just do." We swim harder and faster. My legs kick with as much force as I can muster. My lungs feel like they might explode.

"Jenna, we're not getting any closer," I say, squinting to see the boat, a tiny white dot in the massive sea. I spin around, but there's no sign of land. All I see is an endless ocean. Panic rises in my throat as I realize that I'm not sure which direction we even came from anymore. "We should try to swim back."

But Jenna is determined. We keep swimming and swimming and finally, just when I think I'm going to faint from overexertion, the boat is an enormous shadow looming over us. Rock music blares from the deck.

"Dad!" Jenna yells, waving her hands in the air. "Dad!"

No one hears us. Laughter and drums and an electric guitar drown out the sound of our voices. I can see Jenna's dad, just a few feet away, oblivious to his daughter's shouts just below.

"Dad!" Jenna yells, and I notice that she has run out of steam. She's struggling to stay afloat, her head dipping beneath the water. I grab onto her, but her body is slippery and sinking fast. I can't hold on. She's drowning.

Finally, someone throws a rope ladder. "Jenna!" I shout, pulling her back to the surface. We climb the rope ladder and collapse onto the deck.

Jenna's father is on stage, his fingers lovingly strumming his guitar strings. We lay on the deck, our chests heaving, soaked and in our underwear. Someone brings us clothes. We dress and join the crowd. Jenna dances, a sundress swirling around her, beaming up at her father. She sings every word to every song, never taking her eyes off of him.

The show ends. Jenna races to the stage. "Dad!" She yells. "Dad!"

He turns, his mouth open in surprise. "Jenna! What are you doing here?" He walks off the stage.

She throws herself into his arms. "I came to see your show! It was amazing!"

"Thanks, sweetheart," he says, and ruffles her hair.

"Come with me to my beach," Jenna says. "It's really something. There's blue sand that sparks beneath your feet and stars that form the shape of the human body and--"

"I can't right now, Jenna. I'm going to the afterparty. And no one underage is allowed."

"But Dad, this is important," Jenna says. "You've been to a million afterparties. This beach… it's *me*. I want to show you who I am."

Her dad checks his watch. "I'm sorry, sweetheart, but I've got to go," he says, and turns around.

Jenna is shaking now. "You suck!"

He turns back around. "Excuse me?"

"You heard me!" Jenna says. "I'm not going to sugarcoat it anymore. I'm not going to pretend this situation is something that it's not. You're a shitty father."

His forehead creases, "Jenna, I'm so sorry…"

"Sorry isn't good enough this time!" Jenna yells. Tears stream down her face. "You're selfish and your actions hurt me and mom. I'm done putting up with it."

"Jenna," He steps forward and spreads his arms as if to hug her.

"No," Jenna moves away. "I know what you're doing. I know you're just going to leave anyway. This time, you don't get to be the one to leave. *I'm* leaving. Come find me when you're ready to be the stand-up father I deserve."

Jenna turns around and takes my hand. We dive off the side of the boat and into the water. We don't have to swim. We cruise along the blue waves. Only minutes later, we're thrust onto the shore. We lay on the blue sand, Jenna sobbing into my chest. We're back in our underwear. I have no idea what happened to the clothes we wore on the boat. I can't tell what's real or not anymore.

"I didn't even realize how angry I was," she says. "I don't like being angry, but sometimes it's necessary. From now on, I'm going to let myself feel all of the things, not just the good things. It's time for me to start being honest with myself."

We lay there for a long time, listening to the waves crash onto the sand. After a while, she says, "I'm not going to let it make me jaded. I still believe there's more beauty than pain in the world."

I run my finger along her jawline. The indigo sky and stars light up inside her brown eyes. "Do you think that he'll stay this time? When we get back to the real world, I mean."

"I don't know," I say, running my fingers through her hair. "But I know that no matter what you'll be okay. You're strong, Jenna."

Jenna sits up and flexes her bicep. "That wasn't easy, but I think that things will only get better from here."

I smile. "Agreed."

Then, I see the cheetahs. Three big cats saunter along the shoreline, heading in our direction. "I take that back." The cheetahs' muscles ripple, their claws piercing the sand, igniting blue sparks with each step. "Jenna!" I reach for her hand, but she's already out of reach.

Jenna skips toward the cheetahs. She glances back, grinning. "Come on!" she says.

"Jenna, I don't know about this," I say, my pulse pounding at my temples. "I think that we should be more cautious..." But now she's out of earshot, dashing down the beach. I may be a coward, a giant wimp compared to her, but I'm not going to let Jenna face those creatures alone. I race to catch up.

Jenna runs to the cheetahs, arms outstretched like she's reuniting with old friends. She loses her footing, trips, and falls onto the sand. The cheetahs close in on her.

"NO!" I shout. I'm still too far away to help. I'm going to have to watch, helpless, while my girlfriend gets mauled and torn apart by beasts.

My lungs are about to burst, sand spraying from my heels. One of the cats mounts Jenna. I'll go for that one first. Jenna turns to face me. I'm finally close enough to see her face.

She's smiling. The cheetah leans down and licks Jenna's cheek. Jenna strokes behind its ears, her fingers massaging the spotted fur.

Another cheetah plops down beside her and nuzzles against her neck. The third cheetah stretches out on her other side. The cat rolls over to show its stomach, paws in the air. Jenna rubs its belly.

I stop in front of her, my chest heaving. I hear the sounds: like the rumble of an idle engine, the soft hum, the soothing vibration. The cheetahs are purring. Their purrs combine with the rhythmic crashing of the waves, the trickle of water running across the sand. It's a melody I know well: Jenna's soul sound.

All of a sudden, it makes perfect sense. A cheetah watches me through big brown eyes flecked with green. A cheetah stands and walks to my side. Sweat trickles down my back. "She wants you to pet her," Jenna says.

"Um, I don't know if I feel comfortable."

"She won't bite. I promise."

Petting a cheetah wasn't ever on my to-do list, and the creature's proximity makes my heart bang against my rib cage. I wish I could be fearless like Jenna. I hold out a sweaty hand. The cat nudges her head against my palm.

"Come lay with us," Jenna says. I sprawl out on the sand. The cheetahs scamper about, rolling on and over each other, wrestling.

"They're magnificent," I say. "Like you." Beautiful and playful. Captivating and strong.

The sun's rays dive into me, a comforting warmth seeping into my bones as stars glisten in the perfect indigo sky. Jenna is neither day nor night. She is the best parts of each because Jenna chooses to focus on the best parts of everything.

I take a few moments to marvel over the beauty of being Jenna. She can look past the mundane or destructive and find something brilliant and wonderful. Even with me. Where everyone else had seen a freak and a loser, she saw someone worth falling in love with. I'm still not sure why.

"This is unbelievable," I say. "I'm not sure how we got here, but I wouldn't mind if we stayed forever."

"We can't do that."

"Why not?"

"Because this is my soul," Jenna says. "Now I want to see your soul. When do we go there?"

I don't know how to tell her that my soul doesn't exist. Not anymore. When I was younger, I saw colors when I looked in the mirror: honey and emerald and chestnut. But that was a long time ago. For years now, every glance in the mirror revealed only one thing: a colossal gray wall, composed of slate rocks and massive boulders. Whatever was behind it is gone. Long gone.

Before I can respond, a train's whistle cuts into my thoughts, wheels clattering along a metal track. "Huh?" I jolt upright. "I didn't see a train station." But sure enough, a silver subway car barrels towards us on tracks that seem to materialize on the beach, foot by foot. "What the—"

A few yards away, the train screeches to a stop, the doors gliding open. Jenna jumps to her feet. She steps into her jeans and then pulls her t-shirt over her head. "Let's go!" she says, reaching for my hand.

I stand back. "Where are we going?"

Jenna shrugs. "We'll find out."

I throw on my clothes. A few steps ahead of me Jenna hops onto the empty train. She twirls around a silver pole. "You coming?" she asks.

I'd go anywhere with her. And this time, that's exactly where we're going. I take in a deep breath and step onto the train.

One of the cheetahs leaps through the doors and stands next to Jenna. My girlfriend looks like a mystical queen: her hair windblown, her eyes bright, standing tall and regal with her loyal beast beside her.

"Does the cat have to come too?" I ask. As tame as the animal seems, I'm still wary of anything with the teeth, claws, and strength to tear open my throat like Papier-Mache.

Jenna strokes the cheetah's head. A low rumble fills the subway car. "If she wants to, I don't see why not."

An automated voice comes through the intercom. "Stand clear of the closing doors."

The doors clamp shut. From the beach, the two remaining cheetahs stare as our subway car starts to move. As the pace picks up, I watch them through the window, their spotted bodies growing smaller against the blue sand.

The voice speaks again. "Next stop, Ethan's soul."

I swallow hard.

21

Ethan's Soul

Jenna

The train rolls to a stop and the doors slide open. A computerized voice drones through the speakers. "Last stop, Ethan's soul," as though this is an ordinary destination and not the most extraordinary day of my life. In all of the hundreds of hours that I've spent imagining all of the mystical things, I never dreamt up anything close to this.

My whole body thrums with excitement. I can't wait to explore every nuance of Ethan's being. "This is the last stop for this train. Everyone, please leave the train."

I enter into a world of gray. There is no sky, no clouds, no sun or moon. Just gray. As soon as we all step out of the train, it disappears, tracks and all. There is no way back. We are in the middle of nowhere without a map or a clue, and I'm totally psyched.

My cheetah darts past me, running like only a cheetah can, her limbs a blur. "Nala, wait up!" I shout.

Ethan looks amused. "Did you name the cheetah Nala?"

"My familiar needs a name," I explain.

"Doesn't a familiar belong to a witch?"

"A girl can dream," I say. "Although I'd only use my powers for good."

"Still, shouldn't a familiar have a more sinister name? I don't think that most witches would name their familiar after a character from the Lion King."

"I'm not most witches," I say. "If it makes you happy, I'll name the other two 'Ghost-Face' and 'Killa.'"

Ethan laughs. Nala trots back to me, her tail in the air. She rubs her cheek against my leg. "You're right. I think Nala is a perfect name," Ethan says.

"Don't ever doubt me," I tease, surveying the vast gray fog ahead. "Where are we?" I ask. "The train was supposed to bring us to your soul."

Ethan's expression turns grim. "This is it." He stuffs his hands in his pockets, his gaze falling to the ground.

"That's not true." I reach into his pocket and intertwine my fingers through his. "Let's go. Your soul is around here somewhere."

We walk hand in hand through the gray fog until a stone wall comes into view. It's taller than any skyscraper that I've ever seen, constructed of pebbles, boulders, and sediment. When I curve my neck up to the sky, I can't see the end of it. "What's this?" I ask.

"It's what I've seen in the mirror for the past decade," Ethan says.

"And before that?"

"When I was really small, I used to see colors. Green and brown and yellow," Ethan pauses. "But that's long gone."

"Or maybe it's just beyond this." I run my fingers over the smooth stones, the long slabs of concrete rough against my palms. This wall is rock solid (pun intended). I either need to become a sorceress or hire a demolition team with the world's largest wrecking ball to knock this thing down. "You built this barrier to protect yourself," I say. "From all the scary things that you saw as a kid."

"Maybe. I'm not sure how."

"Brick by brick, stone by stone. The same way anything gets done." Out of a sudden impulse, I punch the wall as hard as I can. Pain shoots through my fist and up my arm. "Ouch!" Apparently, I don't have superhuman strength in this realm. I'm also not invincible or immune to pain. Bummer. Unless a helicopter magically materializes, our options appear to be limited.

"Are you crazy?" Ethan asks, taking my hand and examining it. "You could've broken your hand."

"Do you have any better ideas?"

"Yes," Ethan says. "We should go back. Do you remember the Mind-Merge instructions? All we have to do is say—"

"Stop!" I shout before he could get the word out. "I'm not leaving until I see your soul."

Ethan plops down on the concrete ground. "You already have."

"I refuse to believe that," I sit on the ground beside Ethan. "Hey, wasn't Mind-Merge supposed to self-abort after thirty minutes?"

Ethan's eyes widen. "It's been a lot longer than that. Do you think we're stuck here?"

"We'll find our way back," I say. "The first step is getting past this wall." Nala lays down beside me, resting her chin on my thigh.

"I'm sorry," Ethan says. "I always ruin everything."

"That's not true. Maybe once you start believing that, this wall will come down."

"What do you mean?"

"You built it, so I'm pretty sure that you can take it down," I say.

"How do I do that?" Ethan asks.

"First, you have to want to. Truly, sincerely, deep-down want it to be gone."

"How do you know all of this?"

"The voices are telling me." I cup my hand around my ear and lean towards the sky, my brow creased as though I'm listening intently. Ethan's jaw hangs open. I laugh. "The truth is that I don't know anything," I admit. "This is what my gut is telling me. And I trust my gut."

"I have to want to get rid of it," Ethan says. "But I put it up for a reason. I needed protection."

"Was it effective?"

"I guess not. I still struggle every day."

"The demons and ghouls of the world aren't going to let a wall deter them. They'll seep through even the tiniest crack."

Ethan puts his head in his hands. "I don't know what to do."

"You can't hide anymore. The only way to overcome fear is to face it head-on."

Ethan shakes his head. "This is so embarrassing. I'm not brave like you, Jenna."

"It doesn't take a special talent to be brave," I tell him. "Anyone can do it." He watches me, his lower lip trembling.

The wall begins to crack. I hear it snapping and splitting apart, the fracture lines intersecting like spider webs. Beams of color pour through the cracks, shimmering emerald, and gold.

The sound of breaking ceases. The crevices still aren't deep enough, and now they've stopped spreading. The wall is damaged, but intact.

"I'm sorry," Ethan says. "I tried."

I can't think of the right words to say, so I say the one thing that I know for certain. "I love you."

"I don't know why you love me."

"Your compassion, your strength--"

"I'm not strong."

"Yes, you are. You went to the police for Mia even though you knew that you'd be ridiculed. That one act shows both your compassion and your strength."

"I guess," Ethan mumbles.

"And I'm not done yet. I can come up with an infinite number of reasons to love you. I love your humor; you're witty and goofy and sometimes you make me laugh so hard that I think I might pee my pants. I love how you listen, really listen. Not many people do that. Most people are too busy thinking about what they're going to say next to focus on what they're hearing. I love how you're open-minded even though you're more logical than me. You don't always believe in mystical things, but you don't mock me because I do. I love how you touch me: with the passion of the first time but the tenderness of knowing it might be the last time. Do you want to me go on? Because I can ramble for an eternity."

"But I'm disabled," Ethan says. "Inherently flawed."

"You're different. But there isn't one thing about you that I'd change. Even the things that may make your life harder still make you *you*."

Ethan studies his shoelaces. "Look at me," I say. He looks up. I feel his gaze: probing, pulling, digging, seeing himself through my eyes. "You know what I think of you. Now you just have to believe it yourself." Ethan's bottom lip trembles. "You deserve to be loved. You don't have to be ashamed of who you are."

Ethan rises to his feet and faces the wall. He grits his teeth, his face scrunched up in concentration.

And just like that, the wall crumbles. Rocks and pebbles pelt down on us like we're caught in a hailstorm. Nala jumps to her feet, a growl erupting from her throat. I stroke her side and pull her close. Ethan hovers over both of us, his arms around us, shielding us from the onslaught of pellets. And he says that he isn't brave.

A few minutes later, the sky stops falling. Most of what had been the wall is spread out in miles of knee-deep rubble. The rest was swept away in a windstorm of dust.

Beyond the debris is a glorious expanse of green and gold. Miles and miles of rolling hills, gentle slopes, and valleys, glistening under the shining yellow sun. Ethan grins. "I guess I'm a country boy through and through."

I hold out my arms and spin around like I'm Julie Andrews in *The Sound of Music*. "It's beautiful," I say. "Just like I knew it would be. Let's explore."

Cattle and deer graze on the abundant meadows. A flying squirrel floats between trees. Weeping willow branches sway. Wild brown horses prance across the fields, magnificent manes rippling in the wind, their young following close behind. "Now

I know why we were so drawn to each other. We both have wild souls," I breathe. Ethan pulls me closer, and I rest my head on his shoulder.

Two horses gallop towards us. They stop a few feet away and then bow down, their heads lowering, a front leg stretched out in front of them.

"Pleased to meet you," I say, and curtsy.

"It's an invitation," Ethan says. "They want us to ride them."

We mount the horses and they take off, Nala jogging alongside us. We travel through the grasslands, birds chittering overhead. We trot along, emerald and jade and honey streaming by. I bask in Ethan's essence: peaceful and steady, but full of life and wonder.

A moment passes when I sense that we've crossed an invisible barrier. The sky transforms from sunny blue to ash gray. There isn't an animal in sight. The horses' hooves pound against the landscape, the only sound in the sudden eerie silence. All of this is enough to freak anyone out, but it's more than that. It's an intuition, the way dread twists inside my gut. I don't scare easily. And yet, I'm terrified.

On the plus side, if I'm right, this could mean that I'm developing a sixth sense. I've always wanted psychic abilities; Vegas here I come! On the other hand, if I'm right, we might not make it out of here alive.

The horses come to a dead stop. "I guess this is the end of the road," I say, swinging one leg around and sliding off the horse. I stand up tall, chin jutted out, pretending to be braver than I feel.

As soon as Ethan dismounts, the horses dart back in the direction we came. They disappear over the hills like bats racing out of hell. "I think this is the part where a horde of zombies try to eat our brains," I say. Nala rubs against my legs, reminding me of Purrscilla. A cat is a cat.

"Now what do we do?" Ethan asks.

There are no bright colors in this barren wasteland. Dead, dried-out grass crunches beneath my sneakers. An old barn is straight ahead, its brown paint peeling off the wood boards. "We kick ass," I say.

With each step, the unexplainable fear intensifies. Just outside the barn, evil is palpable in the gray air. I breathe it in and my heart rattles. Nala whimpers, her ears pressed back.

"Let's go back," Ethan says. "Or we're going to get killed."

I take another step forward even as every cell in my body tells me not to. My arm seems to move in slow motion as I reach toward the barn door. I curl my fingers around the rusted metal handle.

"Jenna, we can't do this," Ethan says. "Do you even know what's inside there?"

"No," I admit. Whatever is in there is evil. It doesn't take a fortune teller to figure that out. It's hateful and vile and strong. Walking away would probably be the smartest course of action if we want to live to see the light of day.

But if we leave now the heinous demon-beast or whatever from hell is in there would survive. I'm not a huge fan of heinous demon-beasts surviving in any particular location, but this isn't any old place. This is Ethan's soul. I'll be damned if I'm going to let a brutish hellion poison my boyfriend's soul. This expression takes on new meaning knowing that I could literally be damned by whatever creature is inside. It doesn't matter though. This is my opportunity to save Ethan from himself. A chance that I may never have again. Carpe diem.

My sweaty palm slides along the handle as I tighten my grip. A gust of wind blows through, so strong that it almost knocks me off my feet. "I'm going in," I say.

"Jenna!" Ethan shouts to be heard over the gale. "We aren't prepared for this!"

"Preparation is overrated." I pull. The door doesn't budge. I take in a deep breath, muster all of my strength, and yank as hard as I can. The door will not surrender. I wrap both hands around the handle and jerk backward. It must've been some kind of optical illusion. It looks like a flimsy piece of rotting wood but is tougher than Fort Knox.

Sweat drips down my neck, my t-shirt sticky against my back. If only my whole body could morph into a liquid state and slip under the door, then I could kick some soul-invading demon ass. Instead, I'm just starting to stink. Maybe when I finally get inside, I'll scare off whatever is in there with my stench.

"Come on," Ethan says. "Let's get out of here."

I kick the door, my hands clenched at my sides.

Ethan takes my hand. "Jenna, there are some things that just can't be changed," he says. "Some things are what they are and that's it."

I don't believe that. I'll never believe that. I'll never give up on Ethan.

"Let's go," Ethan says. I kicked the door harder. Ethan pulls my arm. "Come on," he says. "You're going to hurt yourself."

Reluctantly I allow Ethan to lead me away from the barn, Nala following behind.

"I think it's time to go back to the real world," Ethan says. "According to the Mind-Merge instructions, all we have to do is say----"

Ethan's sentence is cut off by the most horrifying wail that I've ever heard in my life. It isn't an ordinary cry. Somehow, the sound carries all of the emotions it was born from. Terror, sorrow, and despair echo inside the hollow of my bones.

The high-pitched cry devolves into a sputter of sobs, and I'm certain of one thing. It's a child. A little boy. Ethan turns back towards the barn; his eyes narrowing in sheer determination.

"Do you think it's a ruse?" I ask.

"I don't know." The weeping continues. It hangs in the air, thicker than soup, permeating my every pore, filling me with the boy's overwhelming sadness.

Ethan marches forward, his lips a firm straight line. If this is a trap, we're walking straight into it. I'm steps behind Ethan as he grabs the barn door handle.

He flings the door like it's lighter than a feather. The door flies wide-open, its handle clanking against the side of the barn. For a split second, I wonder if he suddenly developed superhuman strength like when adrenalized mothers lift cars to save their babies.

Then it hits me. (In the figurative and not the literal sense. It was not an ideal time to get knocked out.) Of course, *I* couldn't open the door. It was just like the wall. I could support him. I could even help him. But I can't save Ethan from himself. He has to take the first step. He has to decide that he wants to fight his demons, no matter the chance of failure, no matter how scary they may be.

We step inside. Enormous cockroaches cover every surface, moving on and over each other, their antennae wiggling as they skitter by. In the center of the room, a gargantuan creature towers over a little boy who is curled up in the fetal position on the floor, his hands covering his face.

The monster is more grotesque and obscure than anything I've ever imagined (and I've dreamt up some weird-ass villains). It's a chaotic mash-up of many creatures, like its creator simply slapped on features of different beings without any forethought to the final aesthetics of their product. In this case, the end result is ugly as hell.

When we enter, it spins around, raising its razor-sharp claws, an enormous tail swinging around and clunking against the ground. I follow the curves of its dragon-like shape to its bat-like wings, up to its alien's eyes placed in the center of a rodent's face. Red-eyed spiders crawl across its body, moving through tufts of matted fur and humps of green scales.

The little boy spreads his fingers wide, peeking through the cracks and revealing big brown eyes that I would've recognized anywhere. Ethan. I do a double-take from the young man standing beside me to the small boy curled up in a ball on the floor. Is that how Ethan really feels, deep down inside?

It's time to change that. The creature bares its vampire teeth and opens its mouth as if to roar. Instead, the room fills with hyena laughter. Dinosaur-like feet shake the floor as the monster steps toward us. Ethan flinches, pulling me back towards the exit.

"No!" I say, pushing him away. "I won't run. I'll fight."

The monster takes another step forward. I rest my hands on my hips and raise my chin up high. "I'm not afraid of you!" I shout. It's a bald-faced lie.

Octopus-like arms emerge from its sides, shooting out towards me before I have a chance to react. The slimy tentacles coil around me, lifting me up high and then tossing me aside. I'm airborne for a few moments before I slam into a wall. Gravity thrusts me to the floor, sprawling me out flat on my back.

A growl erupts from Nala's throat: feral, angry, menacing. I turn my head in time to watch her pounce. She sails gracefully through the air and slashes her claws into the monster's chest, her teeth ripping into its neck. The monster flails violently. Nala hangs on, her claws digging deeper. I jump to my feet, ignoring the pain that shoots through the left side of my body. The creature is twenty times Nala's size. Even though the cheetah is a fighter, she can't do this on her own.

Ethan runs to my side. "Are you okay?"

"I'm fine," I say. "We have to DO something."

"I have an idea," he says, his gaze peeled on the far wall. "Come on."

I follow him to the roach-infested wall. He pushes the cockroaches aside frantically, flinging them onto the floor. "What're you doing?" I ask. We don't have time to waste.

"Trust me." He clears out several layers of roaches. I see the glint of metal. Wrist-deep in insects, Ethan unhooks a shiny gold sword. He grips the handle, the blade out in front of him.

"Do you know how to use that thing?" I ask.

"Not a clue," Ethan says. Nala yelps as the creature heaves her across the room. "But someone told me that preparation is overrated."

My heart pounds as Ethan turns to face the massive beast. He takes a teeny tiny tentative baby step forward, the weight of the sword shaking in his grip. The sound of a thousand hyenas laughing fills the space, mocking him.

The boy is still on the floor, feet away from where a battle is about to ensue. I race to him and crouch by his side. He scoots backward, his eyes peeled open. "It's okay," I say. "I won't hurt you. I want to protect you."

Something brushes against my side. I spin around, poised to fight. Nala sits up straight, her stance regal and strong, as though she hadn't just taken a massive hit. The boy watches her, his lip quivering. "She's a friend," I whisper, stroking her fur. "See, she's not scary."

The monster and Ethan are circling each other now, sizing each other up. "Get out of the way," I tell the boy, pointing to the far wall. I glance at the spot where Ethan had found the sword and see another glint of light hidden beneath the moving roaches. How had I missed that before?

I grab hold of the boy's hand and before I can think my legs are pumping. Nala scurries behind us. I dig into the wall of roaches, their little legs and antennae tickling my wrists. My fingers clamp around cold metal. I pull out a golden bow, shaking off the last roaches. I run my hand over its arch and down the string. But there are no arrows. Where are they? Are they hidden deeper in the bug-infested wall?

I glance over my shoulder frantically. I don't have time to search. Ethan and the creature are inches from each other now. The monster takes a swing at him. Ethan ducks, missing the blow by mere millimeters.

"You'll need these," the boy digs inside his pocket and retrieves three golden arrows. I don't have the faintest idea what I'm doing, so I channel my inner Xena Warrior Princess and wing it. I draw the arrow back taut against the string, aim, and release. The shot sucks harder than a starved vampire. My second attempt isn't any better.

The monster swings again. Ethan leaps backward, waving his sword awkwardly as he trips over his own feet. As he falls, his sword slices the monster's hand. The monster roars as blood pours from the laceration. But it's only a surface wound.

If we don't do something fast, Ethan is about to become this monster's appetizer before he moves on to the boy and me for his entrée.

I look down at the bow. It's a bad-ass weapon, a tool I've dreamed of wielding in all of my Katniss Everdeen fantasies. And yet, it doesn't feel right in my hands. I know what I have to do. The bow isn't mine. I hold it out to the boy. "Your turn," I say.

Wide-eyed, the boy takes the bow. He fumbles at first, unsure of how to manipulate the string, but he catches on fast. The arrow sails through the air as the monster lunges at Ethan. The arrow pierces its shoulder mid-lunge. Startled, the creature balks.

Injured and distracted, the creature doesn't seem to notice as Ethan climbs to his feet. Ethan holds his sword overhead and then plunges it into the monster's heart. The monster screams, a lion's roar that evaporates into a long hiss before poof! He disappears. Must've been the vampire in him because he crumbled into a pile of ashes. The barn door swings open, sunshine pouring through, a gust of wind sweeping out his remains.

Ethan and I run to each other. He wraps me up into a hug, my face against his neck, his pulse flittering on my cheek. I'd been so close to losing him. I pull him even tighter, feeling his sticky skin against mine.

"We did it," he says. "It wasn't as hard as I'd thought."

"Most things aren't as scary as they seem," I say. "And you're much stronger than you think you are." We stay like that for a while, tangled up with each other, our breaths in sync, rapid and then slowing to an easy pace. A wave of dizziness washes over me. I hold on.

"Wow!" the boy's voice breaks into our trance. He stands in the doorway looking outside at a magical world that is his own. Animals graze the lush green fields. A blue jay swoops down and perches on a white stallion's head. An eagle flies above the amber trees.

We follow the boy outside, the sun beaming down on us. The boy giggles as he wrestles with Nala in the grass. I notice my temples are throbbing, the feeling of a migraine coming on. But the moment is too beautiful to spoil, and so I say nothing.

Ethan seems distracted, staring off into the woods. "Are you okay?" I ask.

"Yeah. I just…" His voice trails off. "I'll be right back," he says. "Will you be okay by yourself for a little while?"

"I'll be fine. Is everything okay?"

"I think…" He pauses. "I need a few minutes to myself. To remember who I am, who I could've been…without the monsters."

I nod, understanding. "Go," I say, ignoring the pain intensifying at the base of my skull. Wasn't there a warning about adverse reactions when we first logged onto Mind-Merge? It seems so long ago, the memory foggy now. Besides, I'm not going to let a headache interrupt Ethan's progress. "Take your time."

Ethan disappears into the woods. For a while, I watch the boy. He rides Nala's back, jetting across the fields, giddy with laughter, waves of joy emanating from him. I smile through the pain searing through my brain.

When I can't take it anymore, I lay on the grass, the sun soaking into my arms, seeing the intensity of the rays even behind closed eyes. My head pounds relentlessly. I wonder if a microscopic zombie crawled up my nose and is munching away, eating through my skull and into my brain.

The boy and the cheetah hover over me, the boy shaking my shoulders. My eyelids feel so heavy. "Are you okay?" the boy asks. "We should bring her inside. She doesn't look so good."

I lean against the cheetah as I stagger inside the barn. It's different than before. The roaches are gone. Along the back wall, the sword and the bow hang side-by-side, shining against the oak wood.

I sit on the floor, my back against the wall. "I think we're going to have to go soon," I say. "I'm not feeling well."

The boy's eyes well up with tears. "But what will I do without you?" he asks. "The big scary monster will come back."

I pull him close. "You know how to protect yourself now." I glance up at the weapons. "You had the tools all along. You just needed the courage to get up and find them." Even as I say the words, I wonder if they are entirely true. The weapons are hanging up pretty high, probably out of a child's reach. For a moment, I wonder if there are certain things that a child's mind isn't equipped for, if these premature exposures could devastate their vulnerable psyche, if they'd even have a fighting chance.

The boy watches me through Ethan's big brown eyes. Tears stream down his face. "I don't want you to go."

"You'll be okay," I say. Ethan wasn't a boy anymore, but now I know the child we once were lives inside all of us. I felt her deep in my own sapphire ocean, just before I reached the boat. Beneath the waves, her insecurities twisted around my ankles, pulling me underwater and filling up my lungs until I couldn't breathe. I kicked her away. But now I know that she's always there, hovering just below the surface. She'll resurface if I let her.

My stomach churns. Black spots flash in front of my eyes. I would've gotten up and found him myself if I wasn't so weak. "Can you please get Ethan?"

The boy and the cheetah race out of the barn, the walls closing in around me.

22

Baby Steps

Ethan

I don't know what I'll find or even what I'm looking for. I only know that I need to move; I need to clear my head. I should've been celebrating. We defeated the monster. The monster that was all of the scary things…a conglomeration of every creature and goblin and demon that snuck past my barriers, terrorizing the very core of me for all of these years.

I killed it. I won. I wonder if what happened here today will impact my life in the outside world. Even if it does, will the change be permanent? Or will every day continue to be a battle, wearing me down until eventually, the evil reclaims its hold on my soul?

The trail ends. I recognize the playground in front of me. It's the biggest one in Roxbury, the one Mom took me to twice when I was a kid. I hear the children's laughter, echoing like I'm at the bottom of a well. *Freak! Loser! Weirdo!* And more and more laughter. Jokes that I'm not in on. Jokes that are on me.

I spent most of the time clinging to my mom's leg, my gaze glued to the ground. A few times I let go, running aimlessly, afraid to look up, the children's jeers following me as I dashed by. I never dangled from the monkey bars. I never climbed the jungle gym. I wasn't welcome. Even if I was, I wouldn't allow myself to break my concentration for that long, to risk another encounter with the demons.

I wrap my fingers around the cold metal bar and bend my knees so that my feet won't touch the ground. *Freak!* I swing from bar to bar. *Loser!* I run across the wooden drawbridge and dive down the slide. *Weirdo!* I stand on the tire swing, spinning round and round and round, my own laughter drowning out the children's until I can't hear theirs anymore.

"Ethan!" the boy's calls break into my thoughts. "Ethan!" I hear the urgency in his tone. I race back the way I came, bursting through the woods and into the meadow.

"Ethan!" The boy looks taller than I remembered, as though he aged in the time that I was gone. I don't think I'll ever find the words to fully describe how trippy and disorienting it is to interact with a younger version of yourself. "Jenna's sick! Come now!"

In the barn, Jenna lays on the floor, her eyes half-open, her complexion pale as a ghost. "Jenna!" I kneel beside her. "Are you okay?"

Upon seeing me, Jenna props herself up on her elbows. "I'm okay." She offers a weak smile. "Did you find what you were looking for?"

"I think so," I say. "But enough about me. What's wrong with you?"

"Invisible men with invisible swords keep stabbing me in the brain. I don't know what I've done to anger them so."

"We have to go. We shouldn't have stayed for so long."

"No!" the boy shouts, wrapping his arms around Jenna's waist. "I won't be safe without you here!"

Nala nuzzles the boy's shoulder in an apparent effort to comfort him. Jenna looks from Nala to the boy. "I have to go," Jenna says. "But she can stay. Nala will protect you."

"What?" I ask. "Jenna, no. You're not thinking straight. You can't give away your cheetah."

"I can and I will," Jenna says, her voice firm. "As long as she agrees."

Nala stares with wise eyes, seeming to understand. She stands in front of Jenna, places her front paws on Jenna's lap, and licks her face three times. "I'll miss you too, girl," Jenna murmurs. Nala moves to the boy's side, nudging herself under his arm. Jenna nods. "It's decided then."

The boy's eyes widen. "I can keep her?"

Jenna nods. The boy smiles.

"Jenna, I appreciate the gesture, but I don't know about this," I say. We don't know what we could be getting ourselves into, meddling with our souls like this. Would losing a cheetah change Jenna? Could Nala's presence alter some part of me? Would there be repercussions for this, ones that we could never even imagine?

"I'm sure," Jenna says, losing her breath between words. "But we really do have to go."

"Mind-Merge Exit," I say. Nothing happens. Jenna's face starts to take on a green tinge. "Mind-Merge Exit," I say again. Jenna's breathing is labored. Her eyes roll back into her head. "Mind-Merge Exit!" I shout.

Streaks begin to whirl around us: green and gold and orange and sapphire blue. Through the colors, I see the boy, arms around his cheetah.

I blink. I'm inside my bedroom. Blue bedsheets, beige carpet, bare walls, sunlight streaming in through the curtains. It seems crazy that a place this ordinary even exists. And how is it still daytime?

Jenna lays on my bed, eyes closed, tendrils of hair stuck by sweat to her forehead. "Jenna!" I shout. I press my fingers against her neck, releasing a huge huff of relief when I feel the pulsation. "Are you okay?" I ask. She doesn't respond. I reach for my phone and dial 911.

Jenna opens her eyes and smiles. A gigantic, glistening smile that fills the room with heat and stars. I can hear the low rumble, the waves crashing on the sand.

"How are you feeling?" I ask.

"911, what's your emergency?" The operator says.

"Amazing." Jenna grins. "Like a bad-ass, monster-destroying, dimension-traveling, soul-saving demigoddess."

"Hello?" The operator says.

"Sorry. Oh, um, hi," I mumble. "I think everything is okay now. Sorry for bothering you." I disconnect the call.

Jenna's eyes widen. "Did you call 911?"

"Yeah, I was worried. You were sick."

"But you hate hospitals."

"I love you more than I hate anything," I say. "Are you sure you're okay?"

Jenna sits up and then teeters, grabbing the bedpost for support. "A little dizzy," she says, grimacing. "And this headache's brutal."

I lift my phone, but Jenna holds up her palm. "911 is not necessary. I'm sure my mom has a tea for this."

Fifteen minutes later, we pull into Jenna's driveway. Her feet drag as we make our way across the porch and through the front door. She drops onto the couch, slumping against a pillow. "Mom!" she shouts.

I hear laughter coming from the kitchen. Jenna's mom enters the living room, her smile breaking when she sees her daughter. "Jenna, you're so pale! What happened?"

"Mind-Merge sent us to another dimension where we had to free a boy from a ginormous dragon-monster. It was an epic battle from which we emerged victorious and unscathed, although now I feel like I took ten shots of tequila last night."

Jenna's mother is so used to her saying outlandish things that she doesn't even respond to the first half of Jenna's story. Hands on her hips, she faces her daughter. "Are you hungover?"

"No. Mom, I just told you. I didn't have one drink. I've been fighting demon-beasts in another realm."

Jenna's mom rolls her eyes and turns to me. "Could you please provide an unembellished tale?"

"We used Mind-Merge," I admit. "There were a few warnings in the beginning, but I don't really remember… Something about headaches and permanent psychological changes."

Jenna's father enters the room, looking at home in sweatpants and bare feet. I've met him a few times before, but every time I struggle to contain my awe. He is a sight to behold. He is enveloped by trillions of feathers: feathers that stretched to the ceiling overlapped by shorter or broader feathers, pink feathers, blue feathers, gold feathers, feathers with wild designs, peacock-like feathers, etc., etc., etc.

"These kids think they're invincible," Jenna's mom says, throwing her hands up in the air. "I read about this Mind-Merge stuff. You're messing around with your brains! I'm going to call the doctor." She walks back into the kitchen.

Jenna's dad settles on the armchair, his legs stretched out in front of him. The feathers move ever so slightly, their individual barbs fluttering as though they are gliding along a breeze. I hear the whoosh, a peaceful whistle as air sweeps through his wings. Always in motion even as he is seated here in front of us. Always ready for flight.

"I've heard of Mind-Merge," he says, lowering his voice so that Jenna's mom can't hear. "It sounds really cool. How was it?"

"It blew my mind," Jenna says. "Hopefully not literally." Jenna reaches out and holds my hand. "I think Ethan finally saw the superhero that I've always seen."

Jenna's mom reenters the room, dunking a teabag up and down inside a mug. "I spoke to Dr. Bradford. He said to watch out for signs of seizures, but as long as you're awake and alert we don't need to come in." She hands the cup to Jenna. "Feverfew tea should help your head." Jenna takes a sip. "Just promise me that you'll never do anything that stupid again."

"I promise," Jenna says, but her hand is in mine, and I feel her fingers cross just before she responds.

* * *

Weeks pass. I wish I could tell you that now I march into school with my head held high, look straight ahead and never feel afraid. But that would be a lie.

In the hallways, I still see the chaotic mass of images, feel the uncontrollable rush of sensations and sense the danger. And so, I put my head back down and walk to class, my hopes crushed beneath the sneakers that I stare at all day.

It's become too cold to eat outside, so I spend my lunch hours in the recesses of the library. It isn't the greatest place to socialize. Mrs. Feldner is an old-school librarian; she doesn't allow any chatter. When Jenna joins me, we whisper, pass notes, practice our own made-up sign language, and mime laughter. Jenna's attempts at the latter often lead to loud snorts or squeals. Mrs. Feldner does not approve of this "ruckus" and often threatens her with detention. I wish that I could do better. Jenna doesn't belong in the back corner of the library.

It's Tuesday, and so Alex slides into the seat across from me. He opens his notebook and writes in big letters on a clean page: **Mr. Soto nominated me for the Young App Developers Fair!**

I grab his paper and write: **Awesome! You beat Luke!**

Not exactly. We were both nominated. He'll be competing too.

Mrs. Feldner glares at us as she walks by. Alex opens his math textbook and begins copying an equation into his notebook. Although I try, I can't focus on my history project. My mind wanders to a place where I pulverized a concrete wall into a mound of dust, a place where I plunged a sword into a beast's heart.

"Alex," I whisper.

Alex's eyes bulge and he points to the sign on the wall. QUIET IN THE LIBRARY.

I rip a piece of paper out of my notebook.

Have you noticed anything different about me? I pass the paper to Alex. He studies it, his brow furrowed.

`No.`

Well, at least he's straightforward and to the point. I close my eyes and I'm back in that old barn. I was terrified, but I confronted the monster anyway. Maybe that's the only difference between now and then. When I fell in the barn, I got back up.

I'm going to start doing things that I wouldn't before. Even if I'm scared.

`The fight-or-flight response is a biochemical reaction in which the amygdala releases adrenaline in response to a perceived threat. It is the individual's emotional reaction to this mechanism that determines if the individual will feel fear or panic.`

Before the end of this school year, I'm going to eat in the cafeteria. I'll find a way.

`Make a right out of the library. Go to the end of the hallway and make a left. The cafeteria is the third door on the left.`

I read his response and grin. Alex always makes things seem simpler than they are. But it was strangely comforting: the idea that I'm almost there, the notion that all I need to do is take a couple of turns, swing around a few corners, and I'll reach my goal. One step at a time. Even baby steps eventually take you where you want to go.

23

New Year

Jenna

It's a new year. A fresh start. I skip out the front door, barely noticing the freezing cold temperatures that nip at my cheeks. Humming to myself, I lift the trunk, smiling at the last three boxes.

Last night Ethan and I counted down the seconds until midnight, but I couldn't wait. I kissed him two seconds early. Our kiss was so explosive, so dynamic that its energy shot out the window of Ethan's house and singlehandedly caused the ball to drop in Times Square and set off fireworks around the country. Yeah, we're good like that. You're welcome America.

It didn't seem like the New Year could get any better until this morning. I'm giddy as I stack the boxes and lift them from the trunk. I shuffle through the front door, the boxes' contents clattering and jangling as I make my way up the stairs and into the master bedroom.

My vision is obstructed. As I shift my weight from foot to foot the boxes veer precariously, left to right, threatening to topple and spill. Through some miraculous feat which I credit to either my impeccable balance or some unknown divine intervention, I and the boxes arrive in the master bedroom unscathed.

"That's everything!" I say, lowering the boxes to the floor.

The normally tidy bedroom looks like it was hit by an apocalyptic explosion. Half-emptied boxes are everywhere. Clothes, shoes, gadgets, and knickknacks are scattered without any semblance of organization; almost every drawer on every piece of furniture is ajar; lamps and band equipment, and dirty tools are strewn across the king-sized bed.

I raise my eyebrows. If my mother sees this, she might drop dead on the spot. "Did a pack of savage werewolves tear through here?" I ask.

My dad shrugs, kneeling in front of an open suitcase. "It's all part of the process," he says. He tosses a rolled-up pair of socks across the room. They land in a dresser drawer. "Score!" He picks up another pair of socks and takes another shot. The socks miss, bouncing against the dresser and rolling into the corner. My dad's phone chirps. His fingers swipe across the screen as he texts a response.

I drag a razor across the packing tape and spread apart the box flaps. The box is packed with mugs, dishes, and glasses. "This is kitchen stuff," I say.

"Why'd you bring it upstairs?" Dad asks.

I point to the side of the box. In black permanent marker, BEDROOM is scrawled in my dad's spidery handwriting.

"How did that get there?" My dad grins.

"It must've been that mischievous house-elf," I say. My phone buzzes in my pocket. "Hello?"

"Hey, how's the move going?" Mom asks.

I step out of the bedroom, glancing back once at the disaster behind me. I head down the hallway. "Um, great!"

"Glad to hear," my mom says. "Because I'm stuck working a double. Rita and Karen both called out. If I leave, they'll only be one nurse covering the entire ICU—"

"Mom, it's all good," I say. Or will be, very shortly. It's probably better that she isn't home at the moment.

"Okay, great. I've got to go!" I hear the commotion in the background: machines beeping, patients calling her name. "I'll be home as soon as I can." The call disconnects.

My father walks down the hallway, shrugging his guitar case over his shoulder. "I'm heading out for a couple of hours."

"Where?" I asked.

"I'm going to jam with Bobby for a while. You remember Bobby, right?"

Yes, I do. I also remember that my mother hates Bobby with a blazing passion that rivals the fiery pits of hell. "Those boxes aren't going to unpack themselves," I say, and then cringe at how much like my mother I sound.

"Don't worry about that. I'll take care of it when I get back," Dad says. "I've been trying to meet up with Bobby for a while, but we haven't been able to work it out. I can't miss this opportunity. He's got a lot of contacts in the industry. This is big, sweetheart."

"But Dad—" I start.

"I'm doing this for you, sweetheart," he says. "There's nothing I want more than to make it big so that you and your mom will never have to worry about money again." He pats my arm as he passes, taking the stairs down two at a time. The front door opens and closes, his footsteps moving down the front porch. His engine revs up.

I stand in the doorway of the master bedroom, surveying the chaos. A sense of time isn't exactly my dad's strong point. A couple of hours can mean anything.

Everything could be perfect. My dad is finally back. I can't let him screw it up. I sigh, cross the room and pick up the socks in the corner.

As I arrange his clothes in a drawer, I let myself feel angry. I remember a moment on a boat in another dimension and I hear my own voice saying "You're selfish and your actions hurt me and mom. I'm done putting up with it."

And yet I keep unloading boxes and putting his things away, and I realize how easy it is to fall back into old patterns. But he's here, I remind myself. He hasn't left us. He's moving back in. Isn't that the most important thing? No one's perfect, after all. And I'll give him a piece of my mind later, I decide.

A couple of hours later, my dad has not reappeared, but the master bedroom is clean and orderly. A stack of flattened cardboard boxes fills the recycling bin. I unpack the last mug and place it in the cabinet as my phone buzzes.

Mia: Hey, what are you up to?

Me: The King had duties to attend to, and thus departed the castle in great haste. The royal quarters were left in a state of unsightly disarray. The princess, knowing the queen's penchant for aesthetics and cleanliness, took it upon herself to slave like a miserly peasant. As the hours ticked by, the princess has been toiling away, exerting such great efforts that a dewy glaze has become evident across her skin.

Mia: What the hell are you talking about? I've known you for six months, but I still don't understand shit you say.

Me: Most people don't. It can take years to become fluent in Jenna-ese. Allow me to translate for you in terms you may find easier to understand: My dad left his shit all over the house. I've been putting all his shit away so my mom doesn't flip her shit. After several hours of working my ass off, I'm sweaty and I smell like shit. My pits stink like old, rotten cheese that has been chewed, swallowed, and regurgitated twice by a subway rat.

Mia: Haha. Now I get it. When you finish that shit, can you come over? I need to talk to you about something.

Me: Is everything okay?

Mia: No. Not at all. I need a friend.

Me: I'll be there right away.

Mia: Thanks… but it's cool if you take a shower first.

Me: Will do.

A half-hour later, I'm on Mia's couch, my wet hair soaking through the shoulders of my t-shirt. Mia's eyes are puffy, her tablet clenched in her fist. "What's wrong?" I ask.

She hands her tablet to me. As I grab the device, my fingers sweep across the screen, unintentionally clicking a link. An article opens.

Police Continue Search for Missing NYU Student
18-year-old Brittany Shulman was reported missing by her roommate after she failed to return from a date. Brittany had told her roommate that she was going out with someone she'd met on a dating app. Brittany was active on several dating apps, and police are investigating men she interacted with recently online.

"Did you know her?" I ask.

Mia looks over my shoulder. "Wrong article," she says, clicking the back button. "Although that's fucked up too."

The screen changes and another article appears. I feel all of the blood drain from my face like a vampire latched onto my cheek and is sucking me dry.

Florida Man Accused of Molesting Girl

Max Brophy, 40, a wealthy businessman and newcomer to Smalltown, Florida was arrested on accusations of raping an 11-year-old girl. Friends and neighbors are shocked, describing Max as charismatic and congenial.

Clyde Daniels, Brophy's defense attorney, has made the following statement. "My client is an upstanding citizen and innocent. The only victim here is Mr. Brophy, whose life is threatened to be destroyed by the false allegations of a mentally unstable person. I am confident in the judicial process and that my client will be exonerated of all charges."

Tears spill from Mia's eyes. "It's all my fault," she says. "A girl was raped, and it's all my fault."

I wrap my arms around her and Mia sobs into my chest. "It's not your fault," I say. "Another person's actions are never your fault. There is only one person to blame and that's Max Brophy. I hope that he rots in jail for the rest of his life."

"He won't though," Mia says, lifting her head and wiping the tears from her cheeks. "Rich men never do."

I don't know what to say. I don't want to believe that. But maybe my idyllic thinking has blinded me to some of the harsher realities of the world.

"I need to come forward," Mia says. "I know that they're going to villainize me. They'll say that I'm a liar or crazy or saying it for attention, but I'm going to do it anyway. Nothing they say to me is worse than going to sleep another night knowing that I haven't done everything I can to stop this man from hurting another girl." Mia clutches her chest. "If I can manage to get the words to come out."

"You can," I squeeze her hand.

A short while later, I drop Mia off at the police station. "Are you sure that you don't want me to go in with you?" I ask.

"I'll be okay," Mia says. She opens the car door and sucks in a deep breath. "I've got to go before I lose my nerve." She steps outside. I shiver as the cold air sweeps inside my car.

"You can do this," I tell her again. Her eyes are so dark, so full of anguish. I imagine her inside that police station: reopening those fragile wounds, the officer's leery glares splitting them apart, her guts and heart and blood spilling out on the floor silently beside her. "Everything will be okay," I say, even though I'm not so sure.

"Thank you," she says. "For everything." The car door shuts. I watch as Mia strides along the sidewalk, her arms stiffly at her sides. She pulls open the station's door. The door swings closed behind her.

I go home and sit on the couch staring at a blank television screen. I hear a key jangle in the front door and then my mom steps inside. "Hey," Mom says, her brow furrowing in concern. "Happy New Year. What're you doing?"

I shrug. "Just wondering why some people in this world are so evil."

"That's not like you at all, honey," my mom says. She presses the back of her hand against my forehead. "Do you have a fever? You feel cool."

"I'm fine, Mom," I say. "Don't worry."

"Where's your father?" she asks.

"Oh, um," I pause. "He had some business stuff to take care of."

"Um-hum," my mother says, ascending the stairs. A few minutes later, she comes back down. "Everything looks great upstairs! The bedroom is immaculate. He must really want to show me how much he's changed." She moves into the kitchen. I hear the faucet running and then the click-click-click of a burner igniting.

I'm still thinking about Mia when my mom hands me a cup of hot tea. "Drink this. It contains the herbs Ashwagandha and Shankhpushpi."

I raise my brows. "Shank-huh-what?"

"It will elevate your mood," Mom says, half of her words muffled by a yawn. "I've been up for over twenty-four hours. I'm heading to bed."

"Goodnight," I say, flicking on the television. I must've fallen asleep on the couch because it's hours later when I jolt awake as the front door squeaks open. My dad tiptoes inside.

"Is the coast clear?" he whispers.

"Huh?" I ask, still groggy.

"I expected a guillotine in the entry when I got home." Dad settles into the armchair. "I thought I'd only be gone a couple of hours, but the session was going so well. I can't interrupt the creative process when we're on a roll like that. Your mom's probably furious at me."

"You narrowly escaped beheading this time," I say. "Fortunately for you, the organization fairy swung by today. A little pixie dust and boom all of your bags were unpacked. Each item magically transported to its proper place long before Mom got home from her double shift."

Dad smiles, crinkles forming around his eyes. "I guess I owe this organization fairy, huh?"

"She said that she'd come back to collect her gratuity. You can leave cash under her pillow. Interest accrues daily."

He laughs and I can't help but join in. We laugh and laugh, deep, bellowing laughter, laughter that's relief, laughter that's joy. Covering for my dad isn't my proudest moment but it sure is worth it.

The clock strikes midnight; twenty-four hours have passed since the year began. For the past two-hundred-four nights, just before I fell asleep, I whispered the one thing I wanted most in this world. Now, I have that. Dad is back for good. My family is officially together again. Knowing that we're all under one roof, I slip into bed, breathing deeper than I have in a long, long time.

As I fall asleep, I vaguely remember that I wanted to tell my dad off. I feel the strong girl on the boat fading away. He's home, and that's all that matters. Everything is going to be okay. In fact, everything is perfect.

It's very easy to slip back into old habits.

24

Everly's Party

Ethan

Kira slides into the seat next to me. Snakes bite her neck and her cheeks, leaving fang marks. A black tar-like liquid escapes from the tiny holes. It streaks across her aura, smearing and blocking out the fluorescence just below the surface, each streak threatening to swallow the last flickers of her light.

"Kira, I know you're not okay," I say. "Did you read the articles that Jenna sent you? We want to help."

"I'm not allowed to talk to you," Kira says. The black liquid drips onto her hand. I go to wipe it away and a snake strikes at me.

After school, Jenna collapses onto her back in the knee-deep snow. She laughs, puffs of white escaping from her lips as her arms and legs pump wildly. I study the row of snow angels, all touching wings. "How many are you going to make?"

"Seven," Jenna says. She stands up, takes a few steps, and starts the process all over again. "The seven archangels." She's breathless, her stars illuminating the snow beneath her.

Jenna sits up, counting the line of angels. "Done," she says, brushing off her pants as she stands up. I sling my arm over her shoulder. "Each archangel has his own special gift: strength, healing, communication, intellect, love, beauty, and justice. Whenever you need help in any of these areas, you can ask the archangels for guidance."

"You've already mastered them all."

"That's what you see," she says. Tiny snowflakes land delicately on her eyelashes. She shivers.

"Let's go inside and warm up," I say.

"I'll make the hot chocolate!" Jenna says, skipping ahead. "With marshmallows!"

We make our way onto Jenna's front porch. As soon as she opens the door, we hear yelling.

"Don't roll your eyes at me!" Jenna's mom shouts. "This isn't a joke! We're running out of money. Your account's almost empty."

"Everything's going to be alright," Jenna's dad says. "I'm working on a few new songs and--"

"You need to find a job," Jenna's mom says.

"Music *is* my job!"

"It doesn't pay the bills! In two years, Jenna's going to college. Do you know how expensive college tuition is? Are you even living in the real world?"

Jenna slams the front door. The fighting stops abruptly.

Jenna's mom pokes her head into the entryway, a teacup clenched in her fist. "Hi, Ethan," she said. "It's wonderful to see you." Her smile is tight. I notice a few of her tulips are drooping, thick thorny vines wrapped around their base.

"Hi, Mrs. Farrell," I say, careful not to make eye contact. Jenna takes my hand and leads me to the kitchen.

Jenna's dad stands up. "Hey, Ethan." He shakes my hand. "I don't mean to be rude, but I'm on my way out." He zips up his coat.

"Where are you going?" Jenna asks.

"Work."

"But..." Jenna's voice trails off. "You'll be home later, right?"

"Of course, sweetheart."

The vacuum roars in the living room as Jenna and I drink hot chocolate with extra marshmallows. "Are you okay?" I ask her.

Jenna blinks a few times before she answers, almost like she's trapped in a daze. "Yeah, fine." Her phone buzzes. She responds to a text, her fingers sliding across the keyboard. "Everly's parents are going to a wedding tonight. She's having a few friends over. I told her that I'm hanging out with you."

"How many people?" I ask.

Jenna shrugs. "I'm not sure. Why?"

"I, um, I, might want to go."

Jenna's mouth hangs slightly open. "Really?"

"Yeah, I mean, I want to try."

Jenna's eyes light up. "Let me ask her how many people." Her fingers race across the screen. "She's expecting six people, seven if you join."

I nod. "I think I can do that."

A few hours later, Jenna holds my clammy hand at Everly's front door. "Are you ready?" she asks.

"Ready as I'll ever be." I try to sound more confident than I feel.

Jenna rings the doorbell. I keep my gaze glued to the concrete. I hear footsteps and the door swings open. "Hi,

Jenna!" Two female voices greet my girlfriend. One is accompanied by a steady, calming sound reminiscent of a light pitter-patter of rain. The other has a more frenetic energy, a squirrel with its back arched up.

"Hi, Ethan," Rain-girl says. "I'm Shaviah."

I glance up and see an enormous lion. It watches me through its piercing eyes, its teeth bared back. I lift my hands in defense, backing away too fast, tripping over a rock, and falling on my ass. I never should've come here. I made a huge mistake, and now I'm embarrassing Jenna.

"I knew this wasn't a good idea," the other girl says. "I think he should just go home."

"Chill out, Everly," Shaviah says. "Give him a second."

Shaviah takes a few steps out the door. Iridescent yellow light, like the sun on its brightest day, follows her like a spotlight, the shadow of the lion reflected within it. My heartbeat speeds up. "Are you okay?" Her voice is so kind, so soothing, that I can't imagine how this beast is part of her.

I'm terrified. But it doesn't matter. These are Jenna's friends, and I'm not going to quit on her. I raise my chin. The lion looks down at me. It's a beautiful creature: a long, thick brown mane, wise golden eyes. Now that I've taken a second look, it doesn't seem so menacing. "I'm okay," I squeak out.

"Great!" Shaviah says. She reaches out her arm. After a moment, I take it. She helps me to my feet. "It's so nice to finally meet you. Jenna talks about you all the time."

"She talks about you too," I mumble.

"Let's go inside," Shaviah says. "I'll introduce you to the others."

With Jenna on one side and Shaviah on the other, I walk through the front door. Everly grabs Shaviah by the arm and pulls her aside. "I don't know about this," she whispers too loudly. "I don't want my house destroyed."

"I'm far more likely to destroy your house than he is," Shaviah hisses back. I don't doubt her for one second.

I'm introduced to Raven (endless words, a popping sound as more words emerged, as though they were kernels bursting in a microwave oven), Pete (splashes of neon color, flashes of lightning), and Aaron (a mellow island beat, the scent of lemons).

All of the colors, scents, and images swarm around me. When I'm in class, I know to focus on the teacher and attempt to tune out the rest (although that's challenging, and I often record lectures to re-listen to when I get home). At a social event, I'm not sure which stimuli to attend to. I squeeze my eyes shut, taking deep breaths to block out all the commotion that has become static in my head.

Beside me, Jenna squeezes my hand. "Are you okay?" she asks. I open my eyes and look into hers: dark brown, flecked with green, wide, loving. Suddenly, I am.

Raven pulls up a chair next to us.

"Hey, Raven," Jenna says. "How's the novel coming?"

"It was moving along nicely, but now I'm stuck," Raven says. I watch as the words bounce around her, and now that I'm looking closer, I notice details that I didn't before. There are big words, small words, SAT words, difficult words that I've never seen before, and words in every color of the rainbow. They move around and over and into each other until they find the perfect fit. Words string themselves together into beautiful sentences that read like poetry.

"I have a feeling the words will come together for you," I say.

Aaron cracks open a beer and offers it to me. "You need a drink, man?"

I wrap my fingers around the cold glass bottle. "Thanks." I can't believe how nice everyone is being to me.

I ask Raven about her writing. She tells me about the novel she's working on, and then she asks me about my interests. She's easy to talk to, and I find myself easily blocking out the rest of the chaos that surrounds me.

"You know," Raven says. "You're a lot different than I thought you'd be."

I grin. "The rumors of my psychotic tendencies have been greatly exaggerated."

"You'd be a great character for a book," Raven says.

"Ha!" I shake my head. "Me? Who'd want to read that?"

Pete shuffles a deck of cards. "Who wants to play Cards Against Humanity?"

There's a chorus of agreement as everyone gathers around the table. "Do you want to play?" Jenna asks me.

"Um, sure," I say. I've never played before, but I catch on fast. By the tenth round, I'm in the lead. I guess this soul-seeing thing does have its advantages after all.

But even more than that, I'm enjoying myself. There are no demons here; no vile creatures. Shaviah's lion sits back, strong and loyal. All of the other sights and scents and sounds meld together; a moment of disharmonious turmoil before it blends into something beautiful. This group, together, makes sense. And I'm part of that. Me. Ethan Underwood. Incredible.

The doorbell rings. Everly's eyes widen.

"Who's that?" Shaviah asks.

"I didn't invite anyone else," Everly says. "I hope my parents aren't home early."

The doorbell rings again. Everly and Shaviah jump up to answer the door. A group of five guys enter. A rush of new souls assaults me: an eagle soaring overhead, a spinning compass, glowing emeralds, and an electric guitar playing a riff. "What are you doing here?" Shaviah asks, her arms folded across her chest.

A tall blonde guy answers. "We heard there was a party." He holds up a case of beer. "We brought drinks."

"Well, this isn't a party, and you need to go—" Shaviah starts.

Everly cuts her off. She's staring up at the blonde guy the way Jenna looks at me. "Shaviah, it's okay. They can stay."

The new souls disrupt the rhythm; it's like starting from square one. I close my eyes and clench my fists. "Do you want to leave?" Jenna asks.

I breathe deeply, until the trembling in my core ceases. "No," I say. "We're having fun."

"Are you sure?" Her eyes search mine.

"Yes." I force a smile to reassure her. I've come this far. I'm not quitting now.

Word spreads through Roxbury like wildfire. Within forty-five minutes, half of the high school shows up, trampling through Everly's living room, guzzling beers and blasting music. Shaviah picks up crushed solo cups from the floor, shaking her head.

"This is out of control," Jenna says. "We need to stop this invasion before pandemonium ensues."

A guy bends over and pukes into a houseplant. "I think it already has," Shaviah says. "Where's Everly?"

Everly's on the blonde guy's lap, their lips pressed together.

"Everly!" Shaviah says. "Your parents will be home in an hour. Everyone has to leave now so we have time to clean up."

"Chill out," Everly's words are slurred, her eyes half-open. "It's all good."

"Are you kidding me?" Shaviah snaps her fingers in front of Everly's face. "Get with it or you're going to be grounded for life."

As Jenna and Shaviah try to talk sense into Everly, I retreat further into myself. Demons are swirling now. Blood-thirsty critters circle my feet. I lift my feet and close my eyes. I can still hear the screams. I can still smell the stench of rotting meat. Something crawls up my arm. I'm a few moments away from losing it.

"I'm going to the bathroom," I say. I need to get out of this room. Walls don't always keep the demons out. They can slip under the bathroom door, but at least it will buy me some time. Jenna spins around, her hand clapped against her mouth as she looks me over. I guess I look pretty bad.

"Oh, Ethan, I'm so sorry," Jenna says. "Let's get out of here. I'll let Shaviah handle Everly."

"I'm fine," I insist. "I just need a few minutes. Help your friend."

"No," Jenna says. "We're leaving."

I jump to my feet. "No." I know it's stupid, but I don't want to let Jenna down. Everything has been going so well. I want to finish out the night like every other boyfriend in the room. Like I'm normal. "Don't follow me. I'll be right back. Take care of your friend." I stand on shaky legs and walk into the crowd. Head down, I fixate on my shoes like I do in the school hallways, thinking only of placing one foot in front of the other.

I'm steps away from the bathroom when I hear the familiar cackle. My heart rate speeds up. Not now. Not him. Not when I'm almost there. The black tar-like substance floats around my legs. I remember how it felt lodged inside my throat outside of Vinny's pizzeria. Cole McFadden steps in front of me, blocking my path. "What's this freak doing here?"

"Let me pass," I stammer.

"Who's going to make me?" Cole grins.

Winged hyenas spin around me now, cackling, baring their teeth. The black tar wraps around my feet, anchoring me to the ground. I close my eyes, teeth gritted together. Cole's laughter mingles with the hyena's cackles. The tar moves up my legs and over my torso, pressing into my chest, making it harder to breathe.

I have two options. I can run. Every cell in my body wants to. Turn around and book it the hell out of there.

Or I can fight. The hyenas move in, snapping at me, their spiky teeth inches from my flesh. My heart feels like it might explode out of my chest. Sweat drips down my back.

My eyes flick open. "I am," I said. A gold sword appears, its blade slashing through the air, instantly decapitating three hyenas. I stand up a little taller. An onslaught of golden arrows sail through the air, poking holes in hyenas like Swiss cheese. They shriek, writhing as they drop to the floor.

The black tar fades away. I can move my feet again. I'm winning. *I'm winning.*

But the hyenas don't stop coming. More and more appear, each one more vicious than the last. One maneuvers past my defenses, its teeth digging into my arm. Mind-blowing pain sears through me. Another hyena chomps into my thigh. My knees weaken.

I can't take the pain any longer. I have to get out of here. I'll run away with my head down like all of the other times before. Except for one time. The time I defeated the monster in my soul. I remember the scene: the grotesque monster, the scared little boy, Jenna's voice saying, "You're much stronger than you think you are."

I'm not giving up, not yet. Not ever. A flash of spotted fur breaks through, claws swiping, inflicting deep wounds on several hyenas. The cheetah's face appears, brown eyes glowing as she sinks her teeth into the hyena that's latched onto my arm. After she defeats that hyena, Nala moves towards the hyena on my thigh.

More and more hyenas materialize, but my arrows come faster now, spraying like bullets from an automatic weapon. My sword and Nala take care of the rest. There are only a few hyenas left. They eye me, hanging back, keeping a careful distance.

All of this happens in less than half of a split second.

I lunge at Cole and shove him as hard as I can. He stumbles and falls backward, landing on his ass. There's laughter, but this time it's mine.

His face is bright red as he gets to his feet. "Fucking freak!"

"What the hell's going on?" Tav darts into the hallway, stepping between me and Cole.

"The psycho pushed me," Cole says. "And now I'm going to kick his ass!" But he doesn't sound too confident. He also doesn't resist very much when Tav holds him back.

"The neighbors called the cops. They're on their way," Tav says. "Relax, man, or you'll end up getting arrested."

"Oh, shit," Cole says, moving past me. "Guess you got lucky this time, freak!"

Partygoers move out the front door in hordes. Within ten minutes, Shaviah, Jenna, and I are the only conscious people left inside the house. Everly's asleep on the couch.

"Shaviah, you're brilliant," Jenna says, picking up a beer can and tossing it into a black garbage bag.

"The police ploy works every time," Shaviah pokes Everly. "Wake up."

Everly mumbles something incomprehensible and half sits up. Shaviah puts her arm around Everly's waist and helps her to her feet. "I'm going to put her to bed," Shaviah says. "You guys keep straightening up."

Twenty minutes later, Everly's tucked in, and the house is pristine. As we drive away from Everly's house, a car rolls into the driveway. "I think her parents just got home," I say.

"The nick of time." Jenna reaches over and holds my hand. "Thanks for helping clean up. I'm sorry that everyone in the galaxy showed up in an unexpected invasion. Even so, you did great tonight."

I smile. "I stood up to Cole McFadden."

Her eyebrows shoot up. "You did what?"

"I'm stronger than I used to be," I say. "And it's because of you."

Jenna shakes her head. "Not me. You." She parks in front of my house. "I had a great night."

"Me too," I say as her lips meet mine.

25

Secret Tickets

Jenna

Over the next two months, Ethan metamorphosed from a recluse to a social butterfly. Okay, I'm exaggerating. But comparatively speaking, he came a long way. (I'll admit the bar was low.) On Valentine's Day, we went out to a crowded restaurant, and he got through the entire meal, even dessert. He also attended three gatherings with my friends, and each time he seemed a little more comfortable. After the last event, he didn't even need to change his shirt when he got home. It was completely dry.

When Saja and Javi came to visit, the four of us hiked through the woods. Ethan led the way, guiding us through a labyrinth of trails. We walked over a creaky wooden footbridge, a stream gurgling beneath us. Something slithered through the mud and disappeared into the water. My heart pounded as we made our way up the incline, step by step, my thighs burning. It wasn't until we reached the top that I realized how far we'd climbed. We stood side-by-side at the precipice, the sky impossibly light like we'd wandered into a cloud.

Below us, the world was endless slopes and valleys: hills and fields, waterfalls and ravines, trees that towered and bent and grew from rocks. It was a magical place, ripe for the meanderings of otherworldly creatures. If I blinked super-fast, I could see them: a silver-horned unicorn rolling in the grass, a purple-scaled dragon beating his wings against the white sky.

When we returned to my house, the four of us lounged in the living room. For hours, we talked and joked. Ethan joined right in, the witty boy that I love on display right in front of them. And they loved him too, just like I knew they would.

Everything was perfect. Saja and Javi were coming to visit again next month. I somehow even managed to defy all of the laws of nature and scored an A on my last two pre-calculus exams. Pre-med, here I come!

"GREGORY EDWARD FARRELL, WHAT IS THIS DISASTER IN MY KITCHEN?"

Well, except for the demon that's been possessing my mother every other night for the past three weeks. Even though I'm in the living room with one ear pressed against a pillow and the television on, I can hear every single word. The demon does not use her inside voice.

"GREGORY COME DOWN HERE AND CLEAN THIS UP RIGHT NOW!" My mother yells up the stairs.

The bedroom door opens and shuts. "Linda, will you chill out? I needed a snack. Maybe you need one too. Seems like someone is hangry." His footsteps clap down the stairs and into the kitchen.

"Don't start with me! You're not cute!" My mother hollers. "Why did you feel the need to put half of the refrigerator on the table?"

"I couldn't decide what I wanted."

"How long has all of this been sitting out?"

"Um, I'm not sure. Maybe a couple hours."

"HOURS? These are perishables! Now everything has to go in the trash!"

"Oh, relax, it's fine," my dad says.

"It is NOT fine!" Plastic rustles and I hear thump-thump-thump as items hit the bottom of the garbage can. "We can't afford to be throwing food away! We can barely pay the bills."

"I have plenty of money in my account."

"Gregory, no you do not, and we've already discussed this. You've somehow managed to blow through almost all of your massive trust fund. Whatever's left is for Jenna's college education and is NOT to be touched!"

I turn up the television volume, hoping to drown out the bickering. My chest is tight. No matter how hard I suck in a breath I can't get enough air like my lungs have sprung a leak. How is it that I can be quirky in public, follow strange boys into the woods and fight demon beasts but I can't stomach my parents fighting? Why does nothing else get to me the way this can?

My stomach churns and heat rises into my face. I force in a shallow breath and focus all of my attention on the television. I'm fine, fine, fine, fine, fine. Really, I'm fine. I'm so enraptured by the news that I don't even hear the cabinet doors slam. I don't even notice my dad's fist bang against the table. Nope. The news is so so so interesting. Yup, yup, yup, I love the evening news.

The anchorwoman's expression is solemn. "Another college student went missing last week in New York City. Twenty-year-old Rachel Gallagher was last seen at a local bar on a date with a mystery man she met on the internet. Rachel is a political science major who is passionate about helping others, particularly those who come from impoverished and underrepresented communities. Friends describe her as a person who is determined to make a positive impact on the world." A photograph appears on the screen. Curly red tendrils frame Rachel's soft features.

"At this time, police are unsure if this case is connected with eighteen-year-old Brittany Shulman who disappeared over two months ago. Some fear that a serial kidnapper or worse could be on the loose." Brittany smiles in the photograph displayed on the screen. Her blue eyes shine behind horn-rimmed glasses.

The picture fades and the anchor-woman moves on to another story. "Another accuser has come forward in the Max Brophy case. The twenty-two-year-old woman alleges that she was sexually abused by Brophy at just nine years old. Ever since a Roxbury teen reported that she had been his victim years ago, several new accusers have come out. The teen, whose identity remains undisclosed, seems to have encouraged others who may have been too afraid to bring up incidents from so long ago."

Her co-anchor shakes his head. "This isn't looking too good for Max Brophy."

I grab my phone and text Mia.

Me: You're a bad-ass, kick-ass, brave-ass, inspirational-ass, justice-getting-ass sorceress.

Mia: I don't know that my ass has ever been complimented so much.

Me: Then you must be hanging out with the wrong people.

In the kitchen, the battle rages on. "I don't know what you're smiling about!" My mom shouts. "Our finances are not a joke! At least now we're not paying for that stupid cabin—"

"Oh, is that why you asked me to move in?" My dad asks. "Money?"

"We can't afford two rents, Gregory!"

"Silly me," my dad says, his tone bitter. "I thought you wanted to work on our marriage."

"I do," my mom sighs. "Of course, I do. But we need money! You need to get a job!"

"I have a job. I was up all night working on some new songs—"

"It's not a job if it doesn't bring in a steady paycheck. I saw a music teacher job posted online today. I emailed them your resume."

"Why would you do that? I've told you a million times that I don't want to teach! I want to create!"

"You're going to have a hard time creating anything in the dark when our electricity gets shut off."

"You're so dramatic, Linda. If we need money, I'll take care of it."

"I'm not accepting any more handouts from your daddy! We're not children, Gregory."

I press my fingers into my ears as I climb the stairs. I need to get away. At this proximity, my soul is in jeopardy of becoming possessed by whatever malignant spirit has infected my parents. I'm not sure how to help them. Dousing them with holy water might provide some short-term relief, but this possession was far too advanced for that to last. At this point, I need to learn how to perform a full-blown exorcism; rotating heads, projectile vomit, and all. Hopefully, I can find a tutorial on YouTube.

I slam the door to my bedroom, not that anyone notices over the screaming downstairs. I blast pop music and open my math textbooks. I'm almost finished with my homework when someone knocks on my door. "Jenna?" My dad says.

"Come in." I turn off the music and push my books aside.

My dad sits in my fluffy chair and folds his hands. My heart speeds up. I know what this is about. He's going to tell me that he's leaving again. I swallow hard. I didn't expect this to happen so soon. As much as I hate the drama, I don't want him to go. Hot tears burn behind my eyes.

He smiles. "Sweetheart, I have a surprise for you," he says.

"A... surprise?" Maybe I'm wrong. Maybe he's not leaving.

Dad reaches into his pocket. "I was going to wait to tell you until it got closer, but I'm too excited." He holds two slips of paper in his hand. "There's a very important day coming up next month."

"In April?" I furrow my brow. "My birthday?"

"That's right." Dad smiles. "I got us baseball tickets. Yankees vs. Red Sox. Front row."

I grab the tickets from his hand. "Oh my God!" I squeal, jumping up and down like a little kid. I throw my arms around my dad's neck, scanning the details over his shoulder.

My jaw drops so hard that I'm surprised my jaw-bone didn't dislodge from my skull. The number in the corner... is that the price or the box-office phone number? My heart sinks like a boulder air-dropped into the ocean. I pull out of my dad's embrace. "Um, Dad, these were a lot of money."

"Nothing is too expensive for my daughter's seventeenth birthday present."

"But..." I don't know what to say without taking my mom's side. I hate having to choose. "But Mom is worried about money."

"It's no problem," Dad says. "I'm going to be making a whole lot of money really soon. I'm so close to signing with a big record label."

I've heard that line before. I stare at the tickets in my hand like they're kryptonite.

"Jenna, listen," my dad takes a deep breath, his expression serious. "I know in the past I haven't always been around for your birthday. This year I wanted to make it up to you by doing something really special."

My vision blurs as emotion rises up my throat. My dad always knows the exact right thing to say.

"What do you say, Jenna? Me and you, sitting front row with the celebrities, watching the Yankees destroy the Red Sox, making memories that will last a lifetime. You can't put a price on that."

"Well, when you put it like that..." I surrender.

"You hold on to the tickets," he says. "You know I lose everything. Put them somewhere safe."

"I will lock them inside my dragon-guarded secret vault," I say.

My dad grins. He starts to open the bedroom door but turns back around. "Also, Jenna, I'd appreciate it if you didn't mention this to your mom."

"But..." I pause. "You're going to tell her, right?" I don't like keeping secrets from Mom.

"Yeah, of course," my dad says. "I just don't think right now is the best time."

"When is?" I ask.

"I'll figure that out. Don't worry about a thing. I'll handle it."

I swallow and bite the inside of my cheek.

"Do you trust me?" Dad asks.

I'm not sure if I do. After everything from the past, I shouldn't. But I want to. I want so badly for my dad to be someone that I can trust, someone that I can count on. So I say, "Yes." At that moment, I make myself believe it.

"We're going to have a blast, sweetheart."

26

Free

Ethan

I'm upstairs when the doorbell rings. I hear my mom's footsteps patter across the entryway and the door swings open. It must be a package or something.

"Ethan, there's someone here for you!"

I walk downstairs, my brow creased. On our front patio, I see a flash of golden light. A burgundy sparrow flies into the entryway and lands on my wrist. Her feathers are smooth; her eyes are bright. She looks in much better condition than the last time I saw her.

"Hi, Kira." I lean against the doorjamb. "I'm surprised to see you here."

Her hands are stuffed inside her pockets, and she shifts from foot to foot. "Well, um, you know I haven't been in school all week. I was hoping you could catch me up on what I missed in Chemistry. Sorry I didn't call first. I don't have your number."

"Oh, no problem," I say. "How are you feeling? I heard you had the flu."

"I'm feeling better." I show her into the living room where she sits on the couch.

"I'll be right back." I run upstairs, grab my science notebook, and then come back to join her on the couch. "Um, you look more like your old self." I can still see traces of snake bites around her neck, but they're healing.

Kira stares at me. "How can you tell, Ethan?"

"Tell what?" I laugh uncomfortably, dropping my gaze to the floor.

"What's going on inside of people."

I shrug. "Lucky guesses?" Kira studies me; I can feel her gaze burning into my cheek. The sparrow tilts her head and winks at me. The bird knows I'm different, that I can see her, which means deep down, Kira knows too. "Um, here's my chemistry notes." I hand her the notebook. "You can take them home and copy them. I'm done with them for tonight."

"Thanks," she says, placing the notebook on her lap. "I didn't come here for the notes." She takes a deep breath. "I wanted to say I'm sorry."

"You don't have to—"

She cuts me off. "You were right, Ethan. About everything. About Luke." A tear slips out of her eye. She wipes it away. "I should've listened to you."

I'm not sure what to say. Being right doesn't feel good like it's supposed to.

"I didn't have the flu. I was too depressed to get out of bed. I spent a few days in the psych ward."

"Kira, I'm so sorry." I know firsthand how awful the psych unit can be.

"It was the best thing for me. The therapists made me see how toxic Luke is. I still have a lot to work on. If I'd been stronger and more secure, he couldn't have broken me down as easily as he did. I'm going to continue therapy once a week to work on myself."

"That's good," I say.

"I feel free." She tosses her hair; it tumbles loosely down her back. "I allowed myself to be imprisoned, but at the time, I didn't even realize it. When you're feeling weak, you forget how strong you are." She shakes her head. "I'm not sure if I'm making sense."

Everything she's saying makes perfect sense to me, but I'm not sure how to tell her that. She stands up to leave, my notebook in her fist. We say goodbye, and she's almost through the door when she suddenly turns around and hugs me. I'm stiff for a few moments before I lightly place my hands on her back.

"Thanks for looking out for me. You're a good friend." Kira says.

An hour later, I'm finishing my homework when there's a light knock on my bedroom door. "Come in."

The door creaks open. "The diner is closed for renovations, so I'm home tonight. What would you like for dinner?" My mom asks.

I put my pencil down. "Actually, I'm going to Jenna's for dinner, then we're going bowling with friends."

"That's great," Mom says. She sits on the edge of the bed and watches me. Why do parents sometimes think they can just stare at you, and it's not supposed to be awkward at all? I avert my gaze back toward my History book, rifling through the pages.

"Who was that girl who stopped by earlier?"

"A friend," I say, keeping my eyes on my book.

"Ethan," my mom clears her throat. "I just wanted to say…" She pauses. "I'm so proud of you. Jenna is so wonderful, and you have all these new friends… And I'm just really happy for you, is all."

I swallow hard. "I'm glad you're finally proud of me."

"That's not what I meant."

"It's okay." I shrug. "I understand I haven't made it easy for you. I wouldn't have been proud of me either."

"You're wrong. I've always been proud of you. I know how difficult life has been for you. I know how cruel kids can be. Yet you've always had an amazing heart and great grades at school. Why would you think I wasn't proud of you?"

I shrug. "You were always trying to fix me, reading self-help books on parenting and bringing me to doctors and therapists. Honestly, I thought you were ashamed of me."

"You have it all wrong. I just wanted to see you happy. Being your mom brought so much joy into my life and I wanted the same joy for you."

"I'm happy, Mom," I say. "Happier than I've ever been."

"That's all I ever wanted." The heaviness that always surrounds her lifts, the scratchy surface of worry peeling away. Her pastels encompass me, softness like velvet resting against my skin. It feels stronger than before, now that my walls are down.

When she leaves, I stretch out, my hands folded behind my neck. Even though I've made some progress, I'm far from normal. I'm getting better at navigating social situations, blocking out the noise, and zoning in on conversations. Still, my only attempt to eat in the cafeteria was a complete failure.

When Jenna saw me turning green, she suggested that I take a break. I'm lucky I made it to the bathroom in time to vomit all over the sink. I don't think retching on everyone's lunches would've earned me any friends.

I still have a long way to go, but I'll keep working on it. I think about what my mom said, about always being proud. I don't know if that's true or just some mumbo-jumbo that parents are required to say, no matter how much their kid sucks. It certainly isn't true for my dad. I picture him in my mind: the hard gaze in his eyes, the exasperated sigh when I had another fit, the hard shock of his hand against my bottom like he could beat the craziness out of me.

I wonder what he would think if he saw me now. I wonder if he would be proud of me. On second thought, fuck him. I hope he's happy with his replacement family.

An hour later, Jenna's mom places a tray of chicken and a big bowl of corn on the dining room table. "Do you two have anything fun planned for this weekend?"

"On Sunday we're going to the Young App Developers Fair." My heart speeds up when I think of the fair. It's going to be loud and crowded. Luke will be there, his snakes ready to strike if I come too close. Hundreds of unknown souls will be there, so I'm forecasting at least a few nefarious amongst the benign. Yet, I want to go support Alex. Jenna assured me that we'll leave as soon as I feel sick. I just hope it doesn't come to that.

A phone buzzes and Jenna's dad lifts it to his ear. "Hey, man," he says, raising one finger towards us to indicate that he'll be off the phone in one second. "I can't really talk right now. I'm having dinner with the fam." He pauses while someone talks on the other end. "Definitely, man. We'll meet up tomorrow and go over some ideas. I want you to listen to this new song I'm working on. It has a reggae-funk and hard-rock twist. I think you'll really dig it." Jenna's mom glares. "Listen man, I got to go. I'll see you tomorrow. Alright, bye."

"What do you mean you'll see him tomorrow?"

"Oh, um, I'm meeting up with Eddie for a couple of hours to work on some things."

"You mean, *after* your job interview?"

"Yes, of course."

"What job interview?" Jenna asks.

"Oh, your mom sent my resume in for this music teacher position."

"It's a wonderful opportunity," Jenna's mom says. "Steady salary, great benefits…"

"Yeah, yeah, yeah," he responds. "All of the things I've been dreaming of." His sarcasm can't be missed.

"*You're going*," Jenna's mom says.

"Yep, I'm going." I glance up at her dad. The feathers that encompass him are even more marvelous than I remembered: all of the colors, bright blue and pink and silver and gold, the wild designs and shapes. The feathers move faster than before, flapping furiously, the wind blowing the barbs like a hurricane is blasting through the country kitchen. It defies all laws of gravity that his feet remain on the ground. I don't know if they will for much longer.

Not long after, I follow Jenna inside the bowling alley. I can sense the souls ahead, a few unsavory ones in the mix, but I'm prepared. I can almost feel the hilt of my sword against my thigh, ready to be drawn at a moment's notice. Like Kira, I feel free. Liberated from the chains that held me down for so many years. At least freer than I've ever been before.

But not everyone is free.

I'm drawn towards a flyer in the lobby, my fingertips tracing its edges. MISSING is stamped above Rachel Gallagher's headshot: sky-blue eyes, red curls framing her delicate features. It's not often that I sense someone's soul through a photograph, but Rachel's essence seems to emanate from the paper. A neon polka-dotted butterfly pops off the page, hovering beside me for a few moments before dissipating. IF YOU HAVE ANY INFORMATION ABOUT RACHEL'S WHEREABOUTS, PLEASE CALL THE ANONYMOUS HOTLINE.

"Is everything okay?" Jenna turns back. "We need to rent shoes. Our lane is ready."

"Coming," I say, the lobby door swinging shut behind me. My bowling skills aren't half bad. I manage to have conversations even despite the busy environment. A few demons loom nearby, but one slice of my sword and they keep their distance.

I should've been on top of the world. But for some reason, my thoughts keep traveling back to Rachel Gallagher. The appearance of that neon butterfly makes me think that she's still alive. For now.

27

Ghosts

Jenna

"YOU DIDN'T GO ON THE JOB INTERVIEW?" At first, I'm not sure if I'm having a nightmare or if the demon returned again at this ungodly hour. I roll over and rub the crust out of my eyes.

"Whatever, Linda, I told you that I didn't want that stupid job. You never listen to me."

"YOU'VE BEEN LYING TO ME FOR WEEKS!"

"Because I knew you'd flip out! And look, I was right! I wouldn't have to lie if you were a supportive wife who encouraged me to follow my dreams!"

I reach for the package of earplugs on my nightstand. After several failed attempts at exorcism, I realized that I needed a new strategy. At Walgreens, I stocked up on earplugs, Tylenol PM, and an aromatherapy "deep-sleep" candle. If I fail another exam due to sleep deprivation, I fear that the demon could turn homicidal.

A few hours later, my alarm goes off. I groan loud enough to rouse the undead. In a zombie-like state, I press the snooze button far too many times. When I finally open my eyes, I call my clock a liar, a bitch, and a few other names that should not be used around children. My clock doesn't even argue back. She knows I'm right.

I jolt out of bed, brush my teeth, throw on clothes and run out the front door. As I start my car, I realize that my shirt is inside out, and I haven't brushed my hair. Whatever. Maybe I'll start a trend. If anyone comments, I'll say that I'm bringing back grunge and start head-banging.

At least I won't be late. One more lateness and I'll have detention for the next month. As I speed down my driveway, I notice that my dad's motorcycle is gone. My dad never leaves so early in the morning. My heart's chambers seem to go haywire, a fluttering, breathless sensation that makes me cough. I need to chill out. Everything is fine. I'll see my dad later. Everything is fine, fine, fine. If I say it enough times, it will be true.

The day goes by too fast. I'm pretty sure I've never said that about a school day before. I might be losing my mind. Maybe a zombie stuck a straw in my ear while I slept and sucked out the rational portion of my brain. When the final bell rings, I linger in the library working on projects that aren't due for months. At this point, I'm certifiable. When that gets boring, I research pre-med programs and watch surgery videos. I stay until the librarian kicks me out. Everyone has to go home at some point.

There are only two foreseeable options when I arrive home: one, my parents are still at each other's throats, or two, my dad is gone. I don't know which is worse.

I drive below the speed limit, making sure to come to a complete stop at each stop sign and look in all directions. I find myself gazing at the pot-holes longingly, wishing that one would suck me inside its vortex and transport me to an alternate universe. I can only delay the inevitable for so long.

His motorcycle isn't there. I swing open the front door, telling myself that it doesn't mean anything at all. He could be out making music or running errands. He'll pull up the driveway any minute.

The house is quiet. "Mom?" I say. She doesn't answer. "Mom?" I repeat, louder this time.

I turn around and see the back of her head. She's sitting on the couch, her neck bent forward. The television isn't on. "Mom?" I throw my backpack on the floor and rush into the living room.

She holds a crumpled tissue in one hand and a full teacup in the other. "Mom?".

Her chin jerks up like she just registered my presence. She looks at me. Her mouth opens and shuts, but she can't get the words to come out. She doesn't have to. I already know.

"Where is he?" I ask.

She shrugs. "Damned if I know. He flew away. I only know that much because I checked our bank account online. He bought the ticket this morning."

My veins are gas lines and someone flicks a match. Red hot rage flashes through me. Strangely, the person I'm most angry with is myself. For trusting him. For thinking it would be different this time around. For believing in a fantasy world where every story ends with happily ever after.

We order pizza and sip tea that claims to promote positive thinking. It doesn't work.

Ghosts wake me all night long. I hear footsteps on the porch, the strum of an acoustic guitar, the purr of a motorcycle rolling up the driveway. I peek through the blinds at my driveway. No one is there.

Purrscilla curls up next to me, her chin on my shoulder. She watches me with knowing eyes as my tears slide down. As I roll over, something crinkles under my pillow. I reach underneath and find an envelope labeled *For the Organization Fairy*. Inside is a silver pendant, a delicate unicorn with a sapphire eye. As much as I hate to admit it, I love it.

He calls the next day. When I see his name on my caller ID, I decide that I'm not going to pick up. I last two rings.

"Hello?"

"Hi, Sweetheart!" His voice is cheerful. "Guess where I am?"

"Burning in the fiery pits of hell?"

Dad laughs. "Close enough. I'm in California!" He says it like I should be excited.

"That's too bad. I was hoping Satan was stabbing you with a pitchfork right now."

"I guess I deserve that," he pauses. "I'm sorry I left without saying goodbye. A huge record label guru wants to meet with me ASAP. I had to seize the moment. Carpe diem."

"Sure, and Purrscilla jumped over a rainbow and turned into a flying purple goblin."

"Oh, now I see how it is," Dad says. "You're like your mother. You don't believe in my talent."

"No, I do," I say. "You're very talented."

"Then why is it so hard to believe that someone important in the music industry would want to meet with me?"

"That's not what I meant," I say. He always manages to twist things around to put others on the defensive. I'm not letting him get away with it this time. "I meant that it seems like quite the coincidence that this opportunity arose directly following your blow-out with Mom."

"Life works in mysterious ways. You'll learn that as you grow older. Besides, I'm not staying out here long. I'll be back soon."

"You'd better be back next week," I say. "We have big plans."

"Next week?" Dad sounds confused.

"Yes, next week," My voice has an edge to it now. There's a long pause while I wait for him to respond. When he doesn't, I explode. "Yankee tickets, front row, creating lifetime memories with your only daughter! Do you remember now?"

Dad chuckles. "Of course, I remember, sweetheart. I'm just pulling your chain."

"So, you'll be back then?" I say, quietly now.

"Of course," he says. "I wouldn't miss it for the world."

28

Young App Developers Fair

Ethan

Jenna puts her head on my chest. "He left again," she says. "He went up in the sky and landed somewhere new."

I envision his feathers, flapping like tree branches wrapped up inside a tornado. In that scenario, the tree has two possible outcomes, be swept away or reduced to a pile of sticks. "You know I'm the last person to defend your dad," I say. "But now that I know him, I can't help but think that maybe it wasn't entirely his choice. It's… part of who he is. I'm not sure how much we can fight who we are and win."

Jenna nods. "It doesn't make it suck any less."

"No, it doesn't. It also doesn't mean that you need to forgive him or be okay with it. You can't change who he is, but you can decide how much to let him into your life."

"He said that he'll be back next week for the Yankee game."

"Do you believe him?"

"I shouldn't, but I do."

I hold her tighter. We lay like this for a while. I check the clock. "We should get going soon, if you're still up for it."

"Yeah," Jenna says, hopping up. "Moping around all day isn't going to change anything."

I slide into the passenger seat of Jenna's car, and she revs up the engine. "I'm going to get my driver's permit this week," I say. "It's time for me to learn to drive."

"Will that be safe?" Jenna asks.

"I'll never know if I never try."

At the Young App Developers fair, Jenna and I walk through rows of table displays. Students showcase their gadgets and discoveries. I keep my eyes glued to the floor. It's only been fifteen minutes, but I'm already losing it. This place is huge. There are so many people: colors and sounds and objects swirl around me, warping my vision. The wood floor distorts, becoming an open mouth with jagged teeth ready to eat me alive.

Jenna squeezes my hand, and the floor is a floor again. She stops at a booth. I focus on my breath and her hand in mine. "This seems really interesting."

"Thanks!" The booth's presenter steps forward. "I'm Selena Martinez. Please let me know if you have any questions."

"This says that your app is a cure for subconscious racism," Jenna says. "How does that work? I mean, if it's subconscious, how do you even know it's there?"

"That's a great question, and the exact issue that society has faced in combatting racism in the past. Most people don't identify as racists and have little awareness of their implicit biases. So that's why my app has three phases: in phase one, the app identifies latent thoughts the user has while interacting with a person from another race. These thoughts affect how we respond to people in subtle or not-so-subtle ways. Once the app collects enough data, the user can move on to phase two: which involves acknowledging their unconscious stereotypes in a productive way that allows them to make a positive change through app-guided meditations. In the final phase, stage three, significant structural changes to the brain can be observed—"

Wolves howl, a fan blows, and violins play. It's getting harder to hear over all of the commotion: a mixture of soul sounds, conversation, and sneakers squeaking against the floor. An oversized fly lands on my hand. I swipe it away. It buzzes in my ear before it whizzes away. I can't tell if it was real or not. I'm losing my grip again.

Jenna runs her fingers over my palm. I close my eyes and focus on that: the only thing I can be sure is real, her gentle touch, grounding me back into reality. I might look like a total freak right now, but I'm here. I haven't run away screaming yet.

My hearing returns. "What an amazing concept," Jenna says. "This could change the world."

"My mission is to end systemic racism, one individual at a time."

"Your project sounds awesome," I manage to stammer as Jenna guides me away from the booth. Ugh, I'm so embarrassing.

"Are you okay?" Jenna asks.

Okay is a relative concept. I nod. "For now, but I think I'm going to need a break soon. Where's Alex?"

"We're heading towards him now. Just a couple of minutes."

I put one foot in front of the other. When the lines on the floor start wiggling, I take a deep breath and close my eyes. When I reopen them, snakes swirl around my feet. The familiar dread curves its way up my spine. Luke.

"What're you freaks doing here?" His voice is smug. I keep my eyes glued to the floor, my heart rattling in my chest.

"Nice to see you, too, Luke," Jenna says. "I see you've found the cure to cancer."

"That's right," Luke says. "Well, not exactly a cure, but I created an app that can detect early skin changes that may be precursors to cancer."

All of a sudden, the temperature drops fifty degrees. A man's voice booms. "Luke, did you see the app that's designed to combat racism? Everyone is saying that's the favorite to win this year. Why didn't you come up with that?"

I shiver and glance up. A man with slicked-back blonde hair shakes his head at Luke, looking disgusted. The man looks a lot like Luke, just older and angrier. "Um, I don't know, Dad," Luke says. His snakes retreat as knife-like icicles slice into Luke's skin. Some push their way under the surface and stay lodged there, like frozen splinters. I wonder if he's numb from the inside out as his snakes feed on the blue blood that seeps from his wounds.

For the very first time in my life, I feel sorry for Luke Parker.

"Luke, straighten up and stop looking so pathetic," his father says. "The judges are coming."

A few distinguished-looking men and women approach, scribbling notes on their pads. As Jenna and I walk away, I can hear Luke explaining his project to the judges. "When used every day, my app can pick up on slight changes in skin texture or composition which can be indicative of a spreading deadly melanoma…" His voice fades into the background noise as we approach Alex's booth.

"Hey, Alex! How's it going?" Jenna asks.

"There's a lot of great programmers and ideas here," Alex says. "But I think I have a chance of placing in the top three. Do you guys want to try Mind-Travel? It's up and running."

"Yes!" Jenna says. "Can we go together?"

"Of course. Where in the world would you like to experience for five minutes?" Alex asks.

Something roars in my ear. An animate beaker with legs and a smiling face whizzes by on roller skates, reminding me of the teacup from Beauty and the Beast. I shake my head. If this is what I see when I'm sober, I better never use any hallucinogens.

"Um, somewhere quiet and peaceful," I suggest. "Where there aren't a lot of people around."

"I have an idea," Alex says. "How about the rainforest in Costa Rica?"

"That would be incredible!" Jenna says.

Alex presses a few buttons on his phone, dabs some gel and a circular electrode on each of our foreheads, and then we're gone. Lush greenery and tall trees surround us. The air is sticky. Jenna smiles, pointing above where a monkey swings from vine to vine. "Hey, little monkey!" she shouts. "Come here, cutie!" The monkey leaps over the trees and out of sight. Jenna shrugs. "It was worth a try."

I follow Jenna over a rickety wooden bridge that leads us to an enormous waterfall. The water rushes down. A blue and gold toucan watches from a nearby branch. He spreads his wings and flies. Droplets from the waterfall splash against my skin as Jenna leans in for a kiss.

The scene fades away. We're back at the Young App Developers fair. Alex removes the electrodes from our foreheads and cleans off the gel with a wet paper towel. "How did you like it?"

"It was beautiful," Jenna gushes.

"Yeah, man, awesome job," I say. "It felt one-hundred percent real." I wish we could've stayed longer than five minutes. The fair seems to be getting more and more crowded by the moment.

A bouquet of flowers opens and closes its eyes. The smell of smoke and burnt bacon singes my nose. A clown with vampire teeth laughs at me, his mouth so close that I can smell his rancid breath. I retract my golden sword and swing it at him. He leaps backward, missing my blow. Still, he lingers nearby, leering at me. A one-eyed bat tears into my hand. It takes everything in me not to yelp in pain. The whole room seems to spin around me. I take a step forward and I stumble. Jenna catches me before I fall. I'm acting like a freak. I have to get out of here before I embarrass Jenna even more.

"I need a break. I'm going outside for a bit."

Outside, I sit on the curb, my legs stretched in front of me. Jenna joins me for a while but then heads back inside to check out more exhibits. A light rain turns into a downpour. Soaked, I climb into the passenger seat of Jenna's car.

Jenna comes outside to visit me. She tells me about all of the experiments and interesting people she's meeting. I'm glad that Jenna can have fun without me, but I still feel like I suck and she'd be better off without me.

The rain pounds against the windshield. My eyelids feel heavy. I wake up when Jenna opens the driver's side door. "Hey!" she says. "Rise and shine, sleepyhead! In a few minutes, they're going to announce the winners."

Jenna and I go back inside, hand-in-hand. We lean against the back wall. I notice a man in a suit talking to Alex at his booth. As a woman steps onto the stage, the man hands Alex a business card and shakes his hand.

The microphone squeals as it's lifted from its stand. "Good afternoon, everyone," The woman says. "Today I am humbled and inspired by the immense display of talent exhibited by our great nation's young people. I have no doubt that our future's greatest inventors and innovators are in this very room right now.

"With that being said, picking today's winners was an extreme challenge, as the merits of the contestants' projects were far beyond what any of us even imagined. Every single person that participated today should feel very proud of their accomplishments, and I'm sure that each and every one of you has a bright future ahead."

The woman removes a slip of paper from inside her blazer. "Without any further ado, I'm going to announce the top three winners selected today. For third place: Global Warning: An App to Make Each Person aware of their impact on Global Warming, created by Tyrell Bryant of the Bronx, NY." Tyrell makes his way onto the stage and accepts his medal as the crowd cheers.

"In second place from Roxbury, NY" I hold my breath and silently pray that Alex's name will be announced. "Luke Parker with his Early Skin Cancer Detection App!"

Luke saunters up to the stage and a medal is placed around his neck. "Ugh," Jenna rolls her eyes. "I guess sometimes the villain wins." Although I want to, I can't seem to muster up the same level of disgust at his victory. I keep thinking about his father looming over him, the icicles ripping into his flesh.

"And this year's Young App Developer First-Place Winner is Selena Martinez from Miami, Florida with her Eliminate Subconscious Racism App!"

At Alex's booth, his parents and brother clap politely as Selena steps onto the stage. Alex is bent over his table, packing up his pamphlets and supplies. "Hey, man," I slap him on the back. "Sorry you didn't win, but your project is still awesome."

Alex turns around. "The CEO of Mind-Reel wants to invest in Mind-Travel."

"What?" My mouth opens. "No way!"

"In the contract they drafted, they are proposing buying a fifty percent stake in my app, and I'll still own the other fifty percent. Then, Mind-Travel will become part of the Mind-Reel enterprise."

"I don't understand all of the investment jargon, but I'm pretty sure that this translates to, Cha-Ching!" Jenna says, making it rain with her hands.

Alex's father beams with pride. "And that's not all," he says. "They want to offer him a job!"

"A job?" I ask. "But you're still in high school!"

"I graduate in June," Alex reminds me. "They want me to start working over the summer."

"But what about college?" I ask.

"I'm going to do that, too," Alex says. "And the company is going to pay my tuition in full."

"We weren't sure how we were going to manage to pay two college tuitions at once, with our boys being so close in age," Alex's mom says. "This is such a blessing."

"Nice job, bro," Tav says, a huge grin on his face. "You've made us all so proud."

"Yeah, that's awesome," I say, ashamed of the sinking feeling in my stomach. I still have no idea what I'm going to do after high school. Even though I'm only a junior, I can't imagine that I'll ever have any occupational talents that will compensate for my disability. I can still hear that therapist's voice echoing in my thoughts, "Unemployable," she said.

The temperature drops as Luke and his father move down the aisle towards us. Sharp icicles pound down on Luke like a murderous hail storm. His mass of black scribbles deflects some of the blows, but most pass through the barrier, puncturing him. His skin is covered with welts and scars. I wonder why I never noticed them before.

"Congratulations, Luke," I say.

His eyes widen in surprise when he sees me. "Thanks," he mumbles, then turns away.

"I'm surprised you congratulated him," Alex says. "You always tell me what a bad person he is."

As Luke and his father pass by, I can hear his father speaking, "I don't know what he's congratulating you for. Second place isn't shit. It means that you're the first loser."

I think about the time that Luke pummeled me in the hallway and all that he put Kira through. "I still don't think he's a good person," I say. It's easy to put people in boxes: to fit each and every one of us in a neat little category of good or evil. "But I'm realizing it's a lot more complicated than that."

29

Yankee Stadium

Ethan

When Jenna's dad isn't home the night before the game, I know it's not a good sign. If I were a betting man, I would put everything I own on his no-show. I also would give everything away if it would make him come back. But life doesn't work like that.

I can't stand to see Jenna hurting, Jenna still holding onto hope. We sit on her living room couch, her eyes glued to her phone.

Jenna wiggles her fingers as though she's casting a spell. "Unless you're being held captive by mutant aliens from Saturn, you'll respond…NOW!" Jenna watches at her phone. "No response. It looks like we might have to embark on a rescue mission to Saturn." She blows out a breath, slumping deeper into the couch. "Let me try this again." She begins to chant. "Oh, Goddess of Earth, find the man who gave me birth! Oh, Goddess of Air, tell him there's no time to spare! Oh, Goddess of Sea, have him send a text to me!"

I laugh. "Did you just make that up?"

"I'm a skilled witch. Don't doubt my sorcery." She stares at her phone. "Now." Seconds pass. "Okay, fine. In 5, 4, 3, 2…" Her phone lights up. **New text message from: Dad**

Jenna grins. "I knew the goddesses wouldn't let me down!" She opens the text message. Her smile breaks. "He's not coming," she says.

"What did he say?"

"He got 'caught-up' with business stuff." She uses her fingers to make air quotations. "He hopes I have a great time at the game with a friend and he'll be back as soon as he can."

"I'm sorry."

"Whatever." Jenna shrugs. "It's not a big deal." She excuses herself to go to the bathroom.

I wait for a few minutes. Then a few more. I know that she's not using the bathroom. I knock on the bathroom door. "Jenna," I say. "You don't have to hide. You can cry in front of me."

There are a few moments of silence and then the door bursts open. Jenna emerges, red-faced, tears streaming down. I pull her into my arms. Her blues and tangerines streak by slower now, particles separating, dripping like blood falling from an open wound. She sobs into my shoulder, my t-shirt dampening as I stroke her back.

The front door swings open and shut. Jenna's mom walks through the entryway, grocery bags in both hands. When she sees us, she drops the bags, an apple, and a can of chicken noodle soup rolling across the floor. "What happened?" Her mouth hangs open, seeing Jenna cry is such a shock.

Jenna wipes her eyes. "Dad isn't coming back for the game."

"What game?"

Jenna shakes her head, her hand on her forehead. "He never told you…"

"Told me what?" Her mom's hands are on her hips.

"He bought Yankee tickets for my birthday. We were supposed to go together but he ditched, as per usual." Jenna shrugs. "They were too expensive anyways. I'll see if I can sell them online."

"When's the game?"

"Tomorrow. My birthday."

"Tomorrow is a school day!"

"Dad said I don't have to go to school on my birthday."

"Oh, did he?" Jenna's mom rolls her eyes. "I'm going to make a few phone calls and see if I can get the day off tomorrow."

"Why?"

"So I can go to the game with you."

"But, Mom, you don't even like baseball. And these tickets were super expensive. Like, if you saw the price your jaw might fall off, ricochet off the ground, and land on the moon. It's probably better that I sell them and try to recoup some of the money."

"Jenna, forgetting about the price, do you want to go to the game?"

"Do I want to sit front row in Yankee Stadium and watch them play their ultimate rival? Does Superman wear a cape? Is the Hulk green? Does Romeo love Juliet? Does—"

"Okay, enough," Jenna's mom holds up her palm. "Let me make a few phone calls."

A half-hour later, Jenna and I are watching X-Men when her Mom sits on the edge of the couch. "Jenna, I'm so sorry. I called everyone. No one is available to cover for me on such short notice."

"It's okay. You tried." Jenna reaches for her laptop. "Let me see if I can sell these."

"I'll go," I say. The words kind of stick to my tongue as they come out. I know it's crazy. I couldn't even hold it together at the science fair.

Jenna looks at me like I sprouted six heads. "No." She shakes her head. "You hate crowds. They'll be about seventy-billion people at Yankee Stadium."

"Really?" I raise my brows. "I didn't realize that Yankee Stadium's capacity was ten times the world's population."

She opens her laptop. "You can't. The demons will tear you apart."

"I have a golden sword, a bow-and-arrow, and a cheetah," I argue.

Jenna's mom turns from one of us to the other, shaking her head at the bizarre conversation. "I'll leave you two to sort this out," she says, moving towards the door. "Ethan, if you decide to go, make sure you have your mom's permission to skip school."

"Okay," I say, and then to Jenna, "I'm going."

"Are you insane?"

"Yes. Truly, absolutely, insanely in love with you. I want to do this, Jenna. For you. For us. For me."

For her. To show her that not everyone is like her dad. I'll put her first, on her birthday and every day. I won't let her down.

For us. To prove that we can be a 'normal' couple. We'll post photos in our Yankee gear with the field behind us like the best of them.

For me. If I want to become anything worthwhile in life, I need to face the ultimate challenge. I need to believe that I can conquer any obstacle put in my path. I need to know that I'm worthy of Jenna. And also, let's be real, I've been a hardcore Yankee fan for my whole life. Sitting front row at Yankee Stadium will be a dream realized.

"Please," I say. "Let me do this."

The following morning, Jenna pulls into my driveway. I wipe my sweaty palms against my jeans, push my Yankee hat down on my head far enough to obscure my vision, and smile.

"Hey!" She says as I settle into the passenger seat. "How are you feeling?"

"Great!" I lie. The ride goes by too fast. As we enter the city, I feel the air thicken with the density of souls, all different frequencies mashed together in a tight space. It's the buzz of energy that Jenna loves, the chaotic frenzy of the city that revitalizes her. I already hate it.

"Look!" Jenna points to the enormous structure ahead. "There it is!"

What the hell have I gotten myself into?

She retrieves a ticket from the automated booth, the gate lifts and we enter the parking garage. We circle up the ramps and then pull into a parking spot on a middle deck. "How are you doing?" she asks.

"Awesome," I say, hoping she won't notice that the back of my t-shirt is damp.

We hold hands as we walk through the lot and onto the city street. The stadium looms ahead, just a block from where we stand.

The streets are crowded: fans in Yankee shirts moving towards the stadium, men selling water bottles, a homeless woman shaking a paper cup, coins clanging together. All at once, my senses are overwhelmed with sounds, colors, and sensations. Colors flood my vision, every nuance of every shade, colors that I can't name because they don't exist in this dimension, blurring the world around me.

I can't do this. I'm not even going to make it inside the stadium. I panic, losing all sense of reality, being sucked further into this tumultuous vortex where I can't even hear myself think. Jenna squeezes my hand.

I can't let her down. I remember the strategy that I've been utilizing lately: focusing on one thing and tuning out the rest. I zone in on Jenna's hand. How soft it feels in mine, her thumb caressing my palm. I concentrate on my breathing, inhaling slowly, then pushing everything that isn't welcome out with each exhale.

"I'm okay," I say, as the world comes back into focus. The lines sharpen around buildings; the colors subside. "I'm okay." And I am.

We stand in line with hundreds of other people waiting to show our tickets. Demons linger nearby. I flash my sword. I'm okay.

I'm fine. I'm going to do this. In just a few more minutes I'll enter Yankee stadium. What an accomplishment!

Someone new enters the mix. An evil so powerful it embeds itself deep inside my bones. I see red: blood, gore, animals chained up and gutted open, screaming to be free. I know the pleasure of torturing others: the rush of power when your victims fall to their knees.

This person is the vilest, most vicious, most nefarious soul that I've ever encountered. This person makes my encounter with Max Brophy seem like a walk in the park. This person makes Cole McFadden and Luke Parker look like saints.

Every cell in my body tells me to sprint away from this person as fast as I can. To run like the wind until I can't feel these heinous things.

I do the opposite. I walk towards him.

30

Vigilante Dreams

Jenna

"What's wrong?" I watch as his demeanor changes. His body stiffens, his palm is clammy in mine. "What happened?" I look around frantically. There are people all around us, but nothing seems out of the ordinary. I feel blind. Arguably, in this scenario, I am. And he thinks he's the one with a disorder. Maybe it's the other way around. Maybe everyone else has something missing.

Ethan moves his fists to his temples, his brow creasing up like an accordion. He steps out of line. "Where are you going?" I ask.

"I'll be right back. Please stay here. Stay safe. If I don't come back, find the police."

"I'm perfectly safe and there are cops everywhere. What's going on? Is a hell mouth opening or something?"

"No. At least I don't think so. I just… have to see something. Stay here." He's having trouble speaking; his voice trembles. He sounds like a ninety-year-old chain-smoker hiking Mt Everest.

"We both know that there's a higher likelihood of satanic koalas taking over the city than me letting you face whatever this is alone." I step out of line and follow him. He walks a few dozen feet before he stops.

A young couple walks hand-in-hand. The woman bounces with each step. The man looks like he just stepped off the cover of GQ magazine: tall, fit, slicked-back hair, wrinkle-free black t-shirt. He leans close to the woman, says something to her, and smiles. His mouth is wide; his smile reveals rows of pearly white teeth. He reminds me of a shark: shiny and dangerous, untrustworthy, too many teeth. Even though I'm getting a shady vibe, I can see how other women could find him attractive in a bad-boy Johnny Depp kind of way. The young woman flips her curly brown hair and smiles back at him.

Ethan just stares. He's shaking. His face squishes up like he smells something rancid. Maybe he does. "Um, um, excuse me," Ethan says. The couple faces him. Ethan drops his gaze to the concrete. "Um, Miss, do you mind, if, um, I speak with you for a second?"

The man folds his arms across his broad chest, his biceps bulging beneath his fitted t-shirt. "Is everything alright?"

"Um, not exactly," Ethan says. "I'd really prefer to speak with her alone."

The woman arches her eyebrows. "What's this about?"

"Do you know this guy?" The man interjects. His date shakes her head. "Then, you're not going anywhere with him alone. Listen, man, what's your deal? We're trying to see this game and you're holding us up."

Ethan's ears are bright red now; veins burst out of his neck. His breaths are ragged.

"Come on," The man says, resting his palm on the small of the woman's back. "Some weird people in this city," he mutters. They take a few steps, moving away from us and towards the line.

"Wait," Ethan croaks, taking a jerky step forward. "You need to be careful! How well do you know this guy?"

The woman looks back, her brow furrowed. "Um, this is our first time meeting in person. We've been talking online."

"Please," Ethan pleads. "Don't go anywhere alone with him. Please, I beg you." He chokes out the syllables, sucking in desperate breaths every few words.

The man charges Ethan. "Listen, man, I don't know you or what your problem is." He bumps his chest into Ethan. "But if you're going to try to act like a tough guy the least you could do is look me in the eye while you're talking shit."

"Come on, Ethan," I say, tugging his arm. "Let's go. You've done what you could."

Ethan doesn't budge. It's like his feet are glued to the concrete. If he doesn't move soon, I might have to kick this guy's ass myself.

Ethan's chin inches up. First, he faces the ground, then he stares straight ahead. He sucks in a breath and tilts his face up further towards the sky. He looks straight into the man's eyes.

His knees buckle. "No!" I shout, reaching out to catch him. I'm too late. He drops to the ground. Eyes closed, his body convulses like he's having a seizure. I kneel beside him, my hands on his quivering shoulders.

The crowd closes in around us. "Somebody call a medic!" A woman shouts.

"Are there any doctors here?" Another voice asks. "Does anyone know CPR?"

"He's fine!" I shout. The hospital is the last place Ethan wants to go. The doctors won't understand. They won't know how to treat him. All of the chaos and frenetic energy will make him worse.

"Ethan, please," I whisper in his ear. "It's me, Jenna, can you hear me? If you don't get up right now, they're going to make you go to the hospital." I wipe a cold layer of sweat from his forehead.

His body is limp: flesh, meat, and bone splayed out across the concrete. I place a finger on his throat, but I can't find a pulse. My heart climbs into my throat, crowding my windpipe. With every pump, it steals my breath.

My fingers slide up and down his neck. "Ethan, please… Ethan, please, be okay." I don't know if he's alive. Maybe he saw something so heinous, so unfathomable, that it sucked the life right out of him. I press down harder, and a light flutter trembles against my pointer. I heave a sigh of relief.

"Everyone back up!" A police officer and two medics push through the crowd. "Ethan, wake up," I plead, shaking his shoulders. He doesn't even stir.

As the medics begin their assessment, I notice the couple walking away, the woman's curls blowing in the breeze. I push my way through the crowd and grab her wrist. "Please, listen to us," I say. "He's not crazy." The woman stares at me, wide-eyed as she pulls away. "Don't be alone with him!" I shout.

When I turn back around Ethan is being lifted onto a stretcher. "Where are you taking him?" I follow as they roll him towards the ambulance, sirens blaring, red lights flashing on his pale face.

"The hospital," a medic says. "Kid's in bad shape. You can meet us there. We don't allow friends to ride in the ambulance."

I pretend that I don't hear him and climb inside the emergency vehicle. The medic points towards the exit. "I'm not leaving him. Not even for a second." The medics exchange a look. "Please," I say. "He would want me to be with him. I won't get in the way. I promise." One medic nods as the other closes the door. Sirens shriek as the driver runs through a red light.

What feels like an eternity later, I'm perched on a hospital chair, Ethan's cold hand in mine. It's been hours and he's still unconscious, the beep-beep-beep of a monitor the only reassurance that he was alive.

His mother pulls up a chair on the other side of the bed, her face white as a ghost. She brushes his hair out of his eyes. "It's never lasted this long before," she says. "The crowd must've overwhelmed him. I shouldn't have let him go. He just seemed so confident…" She shakes her head.

I wish I could tell her it wasn't the crowd, and it wasn't her fault. Ethan chose to look into that man's eyes. Ethan wanted to know his secrets. I don't know why.

A woman with long, glossy black hair swings open the door, a file in her hand. "How's everything going in here?"

"Hi, Dr. Zao," I say. "No changes."

The doctor's mouth is set in a grim line. She holds up the paperwork in her hand, "The lab results have come back." She addresses Ethan's mom. "Would you mind stepping out?"

As soon as they leave the room, I put my ear to the door. I can hear Dr. Zao in the hallway. "When he first arrived, his vitals were all over the place. Now, he's stabilized, but his EEG is like nothing I've ever seen. I don't know what to make of it, honestly. I spoke to a few specialists, and they're also baffled. At this point, to be frank, we're not sure if there will be permanent brain damage. We're continuing to treat him with anti-seizure and anti-psychotic medications through his IV. Since this is such an unusual case, we're not sure what else we can do."

"He's not psychotic," I mutter. I lean forward and kiss him on the lips, wishing Ethan was Sleeping Beauty instead of a Soulseer. I don't know how to awaken the latter. Grimm's really let me down this time. "I love you," I whisper in his ear.

A few hours later, Ethan's mom heads down to the cafeteria, and I remain at his side. His eyelids flutter. I run my fingers over his cheek. "Ethan?" His eyes are half-open. They are as beautiful as before: coffee brown framed by long black lashes. But somehow, they seem different. Spaced out. Zombie-like. "Ethan?" I ask again, unsure if his soul has returned with him.

Ethan jerks up, his arms flailing, tugging against the slack of the IV line. "Where am I?"

"We were abducted by aliens and now we're trapped inside their secret laboratory spaceship where they run experiments on humans."

Ethan laughs. Some of the light returns to his eyes. "For real," he says. "Did we miss the game?"

My eyes widen. "You don't remember."

He shakes his head, fear entering his eyes. "Oh no," he says, dropping his gaze. "I ruined your birthday."

"That doesn't matter." I place my head on his shoulder. "All that matters is that you're okay."

"The last thing I remember is getting in line outside of the stadium. What happened?"

"You looked someone in the eye. Some young sleaze-ball type of guy."

Ethan squeezes his eyes shut and takes a deep breath like he's willing himself to remember. "Why would I do that?"

"I'm not sure." When he marched up to that couple, he was in pain, but determined. He had a purpose. Now that he couldn't remember what he saw, it all seemed like a waste. "You must've seen his secrets."

"I don't remember anything," Ethan says.

"Has this ever happened before?"

"Amnesia?" Ethan shakes his head. "Never."

"Maybe it was too traumatic," I suggest. "Maybe your subconscious mind repressed it to protect your sanity."

Ethan fingers his IV. "Or maybe the poison they're pumping into my veins is messing with me." He sighs. "I need to get out of here."

The door swings open. Ethan's mom enters, a paper bag clenched between her fingers. "Ethan! You're awake!"

"Yeah, Mom, I'm fine," Ethan says. "I'm sorry I scared you. When can I go home?"

"I'll go get the doctor."

An hour later, Ethan had been examined by two doctors, but discharge was yet to be recommended. Both doctors seemed befuddled by his sudden turnaround. "Perhaps he should stay overnight for observation," one doctor suggested.

"No!" Ethan protested. "I'll recover much faster at home."

As time passes, Ethan's condition worsens. He covers it well, but I can see through his mask. I recognize the stress in his eyes, the sweat beading along his hairline.

In front of his mom and the doctors, I keep my concerns to myself. When his mother goes to get a drink, I seize the opportunity. "What's happening to you? Are there evil souls in our presence?"

"No," Ethan says, his complexion taking on the hue of a dragon. "I'm starting to remember." He gags. "Bag." He points to a crumbled bag on the windowsill. I empty its contents and hand it to him. He retches into the bag, again and again. When he's done, I bring him a wet paper towel to wipe his mouth.

"What are you seeing?" I ask.

"Only bits and pieces. But it's bad, Jenna. Really, really bad." The zombie-like glaze is gone from his eyes, but they still look different from this morning. Older. Haunted.

He hands me the bag. "Hide this, please. If they find out I puked they'll keep me here for another eternity."

More hours pass. Two more doctors examine Ethan, but no one will say when he can go home. Only I recognize the pain in his eyes, the sudden hitch in his breath, the way his nails dig into the sheets. I can't ask him what he's seeing. There are too many people around.

Finally, Ethan is discharged under the strict provision that he follow up with a neurologist ASAP. Ethan's mother drives us to my car which is still parked in the garage near the stadium.

"Mom, can Jenna drive me home?" Ethan asks.

"I'm not sure if that's a good idea. What if you get sick again? I don't want to put that responsibility on Jenna."

"Mom, I'm fine. I already ruined her birthday. It's not fair that she should have to drive back by herself."

I don't mind driving alone and Ethan knows that, but I play along. "Yeah, I get nervous on long trips. I'd rather he came with me."

"Alright," Ethan's mom relents. "But if anything happens, call me immediately, okay?"

As Ethan's mom drives away, I look at him funny. "What was that all about?"

But Ethan doesn't answer. He walks in the opposite direction from my car, his feet moving swiftly across the garage to another row of cars. "Ethan!" I shout, catching up to him. "What are you doing?"

Ethan stares straight ahead, zoned in on his destination, wherever that may be. "I know you're from the country, so I just thought I'd let you know that garages aren't like the woods. There aren't many sights to see, and generally, I wouldn't recommend hiking them for pleasure." It's like I don't exist. If a witch has set a spell on him, I'm not sure how to reverse it. I could try invoking the Goddesses with my impromptu chanting, although my success rate using that tactic only averages around one percent.

Ethan keeps going. We're getting further and further away from my car. I hear a man's laughter behind us. I turn around. Two hulking figures cast shadows, just a few rows away, moving in our direction. My heart speeds up. Although I'm not a fearful person, being raised in the city I've been taught to be aware of my surroundings. Meandering around a parking garage late at night is not advisable. "Ethan, seriously," I say. "What's your deal?"

He rips a flyer off a post. It trembles in his hand. Tears stream down his cheeks. "I saw this when my mom drove in."

MISSING is written in big block letters across the top of the page. Red curls frame the young woman's delicate features. I've seen the picture before on the news.

"I know where Rachel Gallagher is," Ethan says. "I know where Brittany Shulman is too, but she's not alive. At least her family will have closure."

The first name Ethan mentioned is on the flyer. I recognize the second name from the news. The two missing college students. The horror of it all sweeps over me and for a moment I feel dizzy. I place a hand on Ethan's back to steady myself.

"I don't have time to waste. Any minute could be Rachel's last."

I pull myself together. "Okay, I'm in. Let's see, first stop will be to pick up supplies. We'll need all black clothing, must be made from a flexible material so as not to restrict movement, black ski masks, black boots... Some kind of weapons, maybe knives and nunchucks..."

Ethan raises his eyebrows. "Nunchucks...? Are we ninjas now?"

"I was thinking more like versatile vigilantes extraordinaire. What choice of weaponry would you suggest for our rescue mission?"

Ethan points to the bottom of the flyer. "I was just going to call the anonymous tip hotline."

"Way to burst my bubble," I say, then shrug. "But I guess that could work too."

31

Happily Ever After

Ethan

Four Days Later

Jenna nuzzles up next to me and I flick on the television. A scene unfolds on the screen. An older woman embraces the blue-eyed young woman. A man studies the younger woman's face, as if he couldn't quite believe that she's there.

A newscaster narrates, "After over a month in captivity, kidnapped and at the mercy of a madman, Rachel Gallagher is finally reunited with her parents."

Rachel's father holds her like he's afraid she might disappear, her red curls mingling with his grays. Heavy bags hang under the mother's sky-blue eyes that match her daughter's. Still, her eyes shine above the dark circles, squeals of joy erupting from her throat. When I squint, I swear I see a neon butterfly bounce across the screen. It makes me smile.

The screen changes; figures clad in black hover around a casket as it's lowered into the earth. "Another family was not so lucky. Today hundreds of friends and family members said their final goodbyes to Brittany Shulman, another victim of the same madman. We had the opportunity to speak with Brittany's mother following the funeral."

Deep creases mar the woman's sallow skin. "Brittany was the light of my life. I'm not sure how I'll go on without her." Tears roll down her face. "But I'm thankful that she was found and brought home to us so we could lay her to rest in the family plot. She's at peace next to her grandmother now. They were best friends, and I take comfort in knowing they're together now."

The scene changes again. The man from outside of Yankee Stadium looks different in his orange jumpsuit. He shuffles forward, his movements restricted by shackles, his head down as he's escorted across the courtroom. "Phillip Lepore is being charged with first-degree murder and kidnapping and will be held on no bail."

"All because of you," Jenna says, squeezing my hand and gently kissing my cheek.

"Another woman narrowly escaped Lepore's clutches after a complete stranger cautioned her to stay away from him. That woman is Thais Gomez, a student at Fordham University and a lifetime resident of the Bronx."

The young woman I warned outside Yankee stadium sits cross-legged on a beige couch, a reporter beside her. "Tell us how you knew Phillip Lepore."

"I met him on college-match.com," Thais says. "We'd been chatting online for a few weeks when I mentioned that I was a Yankee fan. He told me that he had an extra ticket and asked me to meet him at the game."

"Did you have any hesitations about meeting him?"

She shakes her head. "No, not at all. He seemed like a nice guy, and I was meeting him at a public place."

"But then something very unusual happened," the reporter prompts.

"Yes, I'd just met Phil a few minutes before. We were walking to the stadium when this random guy and girl came up to us. They looked young, like high schoolers. This guy was acting really strange. I thought maybe he was on drugs. Then, he told me to not go anywhere alone with Phil."

"What did you think of this strange encounter?" the reporter asks.

"I wasn't sure what to think. Then, the boy suddenly had a seizure. While he was on the ground, the girl warned me again. Something in her expression stuck with me. This wasn't a prank. She was genuinely concerned."

"And you didn't know either of these people?" Thais shakes her head. "What about Phillip? Did he know them?"

Thais shrugs. "He said he didn't."

"And what did you do next? Did you go to the game?"

"Yeah, we did. We had a good time. He was so sweet and charming that I almost forgot about the weirdness from earlier."

"But then you decided not to get into his car."

"Yeah. After the game, he offered to drive me home. I almost said yes, but I kept hearing the girl's voice in my head telling me not to be alone with him."

"If you hadn't been warned by these strangers, do you think you would've taken his offer for a ride?"

"Yes," Thais says. "It feels strange saying it now, but at the time, I liked him. Later on that night, I was kicking myself for being paranoid and missing out on spending more time with him."

"Now you realize you were one decision away from getting in the car with Brittany Shulman's killer. We also know Rachel Gallagher was kidnapped after accepting Lepore's offer to drive her home. Do you believe those strangers outside Yankee stadium may have saved your life?"

"I do, and I still have no idea who they are. If they're watching right now, I can't ever thank you enough. You're my guardian angels."

Jenna grins. "Guardian angel. No one ever called me that before. It has a nice ring to it."

"A few more good deeds and you'll earn a halo and wings," I say.

Jenna faces me, her eyes probing deeply into mine. "Seriously, though. I didn't do anything. You're the angel here."

"You sure did," I say. "You heard the woman. To her, I was just some weirdo. You were the convincing one."

"I wouldn't have had anything to convince her of if it wasn't for you."

I shrug, heat rising in my cheeks.

"Why'd you do it?" Jenna asks.

"Do what?"

"Look into his eyes."

I shudder, remembering the pure horror that seeped into my being when he arrived at the stadium. "Phillip Lepore is the vilest, most disgusting, most repugnant human that I've ever encountered. I knew he had terrible secrets, most likely criminal ones."

"And you wanted to bring him to justice," Jenna finishes.

"I think so," I say. "I was in a lot of pain and not entirely in my right mind, but I'm pretty sure that was my motivation. I'm lucky it worked out this time. Other times have only led to years of nightmares and a head full of information that I cannot prove, and no one will ever believe."

"It wasn't luck. It was you. It's time to give yourself some credit. You're brave and incredible." She runs her thumb over my cheek, sending jolts of electricity down my spine. "You saved Rachel, Thais, and countless others by getting Phillip Lepore off the street." She kisses me. "You, Ethan Underwood, are a hero."

"Tell that to the good folk of Roxbury. They'll say I'm a loser and a freak."

"If you come out of anonymity, they'll hold a parade in your honor. They'll march through the streets singing your praises. Now that you see what good can come from your abilities, you shouldn't feel ashamed. You can come forward and reveal everything."

I shake my head. "Might as well put a target on my back. No one wants someone around who can see right through them, who can steal all of their secrets with a glance. I'd be a dead man."

"I didn't think of it like that," Jenna says, her brow furrowed.

"I know you didn't. You always think the best of people. I love that about you." I run my fingers through her hair. "You've changed me too, you know? Before I met you, I thought that pretty much everyone sucked. Now I see that most people are good. You've helped me see that." This new perspective, this positivity, even after seeing firsthand the cruelty and violence humans are capable of, would never have been possible without Jenna. I'll be eternally grateful to her for that. By seeing the best in me, she brings out the best in me. "Besides," I say, returning to the previous subject. "Even if I wasn't afraid of the public's reaction, I still wouldn't reveal my secret to the world."

"Why's that?" Jenna asks.

I shrug. "Why doesn't Clark Kent tell the world that he's Superman? Why doesn't Peter Parker announce that he's Spider-Man?"

Jenna grins wildly, her eyes lighting up like the North Star, the cute dimple indenting her right cheek.

"What're you so happy about?" I ask.

"You admitted it," she says. "Indirectly, but it still counts."

"Admitted what?"

"That you're a superhero," she says.

She got me. I guess I had. Now I'm grinning stupidly as well.

"So, does that make me Lois Lane or Mary Jane?" she asks.

"You," I say, cupping her chin. "Are Jenna Farrell. There's no other like you. There are no comparisons. You are unparalleled."

She kisses me, and my whole world is set on fire. It doesn't matter if it's our first kiss or our five-thousandth. Every time, the combination of heat and tenderness blows me away.

Jenna changes the channel. The Yankee game has just started. The opposing team throws the first pitch. Strike one. My heart sinks as I remember how I've let Jenna down. She was so excited to sit in the front row. Now she may never have that chance again.

"Maybe I'm a superhero, but I'm not a superhero boyfriend. We missed the game. I disappointed you on your birthday. Just like your dad." I look down. "I'm sorry. I promised myself that I'd never be like him, that I'd never hurt you."

"You can't be serious right now," Jenna rolls her eyes. "If my dad bailed because he was saving women's lives, I think I'd let that slide. He's just… selfish. It's not the same at all."

"I guess," I say. "But there's more bothering me. I don't know if I can ever truly make you happy."

"I'm happy. What're you talking about?"

"I don't know if I could ever live in the city. It would be too much for me," I say.

"So what?"

"So, you love the city! Don't you want to move back?"

"I can visit. And if you don't want to visit with me, I'll go without you. I'll survive."

"You deserve someone who can give you everything, who can be there for you through everything, who can be everything you ever wanted."

"Ethan, I think we just reversed roles. Right now, you're the one living in a fantasy and I need to give you a dose of reality. No one can be *everything* that anyone ever wanted. That's just not how relationships work. Real-life relationships require some level of sacrifice and compromise."

"But how many sacrifices? At what point does it become unfair?" I ask.

"We don't need to be attached at the hip. I'm part-cheetah, remember? I'm strong and independent. I'm perfectly comfortable doing things alone or with friends." She pauses. "If I'm being honest, I didn't like it when you were a total hermit. But ever since you've started hanging out with my friends sometimes, I'm happy." Her phone buzzes. Jenna glances at the screen and then tosses her phone to the side. "My dad."

"You're not picking up?" I can't conceal the surprise in my tone.

"Nope. I don't feel like talking to him right now." She takes a deep breath. "I'll call him when I'm ready. He can be the one to wait for once." She fiddles with a string hanging from her jeans. "I told my mom she shouldn't forgive him when he comes crawling back this time. I think she was... relieved. I know a lot of the reason she's tried to make it work is for me. I've finally realized that as much as it sucks, it's better for them to go their separate ways. They aren't going to find happiness with each other." A crease appears between Jenna's brows. "He expects my mom to sacrifice for him, but he isn't willing to compromise at all." She shakes her head. "You, on the other hand, are the complete opposite. You may try to hide it, but I know that being social is still a struggle for you. I can tell when you're uncomfortable at parties. And yet, you were willing to go to one of the busiest, noisiest, most chaotic places in the world for me, knowing how painful it would be for you. I can't imagine a bigger sacrifice than that!"

"I guess," I say.

"There's no guessing! These are facts. Now you need to stop with all the guilt and questioning yourself and our relationship. That's an order!"

"Yes, Ma'am!" I salute her.

She straddles me. Her warmth and sunset-orange and royal blues enveloped me. She kisses me. Electricity jolts up and down my spine. Stars spin around us.

"Jenna, do you remember when you asked me what I wanted to do as a career?"

She smiles. "Yes."

"Well, I think I've figured it out."

"Let me guess. You're going to open a private investigative firm that single-handedly captures all of the serial killers and homicidal maniacs of the world."

"Well," I laugh. "Close. I was going to say that I want to study criminology and maybe move up the ranks in a police department and become a detective one day. I may have special… assets that can help solve cases."

"That's cool, but I still say that we should open our own business. We'll have more freedom. We can travel and experience all different cultures and lifestyles. We'll solve so many cases that we'll become rich and world-famous."

"We? I thought you were becoming a doctor?"

"Well, duh, obviously I'm going to be a doctor. I'm not giving that up. I'll do both."

I raise my brows. "Both?"

"Yeah, why not? Neurosurgeon by day and crime-solver by night."

"Ambitious, but neurosurgeon? I didn't know you decided on that specialty."

"The brain fascinates me. There are so many mysteries about it yet to be discovered. And who knows? Maybe I'll start a new field of study: the connection between the brain and the soul."

"You'll be the laughingstock of the medical community."

Jenna shrugs. "Let them laugh. Many of the greatest discoveries were ridiculed at some point. It's impossible to make progress without a little risk."

She's right. "Maybe I'll minor in psychology. I can write a book about the development of the soul throughout childhood, specifically studying individuals who eventually resort to a life of violent crime."

"Now you're talking."

Before Jenna, my future was bleak. Now the possibilities are limitless. I imagine making our dreams a reality: scouring the globe together vigilante-style, hunting and maybe even finding ways to rehabilitate the souls of criminals. Whenever I need a break from society, we'll hole up together in a cottage at the end of a country lane, waking up to birds chattering as I hold her close to my chest. Wherever I end up, there's one thing I know for sure. I want Jenna by my side.

She's the only one who knows all of me. She makes me see that my differences don't make me a freak or a loser or unworthy of her.

"I love you, Soul Seer," Jenna says. She loves me. And now I know that I deserve to be loved.

I love her back with every ounce of my heart and soul. "I love you," I say, but I can't tell if I said it out loud. All the sounds of this dimension are drowned out by Jenna's soul song. I close my eyes and bask in it: the rhythmic waves crashing on the beach, the soothing melody, the rumble-like purr. I hold her so close that I can't tell if the purrs are hers or mine.

I never used to believe in fairy tales. Now I believe in everything: soulmates, destiny, magic, and all. I'm not quite sure how to end this, and the truth is, it doesn't end here. For us, this is only the beginning. But I know how Jenna would want me to finish it off, so here you go.

And they lived happily ever after.

Want more YA fantasy romance by Faith Prince?

The Crowe Sisters Trilogy is available now!

Where Magic Begins: https://www.amazon.com/dp/B0BZZ6HZC1
Magic Coming Undone: https://www.amazon.com/dp/B0CXN18C8G
Twin Flames: https://www.amazon.com/dp/B0F788SSZ1

Faith Prince is the author of The Crowe Sisters Trilogy (Where Magic Begins, Magic Coming Undone, Twin Flames) and the stand-alone novel Wild Souls.

Besides writing, some of Faith's favorite things include: spending time with her family, reading, country music, cats, chocolate, coffee, traveling, and concerts, in that order.

Visit Faith's YouTube channel at
https://www.youtube.com/c/FaithPrinceAuthor

Signed paperbacks are available for purchase on my website. www.faithprinceauthor.com

Follow me!

Instagram: https://www.instagram.com/faithprincewrites
Twitter: https://twitter.com/FaithPrinceAuth
TikTok: https://www.tiktok.com/@faithprinceauthor
Amazon: https://www.amazon.com/author/faithprince

www.ingramcontent.com/pod-product-compliance
Lightning Source LLC
Chambersburg PA
CBHW070452300726
48975CB00007B/2135